A Good Day
to
Pie

Also available by Misha Popp

The Pies Before Guys Mysteries
Magic, Lies, and Deadly Pies

A Good Day to Pie

A PIES BEFORE GUYS MYSTERY

Misha Popp

NEW YORK

This is a work of fiction. All of the names, characters, organizations, places and events portrayed in this novel are either products of the author's imagination or are used fictitiously. Any resemblance to real or actual events, locales, or persons, living or dead, is entirely coincidental.

Published in the United States by Crooked Lane Books, an imprint of The Quick Brown Fox & Company LLC.

Crooked Lane Books and its logo are trademarks of The Quick Brown Fox & Company LLC.

Library of Congress Catalog-in-Publication data available upon request.

ISBN (hardcover): 978-1-63910-232-7
ISBN (ebook): 978-1-63910-233-4

Cover illustration by Stephanie Singleton

Cover typography by Meghan Deist

Printed in the United States.

www.crookedlanebooks.com

Crooked Lane Books
34 West 27th St., 10th Floor
New York, NY 10001

First Edition: February 2023

10 9 8 7 6 5 4 3 2 1

To all the readers
who came back for seconds

Chapter One

This is the pie that's going to kill me.

No, not the pie.

The process.

It's one thing to bake a honey crunch pie, but it's a whole other thing to bake it in the glare of studio lighting with a pair of cameras tracking my every move.

I know it's my own fault.

I have no one to blame but myself.

And Noel.

I'm definitely blaming Noel too.

I keep that thought out of my head as I work my hands into the flour and butter in front of me, though. Yes, I'm out of my comfort zone, but that's no excuse for accidentally working a bit of magical vengeance into this pie dough.

Especially with cameras watching.

So I smile and bring my hands up for the cameras. One zooms in on the flakes of flour-coated butter I'm holding, and I turn to the other and say, "I wish I could say I learned this from my mother, but the truth is, she could barely handle boxed brownies." I laugh, and the memory of smoke alarms cheering on my mother's baking efforts makes it even feel natural.

I stir water into the dough and continue narrating. "Baking just makes sense to me. It's like some people are naturally good at art, or sports, or languages." I gather the dough into a ball and flatten it into a disk, prodding a few of the visible lumps of butter out of habit. "For me, pie is my language, or my art, if I want to be extra pretentious about it." I shoot a look at the camera that I hope makes it clear I do *not* want to be pretentious. "Baking is my life. It's my identity. It's what I'm good at." The woman behind the camera holds a hand up in a *stop* gesture, and I wait, keeping my eyes on the camera like we discussed, and can practically hear the dramatic music they're going to add in when this airs. Then she drops her hand, and I have my signal to wrap it up. "And that's what I want to show the world on *Bake My Day*."

There's a silence as the cameras record their final seconds, and I hope the smile on my face doesn't look too deer-in-headlights. I have a flash of panic that I said the wrong title—the show has already gone through four puntastic iterations since I applied—but Kate looks pleased when she calls wrap and steps out from behind her camera.

Her assistant lowers his handheld and nods. "Plenty of close-ups," he says, swiping a hand across his forehead.

"Good. Get these goddamned lights down. This place is like a sauna." Kate starts packing her camera away and, at that moment, the door swings open and Frank, owner and official curmudgeon of Frank's Roadside Diner, stomps into the kitchen.

"We done in here?" he barks. "I got a business to run, you know. This ain't Hollywood."

"It most certainly isn't," Kate agrees, matching his tone.

"You saying my diner—"

I jump in before he can continue and get me kicked off the show before it even begins. “Frank, we’re clearing out. I’m sorry we couldn’t do this in the van. Kitchen’s all yours.”

“Damn right it is,” he grumbles, and jabs a finger at the pie dough resting on the stainless worktop. “I assume you’re making more of that?”

I snap a salute at him. “Of course. You’re going to be well stocked in both pie and pie components. I’m sure Juan can handle assembly if stock runs out.”

“Don’t know what I pay you for,” Frank huffs, brushing past the camera operator, who is breaking down lights in front of the flattop. “Son, unless you’re volunteering as my new grill cook, you have two minutes to get off my line.”

I shoot the kid an apologetic look before turning a beaming smiling on Frank. “You still don’t pay me, Frank.”

And it’s true, he doesn’t. In exchange for all the pies the diner can go through, I get to park Penny, my vintage pink RV, out back and tap into the water and electricity. It’s an arrangement that’s served us both well, and even though Frank likes to talk tough, I know it’s all bluster.

Unfortunately, Kate does not.

“Mr. Harrow, you signed a release granting us access to this establishment to film promotional materials as needed. At some point, I would suggest you get your attitude under control, because if Daisy makes it past the first week, I can guarantee we’re going to be back here getting more footage.”

Frank harrumphs again. “Of course she’s making it past the first week.”

I feel my cheeks flush, just a little, at this extravagant display of affection.

"We'll see," Kate says, zipping her wheeled camera bag closed. She offers me a pointed look. "Remember, nine outfits for shooting, plus something for the reception. Specific requirements are in your packet. We'll see you in a week."

Without a word to Frank, she strides out of the kitchen, leaving her assistant scrambling to gather the rest of the equipment and scurry after her.

Frank cranks the knobs on the flattop and fires up the fryer, the soft whooshes of ignition louder than usual in the sudden quiet.

"I hope you know what you're getting yourself into," Frank mutters. "Can't trust these damn show biz types."

"It's just a baking competition," I say. "Same as the pie contest."

The swinging door to the dining room bursts open, and Juan, the diner's head cook and one of my very favorite humans, crashes in with a pile of servers on his heels. "Except this time you're going to be properly famous," he says, adding a terrible posh British accent to the last two words before grabbing me in a hug. "How'd it go?"

"You know those scenes in old detective movies, where they put the suspect in a dark room with a spotlight? It kind of feels like that, only with more butter."

"I'm sure you were great," Juan says. "The camera's gonna love our Pie Girl."

"We'll see." A mix of excitement, hope, and panic swirls in my chest like meringue.

"Well, Ana's already jazzed. You would think it was her going on TV."

"If I make it to the finals, it will be." I flush, the many implications of that statement hitting me all at once. "I mean, if you want to. If she wants to." I steal a look at Frank, who's busy haranguing the servers about side work but also has an eye in my direction.

"You don't have to. None of you. I mean, it's just that, if you're in the finals, they do this whole meet-the-family thing. And you guys, well, you're the closest thing I have to family, so I think that means it'll be you they're coming for."

I know I'm babbling, but I can't help it. I spent the morning psyching myself up for cameras and repetitive takes and intrusive lighting, not stark emotional confessions in a barely open restaurant.

But here we are.

"Oh, I already have my whole spiel planned," Juan says, like it's an absolute given that I'll make it past the first week. "Ana's making signs, Eric's overseeing, it's going to be a thing."

Juan adopted Ana last year, and in that time she has already become my unofficial biggest fan. Getting to the finals will be as much fun for her as it will be for me. Maybe more so, since she's six and won't actually have the stress of, you know, actually being in the finals of a nationally televised baking competition.

The whole thing started as a lark. The invitation to audition for a new FoodTV show had been extended after I won the state pie contest last year. It was being billed as America's answer to the popular British baking show, and if I'm honest, I don't think I really believed I'd be chosen, but Noel was so excited about the prospect that I went ahead and applied.

Which is why he's square in my blame cross hairs. If it weren't for him and his sweet, rumpled earnestness, I wouldn't be faced with the mountain of pies I need to make Frank to cover the two weeks I'll be away filming, I wouldn't be worried about which of my vintage swing dresses will look best on camera, and I wouldn't be mentally planning how I'll spend the prize money.

It's going to sound materialistic, but that's the real reason I've thrown my hat into this ring. I don't care about fame, I don't care about competition, but I do care about that hundred grand. I care about how it can fund Pies Before Guys, the darker side of my RV-based baking business that delivers flaky-crusted justice to the worst men out there.

It's a mission that was almost taken from me once, and if I can expand its reach by winning that prize money, it's worth every camera and scripted take in the world.

Chapter Two

I've just finished a lunch rush of pie sales at my new spot downtown when Melly appears at the van's window, all energy and fuchsia-haired enthusiasm.

There's also an edge of something that looks suspiciously like nerves, which immediately has my stomach tightening. Melly does a lot of emotions, but nervous isn't one of them.

"Pie?" I ask, as if there's nothing amiss.

"Only if you're serving inside," she says with a cheeky grin.

I tilt my head toward the door in assent, and she clambers in, stepping over Zoe, my brown-and-white cream puff of a pit bull, to park herself at my small counter. I slide my serving window closed and suction cup the *Be Back Soon!* sign to it. I take a pair of leftover lemon cutie pies off the tray and slide her one. The little round pastries are infused with my zingy workday blend of motivation and energy, which I realize may not be what this situation calls for, but it's sugar and it's handy, and sometimes that's what matters.

"Okay, don't be mad," Melly says, pressing her steepled fingers against her full lips like it might hide the mischief there. "But I've been doing some recruiting."

"You've been doing what?"

"Outreach. Feelers. Just seeing what's out there. I mean, since you've got this whole road trip planned, I figured it wouldn't hurt to line up some murder pies on the way down, right?"

I bite back a groan, regretting, not for the first time, that I didn't actually watch to see if she ate the forgetting pie she was supposed to eat after the shenanigans from last year. Shenanigans she was, in no small part, responsible for, what with duct-taping a man to a chair and all that. That pie would've wiped that memory clean, along with all knowledge of my little side business.

Of course she didn't eat it.

I notice she's not eating the pie in front of her either, but that's far from my biggest concern right now.

"I have a system," I remind her. "One that works. The client referrals are word-of-mouth so everyone involved has the same stake. This isn't some multilevel marketing scheme where you recruit members for pie parties."

"No, but it should be!" she says, eyes sparkling. "You could have a whole army of murder-pie bakers, each with their own clientele, and they could even train more bakers. It'd be like the pie-pocalypse!"

I laugh because it's impossible not to. Melly's enthusiasm is like a living thing, and even though I'm concerned, I'm also curious. "Recruiting how, exactly?"

She settles down, pushing all pyramid pie schemes aside. "Online," she says, already holding up a hand to stop my protest. "Completely safe and anonymous. When I was interning in DC last summer, I made friends with this computer wizard when I was researching that article about dark web conspiracy rings. She taught me some tricks to cover my trail. And before you ask, no, she doesn't know about you." She arches a pierced eyebrow. "That makes it sound like we're having an affair."

"You wish."

"Obviously. But anyway, there are forums, places people post about all kinds of shitty situations they're in. There's even a board where people can arrange for hitmen."

A bolt of panic shoots through me that, for the first time in weeks, has nothing to do with my impending fifteen minutes of baking show fame. I drop my half-eaten pie on the counter. "Please, please tell me you're not advertising me on hitman Reddit."

"Dude. I'm not an idiot." She levels me with a look that's zero-bullshit and holds it until I nod.

"So what, then?"

"Some of the people who post there are really desperate. In all the places, not just the hitman board. I dig around, get a feel for what they have going on, and if it's something I think you can help with, I get to know them, and they either end up on the maybe list or the not-our-division list."

"So you're basically my murder middleman?"

"I like to think of it more as criminal concierging. I connect people who provide valuable services—you—with the people who need servicing."

"Anonymously?"

She nods and pulls a pair of phones out of her messenger bag. The one with the purple case I recognize as hers, but it's the second one that she swipes through and slides over to me. On the screen is a graphic rendering of my PBG button, a kitschy slice of cherry pie wrapped in a Pies Before Guys banner. Whereas the ones I give out have contact information stuck on the back, this graphic has a phone number—presumably the burner's—on the front along with a string of letters and numbers I don't recognize.

She takes the phone back, saying, "So obviously we don't want this floating around all willy-nilly, so I've added identifier codes to each one that links it to the recipient. That way even if it's forwarded as a referral, it can still be traced back to the original client."

It's more of a digital trail than I'm comfortable with, but at the same time, it's not the worst option either.

She taps the phone. "All communication is through here. It was bought with cash and only topped up with prepaid cards, also bought with cash. The number is only used for this, so no cross-contamination."

There's a hopeful eagerness in her eyes as she watches me digest the information.

"You definitely should've talked to me about this first," I say.

"Would you have stopped me?"

"Yes."

She shrugs merrily. "Well, I'm a firm believer in asking forgiveness rather than permission."

"Yeah, I'm aware," I say wryly, remembering the trouble that attitude got us all into a year ago.

"This was more efficient. We didn't have to argue about it, I did it the safest way possible, and now you have a whole list of people who need help who wouldn't have been on your radar without me."

She's not wrong, and when I tell her so, she beams.

"I'll forward all the details to the PBG account. Unless you want to give me your contract and I can wrap it up for you, make you a whole itinerary."

"Nope, that's where we're drawing the line," I say, hoping to rein her in before she incorporates my whole business and appoints herself CEO. "I'm willing to count you as the referral on these, but official order communication has to be through me. And I can't promise you I'll take everyone on your list."

"As long as you promise to look at them."

"I will. And while I'm obviously happy to help whoever I can, I think it's best if you hold off on recruiting for a while."

"Well yeah, obviously. It's not like you can be making murder pies while you're becoming the next FoodTV star—"

"I'm not becoming a star," I interrupt. "This is one and done. I want to get that money and get out. It's not like I'm going to become a household name. Seriously, can you name a single non-celebrity contestant of a FoodTV show? Exactly. And if I don't win, it'll still be like the pie contest—I'll get a nice spike in orders from the publicity, and that alone will be worth it."

She waves off my protest. "But just think, if you win and you don't have to keep doing the farmers' markets and Frank's, you can travel all over the country and we can line up pie orders wherever you want to go. The word-of-mouth is awesome, don't get me wrong, but it has a short reach." She waggles the phone at me. "But online we have the whole world at our fingertips."

It's a scary thought, not least of all because it feels dangerous, being so proactive. It's one thing to let clients come to me, but it's another thing to seek them out. I have a list of lines I never cross, and choosing targets on my own is one of them. That feels like a slippery slide to serial-killer-ville.

I know what I do isn't exactly wholesome, but it's not wrong either. Like the other women in my family, I've been given a gift. While they could work helpful, uplifting magic into hairstyles or sewing projects, I work magic into pies.

And it's definitely helpful.

Sometimes it's a hit of comforting nostalgia or sharpened focus. The magic is usually tailored to the place I'm serving the pies, positive punches of emotions that work on anyone, but PBG pies are different.

Those pies are for women who are out of options, and like Melly said, it's a valuable service. But it isn't without gray areas.

It would be easy to mistake what goes in them as poison, but it isn't. Poison is tangible, it's dangerous, and it doesn't discriminate.

A murder pie does.

The magic that goes into a murder pie is specifically tailored for an individual recipient, a blend of the most potent pleas to stop that exists.

And for some men, the kind of men I'm called to bake for, the only thing that can stop them is death.

Chapter Three

The nice thing about living in an RV is you don't have to pack in advance.

I give Zoe a nudge with my foot to dislodge her from her spot in front of the fridge and open it.

The only thing I need to worry about bringing is ingredients, both for the pie deliveries Melly arranged and for the show.

Part of the application process included deciding in advance what we would be baking for the craft and creative challenge so they could have everything ready. This was, of course, revealed only after we signed the mountain of NDAs stating we couldn't discuss any of the challenge categories, components, or even our own bakes. But that's okay, because it means we aren't going in blind, and for me, that's making all the difference.

The majority of the ingredients I'll be using for the two weeks—assuming I last the full two weeks—are things the show could easily source, but there are a few I'm bringing with me.

Noel's cider, for one.

When he first inherited Hollow Hill Orchard, it was a failing money pit his uncle, the co-owner, wanted to sell. But Noel had a vision and grew the rambling orchard into a thriving business, part New England farm stand and part craft cidery. It was his apples that took my pie all the way to the state finals last year, so it's only natural that I take his apples all the way to TV stardom.

I check the prepped pie crusts and decide I have enough to get through deliveries. Several of the pies are already waiting in the freezer along with a bag of frozen currants, but a few will be made on the road.

The drive to Longborough Estate, a sprawling historical manor house in North Carolina, is thirteen hours without stops, but thanks to Melly's legwork, we have a lot of stops.

A knock at the door pulls my attention from the fridge, and Zoe's happy woof lets me know who it is.

"It's open," I call, and Noel climbs the narrow steps into my tiny kitchen. At six foot three, he seems to fill the space despite being all arms and legs and lank.

"I come bearing honey," he says, depositing a box on the counter.

I riffle through the jars of liquid amber and pale yellow granules. "You're the best." I stretch up on tiptoes to kiss his cheek, and he grins.

"I try." Zoe plonks herself between us, and Noel bends to ruffle her ears. "Is there anything else you need from the orchard?"

"Nope, I think we're good." I tuck the honey into one of the locking cabinets so it won't slide around during the drive. "You're sure you still want to come?"

He gives me a mock-offended look. "You doubting my road trip worthiness? You wound me."

"I'm just giving you an out in case you want it," I say. "You've barely managed two days away from the orchard since the cidery opened, never mind two weeks."

"Work-life balance," he says. "You should look into it."

"Real funny."

He pins me with those warm brown eyes. "Of course I want to go. Plus Zoe and I are going to have all sorts of adventures while you're filming, aren't we, Zo?"

She thumps her tail at her name, and I'm again struck by how lucky I am that he likes her as much as she likes him. For so long it was only me and her, constantly on the road, and I never really expected that to change. But what started as a short stay in Turnbridge, Massachusetts, turned into so much more. I found a community that welcomed not only my pie van but me too.

I found a family, something I thought I would never have again after my parents died when I was in high school. But Frank, Juan, Noel, and yes, even Melly, with her constant meddling, have become my new family. It doesn't replace what I've lost, but it gives me something to hold on to, something that grounds me, keeps me rooted in a way I never expected to want.

"I appreciate you taking her. I know Juan would've, but at least this way I'll be able to see her on Sunday. This is the longest we've ever been apart."

The way he looks at me doesn't make me feel even remotely stupid for the lump in my throat. "We'll be fine," he says. "She'll get to stay in her own home, and you know she's going to have a ball with my cousin's dogs."

When I told Noel where we'd be filming, he jumped at the chance to accompany us. He has family in North Carolina that he hasn't seen in ages and figured this was the perfect excuse to get me to agree. He was mostly right. I would've been happy to have him along regardless, but this way I don't have to feel guilty about wasting two whole weeks of his life just to have someone to share the drive with.

"Okay. We'll set off first thing in the morning."

"You're staying at mine tonight, right?"

“What, you’re not going to have enough of me over the next two days?” He pulls me into a hug. “I don’t think it’s possible to ever have enough of you.”

“You’re ridiculous,” I say, but I can’t help my grin.

“Ridiculously smitten.” And with that, he replaces the grin with a kiss.

* * *

We leave with the sunrise, driving south. I take first shift, because it is my truck after all. Zoe is curled on the bench seat between us. It’s early enough that traffic is nonexistent as we leave Massachusetts. We stop for donuts in Connecticut, at the kind of cheerful shop I’d love to spend the day in. We buy more than we strictly need, and I let Noel drive while I ready the first of our deliveries.

Since we’re only in New Jersey, this one hardly counts as outside my usual range, but Melly was right—this girl needed a pie.

The pie in question is dark chocolate pecan praline, not a summer pie by any stretch, but decadent enough for that not to matter. The crust is infused with ground pecans, and instead of sugar, it’s sweetened with blitzed caramel brittle. A thick layer of dark chocolate ganache is topped with the kind of creamy caramel pecan mixture you’d die for even if it weren’t filled to the brim with magic.

The man in question, well, he’s a special kind of garbage—a local school board member leading a campaign to put cops in the district’s K–12 schools to ensure kids aren’t given access to anything that contradicts his ultraconservative agenda. But that isn’t what earned him a pie. No, he’s getting this pie for what he did to his daughter.

We find a strip mall near-ish to the delivery address and park so I can unhitch Penny. It’s one thing to make murder-pie deliveries in broad daylight, but it's another thing doing it with a pink RV in tow.

"You along for the ride?" I ask Noel.

"I'll sit this one out, let Zoe stretch her legs a bit," he says, grabbing her leash.

"Okay. I won't be long." I kiss him and Zoe both good-bye and place the pie on the passenger seat. The white box is tied with pink-and-white twine, same as my farmers' market pies, but this one doesn't have the identifying Pie Girl sticker that adorns those orders.

I check the PBG account for the address and plug it into my GPS. It brings me to a tan colonial on a street full of different-colored clones, like a builder bought the whole road and only knew how to make one kind of house.

There's an American flag hanging by the front door and a *Back the Blue* sign stuck in the front lawn next to a *Save Our Schools* sign adorned with red Xs over books, pride flags, and black fists.

There is no part of me that feels guilty for this.

I ring the bell, and a woman with a sharp blonde bob and a penchant for too much bronzer answers. I smile brightly to hide my surprise.

"Can I help you?" she asks.

I raise the box. "Pie delivery."

"I didn't order—"

Before she can finish, a teenage girl comes barreling down the stairs. "I did," she says, pushing past her mother. She takes the box from me with steel in her blue eyes. "Thank you." The look that passes between us says everything those two words can't. She turns to her mother, her smile as bright as my own. "It's for Dad's birthday. Chocolate pecan."

Her mother looks surprised. "Oh, honey, that's lovely. It's about time you ease up on him."

As she ushers her daughter back inside, I force myself to keep my feelings off my face until I'm back in the truck. For a split second, I wish the pie would work on the mother too, because she knows. She knows and she's sided with her husband instead of her own child.

But it won't. It's another of the lines I never cross. There are enough people killing women in this world. I won't be one of them, no matter how much they may deserve it.

Chapter Four

The rest of the pie deliveries go smoothly. There's only one left, the North Carolina client who requested a delivery that coincides with the return leg of the trip. It'll be an easy enough stop to make on the way home.

Regardless of how far I make it in the competition, I'll be at Longborough Estate for the entire two weeks. It's supposed to help keep a lid on the results.

Noel and I binged the popular British series this competition is supposed to be an American take on, but it only drove home how different the logistics are going to be. The British show films one episode per weekend, and the bakers are allowed to talk to their families about the results. In fact, they usually use the footage of each week's winner's phone call home as part of the episode. Anyone cut from the competition simply stops showing up.

For us it will be different. The entire season is being filmed in two weeks, with only a single day off, and we are stuck there the whole time.

I can only hope I won't get cut the first day, because I can't imagine having to sit around stewing in that kind of failure.

We find a campground to park at for the night, and after we grab dinner in town, I set about preparing.

I have two suitcases I borrowed from Juan, one for clothes, one for supplies. We need to have enough outfits for nine episodes, which means I'm pretty much taking my entire wardrobe with me. I thought maybe we'd get chef coats with the show's logo or something, but apparently having our own clothes helps to characterize us. So said the packet, anyway.

The dresses take up more room than I'd like, and I'm forced to use the bigger suitcase to accommodate all the full skirts. I chuck in pajamas, toiletries, and a pair of navy Keds. Between those and the white ones I'll wear there, I should be covered.

The ingredient case gets packed with a bit more care. I wrap each jar of honey and bottle of cider in the frilly aprons my grandmother made and nestle them in tight so they won't rattle around. I add a canister of roasted sugar, knowing I'm going to burn through it quickly but wanting it along anyway. I tuck a mutilated whisk and my favorite rolling pin in on the side, the French one with the tapered ends that makes rolling out pie dough a breeze, and zip the case closed.

I'm as ready as I'll ever be.

* * *

The Longborough Estate is a *lot*. To call it grand is an understatement.

"Damn," Noel says as we turn onto the main drive.

"It's like a *Downton Abbey* set. I didn't think we even had mansions like this here."

"Mansion? I think you mean castle."

He's not wrong. The stately stone facade sprawls across expanses of vibrant green lawn, elaborate wings reaching forward to flank the manicured courtyard. We drive past the white fountain in the center and stop in front of the main entrance.

I'm suddenly very self-conscious about the age and state of my battered old pickup.

"Ready?" Noel asks, searching my face.

I plaster on a brave smile. "As I'll ever be."

"You're going to do great."

"Let's hope so." My heart is racing with the reality of what I'm about to embark on. Not just a baking competition. A prime-time FoodTV series.

"Call me when you're settled?"

"Of course."

He gets out and retrieves my bags from the bed of the truck. I turn to Zoe and bury my face in her neck, scratching her all over. "You be a good girl," I tell her, unexpected tears stinging my eyes. "I'll see you soon."

She wags her tail happily at the attention, unaware that I'm about to leave her for two whole weeks.

Part of me wonders if it's too late to back out, but before I can voice it, one of the massive wooden doors opens and a harried-looking woman gestures for me to hurry up.

I recognize her from the diner filming. Kate.

I give Zoe one last pat and get out of the truck, where Noel immediately envelops me in an embrace. "Knock 'em dead," he whispers, then pulls back abruptly. "Not dead-dead. You know. Metaphorically dead."

I laugh, and some of the apprehension drains away. "I promise." I kiss him once, fiercely, and take the handles of my bags. "Here goes nothing."

I don't look back as I climb the steps to the entrance, because I might crumble if I see Zoe's face in the window. I know Noel will understand.

Kate holds the door wider, radiating impatience. "Come along. You're nearly late," she says, shooing me forward. "The next contestant is due any minute, and I'm under strict orders to keep you all separated." She consults a clipboard as she leads me to an elevator tucked into an alcove and hands me a key card. "You're in room two twenty-one, and you're to stay there until called for the welcome reception at five. There will be drinks and apps, and yes, it's going to be filmed, so someone will be by to check your makeup beforehand."

"My makeup?"

"Yes. No one goes on camera without at least a bit of powder. Trust me."

The elevator glides open and I step in, realizing I have no choice but to do as she says. Before the door can close, she steps in with me, pausing the lift. "I'll need your phone before you go up."

"Right." I knew this was coming, but that doesn't mean I like it. Even though there are plenty of access protections on it, it still feels like handing over a bomb that could explode my life.

She pockets it and steps back into the hall. "You'll be briefed about phone rules during the orientation this evening. The landline in your room connects to the rest of the estate, so if you need anything, please consult the extension list provided."

As the doors slide shut, I have the uncomfortable feeling that the estate is about to swallow me whole.

* * *

The room is, without question, the poshest place I've ever been. The thick carpet feels like the densest cloud, and the bed is draped in swaths of luxe bedding. When they said they'd be putting us up at the estate for the duration of filming, I somehow believed that meant servants' quarters or a nearby motel, not the actual lap of luxury. I looked this place up online and know exactly what it costs to rent this place out. I figure there's got to be some kind of deal because of the publicity the show will bring, but I'm not one to look a gift horse in the mouth, especially when I spot a claw-foot tub the size of Penny in the en suite.

I will definitely be soothing my preshow jitters in there later.

For now, I set about unpacking my meager bag. Since I have time to kill, I iron and hang all the dresses so they'll be ready to go. Even the hangers are high-end—padded and wrapped in soft velvet.

Hell, maybe it's worth getting eliminated early just for the chance to swan around and relax in this grandeur.

There's a balcony off the bedroom and I step out, admiring the sweeping back gardens.

"Amazing, isn't it?" comes a voice so out of nowhere that I nearly topple over the railing.

I turn to see another girl on the balcony to my right, and she giggles at the state of me.

"God, I'm so sorry, I didn't mean to scare you. Although I'm glad I'm not the only one jumping out of my skin. It's the nerves, right? Like you thought you were prepared, but now that it's here and we're actually doing this, it's like—aagh!" She makes a face, and I know exactly what she means. "I feel like three anxious Chihuahuas in a trench coat, you know?"

"Same," I say. "I think it'll be better once we start baking, though. It's the anticipation that's hard."

"You're so right," she says, propping her forearms against the railing so she can lean closer. She has white-blonde hair streaked through with pale-blue highlights and teal cat-eye glasses. "Were you greeted by the scary welcoming committee downstairs? I felt like I was back in Catholic school and she was going to whack my knuckles if I did anything wrong. I'm Nell, by the way. Nell Rogers."

"Daisy. And I think we're actually breaking one of the rules by introducing ourselves already, but I won't tell if you don't."

Her hands fly to her face in a comic display of panic. "Oh my god, you're right! I wasn't even thinking! I just saw someone else and thought, finally, someone who understands!"

"Well, I don't think they'll kick us off for this."

"I hope not. Oh, I can't think about getting kicked off. It's going to do my head in."

Before I can say anything else, a polite knock sounds at my door and I get that same feeling Nell described, like we're about to be punished for doing something wrong. "I think makeup's here," I say. "I'll catch up with you later, yeah?"

"Oh, that'd be great. It was nice *not* meeting you yet!" she says with a cheeky wave.

I slip back into my room and open the door to find the prettiest man I've ever laid eyes on.

"Okay, darling, let's get you set," he says, pushing past me with an air of competent authority. He drops a black bag on the desk and gives me a very obvious once-over. "I'm Julian, and first, love the style. The dress is divine. Second, we're mostly camera-proofing everyone's regular style, but for a price, I'm willing to take requests."

I laugh. "I think camera-proofing should do the trick, unless you want to be paid with pie."

"Honey, by the time these two weeks are over, I'll never want to see another pie as long as I live." He points to the desk chair. "Park your buns."

I do, and he gets to work dusting powder across my face and giving my eyeliner a boost.

"We'll do this every morning before the first portion starts, nice and quick," he says, "then a touch-up after lunch if needed. Once you're baking, if you cry or sweat or in any other manner destroy my work, that's on you. Filming will not stop for makeup mishaps."

"I'm not planning to cry over cake."

He gives me a pitying look and shakes his head. "Honey, someone always ends up crying over cake."

Chapter Five

The welcome reception is choreographed to within an inch of its life.

A phone call to our rooms signals we're free to make our way to the atrium, and we all converge at the top of the stairs at roughly the same time. Camera operators wait on the landing to film our first looks at each other, and we exchange all the nervous, hopeful, guarded glances they expect.

The first thing I notice is that this is most definitely not cast the way the British show is. Part of the charm of that one is that the contestants all look like real people, from all walks of life, ranging in age from high schoolers to retired grandparents.

This is not that.

The twelve people surrounding me have a polished, TV-ready air that has more to do with their natural good looks than any camera-proofing makeup.

I can't help feeling like the odd one out, but I realize that with my blue-and-white swing dress, I probably look like as much of a character as any of them.

When Nell spots me, she smiles, and it's nice having even this tiny touchstone of familiarity in the sea of strangers.

Everyone murmurs polite hellos and nods of greetings as we're ushered down the stairs in a pack.

At the atrium, we're greeted by staff with trays of drinks, and I don't think I've ever been so relieved to see a glass of wine in my life. I'm not usually a big drinker, but the pressure of meeting a crowd of strangers while cameras are recording every interaction has me quite happily reaching for a bit of Dutch courage.

Nell immediately beelines to my side, both hands clutching the stem of her wineglass. "I don't even like white," she whispers with less subtlety than she's probably hoping for. "I just know if I have red, I'll probably spill it all over!"

"Thanks. That's making me feel real solid about my choice," I say, clinking my glass to hers. I hold out a hand, and after a moment of fumbling, she shakes it. "Nice to officially meet you, Nell."

"You too," she says. "Aagh, this is so overwhelming!"

"Should we mingle?" I ask, eyeing the rest of the competition.

"Do we have to?"

"Probably. Don't think it makes for good TV if we stay standing in the corner."

"I wish there was a dog," she says. "I'm always better at parties when there's a dog. Or a cat. Something to pet. Something not human."

"I know what you mean," I say, starting to move away from our spot at the edge of the room. "This is the first time I've ever left my dog alone for more than a day in my whole life. I wish I could've brought her."

"That would've been great," she agrees, hardly noticing that we're making our way into the fray.

The current hub of activity is the antipasto table, where a group is picking at the offerings and making small talk. One of the men, tall and dark skinned with perfectly tailored dress pants, is asking a pair of women about their baking backgrounds.

"I have a black-market cookie business," the wiry woman with a wild mass of black curls says. Her accent positively screams New York. "If I win this thing, I can move it out of my kitchen into a proper storefront, do some real business." She clocks our arrival and shifts to include us in the conversation. "Hi there. Victoria Rossi, but everyone calls me Vic." She points at the man and light-skinned Black woman in turn. "Derek and Courchesne. Derek's a banker in real life, so that automatically makes him the villain, and we're about to find out where Courchesne fits into the cast."

"I don't think I'm the villain," Derek interjects, offering the kind of charismatic smile that's made for Hollywood.

"No villain ever thinks they are," Vic says with a dismissive wave, and I feel a momentary zing of recognition. I certainly don't think I'm a villain, but I can't help wondering what Vic would say about me if she knew about Pies Before Guys. "So Courchesne, cake girl, I take it?"

Courchesne spreads her arms so her T-shirt is on full display. *The Real Ace of Cakes* is printed in a glittery black, gray, white, and purple ombré across her chest. "I have an online baking channel, and yes, I do cakes, both for the obviousness of it and because cake is the superior baked good."

I laugh, and Derek cocks his head slightly. "Okay, that's awesome," I say. "I'm looking you up for the pun alone."

Derek shifts his weight onto his back leg. "I'm missing something."

"Asexual pride colors," Courchesne says, gesturing to her shirt. She sweeps an arm down the length of her. "Asexual person. Asexual cooking show."

"About cake?" he asks.

"Of course! All aces know cake is better than sex," she says.

"It's on the nose," Vic says, "but I'm with Lucy here. I like it."

I realize that it's me she's referring to as Lucy. "Daisy, actually. And this is Nell."

Nell gives Derek a shy smile. "Don't worry, I didn't get it either."

Vic shakes her head, still focused on me. "Nope, in my head you're Lucy, as in *I Love*. It's not changing, not if you keep dressing like that."

Her brash New York accent makes it sound harsher than the twinkle in her eyes indicates, so I cock a hip and say, "Fair enough, Brooklyn."

"So what's your deal?"

"Pie. Although I don't have a fun name for it, just Pie Girl Productions." Something tells me they'd appreciate the Pies Before Guys moniker, but that's certainly not something I'm sharing while camera operators are roaming around, catching our introductions. "I mostly sell at farmers' markets around Massachusetts."

"Wait," Courchesne says, flapping a hand. "Tell me about you. As a person. I bet I can give you a punny name."

I'm saved from having to figure out exactly what to share with her—that I kill bad men with good pies?—by Kate.

"If you could all make your way to the dining room and take a seat, we'll get started on the orientation," she calls in a voice that requires no amplification.

We do, taking seats around the single long table that's set for us. Nell settles in on my right, and a white, chestnut-haired woman who quietly introduces herself as Chloe sits to my left. Before we can make introductions with the bakers across the table, there's a piercing whistle and we all turn to the front of the room.

"Welcome, bakers, to the inaugural season of *Bake My Day*. For those who don't know, I'm Kate, the production assistant. I'm here to make sure everything runs smooth as buttercream this week. It is with great pleasure that I introduce the producer herself, Abigail Whitley, and your host, Natalie Stockwell."

The producer is an overcaffeinated woman in her fifties, whose air of perpetual rushing is completely at odds with the relaxed ease with which Natalie moves. The host has a ginger pixie cut, black glasses, and an impish smile.

"Welcome, bakers," she says with a big wave. Her dark jeans are cuffed above black Converse, and she is hands down the most relaxed person in the room. "You're going to hear plenty of me talking over the next two weeks, along with invading your space and sampling your sweets, so I'll leave you in peace for the mo. The best advice I can give you is to relax and enjoy the ride."

She steps to the side to give the producer the floor.

"Everything you're about to hear is extremely important, so pay attention. I have no desire to repeat myself," Abigail says. Around the table, everyone sits up a little straighter. She makes Kate look cuddly by comparison. "For the next two weeks, I own you. You are to adhere to all of the rules, all of the schedules, and most importantly, all of my orders."

I risk a glance at Nell, who looks terrified.

"Filming will start precisely at eight each morning," Abigail continues, pacing as she talks. "Your makeup artist will be at your rooms between seven fifteen and seven forty-five. You must be there; otherwise I absolutely will send you on camera looking like a greasy mess, and that will not endear you to viewers.

"We film one episode per day, so whatever you choose to wear in the morning has to last through the show. If you cover yourself in cake batter, that's on you, and depending on the episode's challenge, you could be in for a long night of filming in filth.

"Every episode will open with the same establishing shot: you lot walking down the grand staircase. Therefore, it's important that you're actually on said staircase in time to roll film. That means seven fifty-five at the latest. Someone from set prep will be around after dinner to collect any special ingredients you've brought with you. You are to bring nothing onto set except yourself, your apron, and your A game.

"While filming, Natalie and the judges will be circulating and asking you questions. You are to answer them directly, without looking at the camera. If you notice you have a camera in your vicinity and no one is asking you anything, feel free to narrate your process, and for the love of god, make sure you're calling your oven pulls. It is critical we have shots of everything that goes in and comes out. This isn't the Disney Channel, so I don't care if you swear, but if you make *fuck* your entire personality, we're going to have a problem. A sprinkle of censored words can add color, but an entire stream of bleeps is unacceptable." She pauses to let everything sink in.

One of the guys across the table, the burly bearded one who looks like he belongs on one of those lumberjack shows, raises a finger as if to ask a question.

Abigail stops midpace. "Are you volunteering to be my problem child, Grant? Because I don't recall asking for interruptions."

He lowers his hand and folds his arms over his broad chest, a stony look on his face as she continues.

"Now, every day one of you is getting cut from the show—and on the wild card day, it will be two. That's a fact. You're allowed to be upset about it, but you're not allowed to interfere, in any way, with filming after it happens. We need you here for the finale, and there are plenty of things to occupy your time, including the on-site gym, indoor pool, and multiple libraries. Meals will still be communal, so you don't need to hide in your rooms; you just need to stay the hell away from the ballroom during filming—and that includes the grounds immediately outside. The viewers will think you've quite literally been sent home after getting cut, and we don't want to spoil that illusion by having you wander into the background of a shot."

As she speaks, kitchen staff begin slipping in to set up chafing dishes on the table running along the back wall. Abigail doesn't acknowledge them, but the scents drifting toward us make it difficult for us to do the same.

"Lastly," Abigail says, "I'm aware several of you are unhappy with the phone policy, but it's strict for a reason. This isn't the first show we've shot on an accelerated schedule, and I'm not having anyone muck things up because their codependent spouse has to know every detail of their day. Calls are permitted when we're not filming, but they will be monitored and they should be limited. Anyone caught breathing a word of the results, challenge details, or anything remotely pertaining to the show will have their entire existence scrubbed from the footage and given the kind of fine they'll have to sell organs to finance. If you have questions about this or anything else, now would be the time."

No one raises a hand, not even the bearded guy who actually did have a question before.

Abigail claps her hands together. "Lovely. Aprons will be delivered to your rooms while you eat. Please confirm they have your name on it. We don't need any confusion in the morning. Laundry will collect them every other day and return them to you the following morning. Enjoy your meal, get some rest, and be ready to bake your little asses off tomorrow."

Chapter Six

Breakfast is a self-serve affair of scrambled eggs, pancakes, bacon, and an array of pastries and cereals. It's basic morning fare, but if last night's dinner was any indication, it will all be well prepared.

I take an almond croissant, stomach already buzzing with nervous bees, and riffle through the tea selection for mint. I brew it strong with extra sugar.

Our table from last night is set with pitchers of orange juice and water, and several contestants are already busy tucking into breakfast. Tony, a quiet library worker in his thirties, sits at the very end, turned slightly toward the door, and is radiating enough introverted stay-away energy that I leave him to it.

I take a seat in the middle, close enough to overhear conversation but with a buffer seat on either side so everyone has a bit of privacy. I'm sure preshow nerves are hitting everyone one way or another.

Chloe, the elementary school teacher with chestnut hair, leans across the table, excitement and fear doing a tango across her face. "Can you believe it's finally here?"

"It still feels a little like I'm showing up to a test I haven't studied for," I admit, breaking off the end of my croissant. "Naked."

"I know what you mean," she says. "I can't wait to just get in there and get to it."

She's pretty in a classic way, with the kind of open friendliness that lives up to her midwestern roots. "I wonder what we're starting with. I don't think it's in the order we had to submit our creative plans in, because I was talking to Matt last night and he said his first creative was listed as pâtisserie, but mine was pies."

"Mine was cake," I say, confirming the theory.

"I hope we get a cupcake challenge," she says, smiling automatically at the girl who joins us. "That's my specialty."

"Oh bless your heart," the newcomer—Ainsley, if I remember right—says, sweeping her honey-colored hair over one shoulder as she sits. "Cupcakes were so trendy."

If Chloe catches the barb in that southern greeting, she doesn't show it, but I can't help but bristle on her behalf.

I point at Ainsley with the end of my croissant. "And what's your specialty again?"

"Oh, I do a little bit of everything," she says, prodding her fruit salad with her fork before settling on a strawberry. "I think a show like this is stacked against the specialists, don't you?"

"I think good baking is good baking."

"Exactly," Chloe says. "It's science, after all. If you can follow a recipe for cake, you can follow one for brownies. But it will be fun to do the things we like best."

"I agree," I say. "Hopefully I make it to pie week."

"I hope I make it to filming," Freddie—a self-proclaimed fondant wizard from Albany—moans, flopping into the chair next to me. He flails his mug around in anguish. "Can you believe they only have mugs? No tumblers, no glasses, and most importantly, no ice. How am I even supposed to function without iced coffee right now?"

"You could probably ask for ice," I point out, but he drops his head onto the table.

"No, I'm just going to die of panic and lack of caffeine."

Chloe giggles and I pat his back. "There, there."

Ainsley stands, leaving her barely touched fruit behind. "Okay, this is too much drama too early in the morning. Besides, makeup is due soon. Don't want to be late!"

"She's the villain, right?" Freddie mumbles. "She has to be."

"I don't think baking shows have villains," Chloe says.

"Not according to Vic," I explain. "She has a theory that we're all typecast and it's just a matter of figuring out who's who. She pinned Derek as the villain, though, because he's a pretty banker."

"He is pretty, isn't he?" Freddie says, sitting up.

Chloe's eyes widen and Freddie groans. "No. No. It can't be my life that he's literally behind me right now."

"He is literally behind you right now," Chloe confirms in a stage whisper. "Don't worry, he's not stopping."

"That doesn't make it better," Freddie says, pushing his chair back and sweeping up his mug with a disgruntled flourish. "I need to go hyperventilate before we start."

After he's gone, Chloe says, "Is it wrong that I feel better for being less nervous than that?"

"Not at all," I say.

"Do you think it's true, that we're all characters?"

"Probably, but I don't think it's that clear-cut. I have no idea who I am."

"Me either."

"You're the nice one, definitely," I say, and she blushes, confirming the casting without question.

* * *

Most of us arrive at the top of the stairs by seven forty-five, and not a one of us looks tired.

Abigail is on the landing below us, consulting with Natalie and a camera guy. She looks up at us and counts us off, marking each baker with a flick of her finger. I do the same, noting that we're still waiting on Ainsley, Chloe, Courchesne, and Grant, the big bearded guy.

Courchesne is the first of the stragglers to appear, a pair of tiny pride flags—ace and trans—pinned on either side of her apron's embroidered name badge. When the last of the group, Ainsley, shows up, Abigail snaps to attention.

"Bakers," she barks. "When I say no later than seven fifty-five, I mean no later than seven fifty-five. I do not mean seven fifty-eight. We are on a bloody schedule here! Split up, half to the right of the stairs, half to the left." She waits while we arrange ourselves. Nell sticks close to my side. "When I say go, you converge on the stairs. No one runs, no one shoves. You follow Natalie straight to the ballroom and find your stations. Your names are on the back of the laminated recipe card on each worktop. Do not touch the recipe card. Do not mess with your equipment. Do nothing but stand there and look pleasant until Natalie tells you otherwise." She says something inaudible to the camera operator and steps down a few steps. "On my mark. Mark!"

As a pack, we make our way down the stairs, the camera operator leading us with backward steps. Natalie scurries ahead, pointing in dramatic gestures where we need to go before stopping in front of a doorway and another camera operator to begin her intro. "Today we're excited to welcome our competitors to the ballroom, where they'll be faced with challenges ranging from the familiar to the exotic." We file past her one by one, and I pray the camera doesn't pick up the pulse in my neck. It's hammering hard enough that I fear it might.

I lose track of her monologue once I'm in the ballroom. Fourteen stainless-steel benches are arranged in two rows, and I'm again hit with the reminder that this is not the British show I binged. Whereas their set is all pastel colors and kitsch, this is sleek metal and hard edges. Each station has a stand mixer, labeled canisters of ingredients, and an assortment of tools. A pair of burners are set into each worktop, and the ovens are tucked below. Industrial refrigerators are placed at intervals along the walls beside each row, and a long table is placed at the head of the stations, with our application photos set in a row along the front edge.

I take a deep breath, reminding myself that the stainless workbenches are the same as what Frank has in the diner, and find the one with my name on it.

I'm two back from the front, with the quiet guy in front of me. I turn to see Gemma, the youngest contestant at only nineteen, behind me. She gives me an excited wave and I smile at her. Derek takes the bench to my left, with Nell in front of him.

While the rest of the bakers find their stations, Natalie takes up her spot at the front and says, "Don't worry, bakers, we're not going to air you flailing around here. Just find your spots and get settled."

Abigail stands in the doorway, looking impatient. Two judges are with her, and I recognize the woman as Juliet Barnes. She's the closest thing to foodie royalty America has. An elegant sixty-five with steel-gray hair, she'd give Martha Stewart and the Barefoot Contessa both a run for their very hefty sums of money.

The other guy is her opposite in almost every way. Leland Graham is younger, for one, with the casual-cool swagger of a chef who's too talented to be labeled a hipster, despite the vibe.

Abigail has a phone to her ear and is gesturing angrily. We were told to look pleasant, so I do my best not to seem like I'm staring, but I can't miss her growled, "Well fucking find him!"

It feels like ages pass while we stand at our stations, exchanging occasional nervous glances. I wonder if everyone else is as tempted as I am to flip over the recipe card for a peek.

Eventually, Kate appears in the doorway with a well-dressed man in tow, and every trace of nerves vanishes at the sight of him, replaced by stone-cold panic.

I recognize that smarmy too-white smile and slicked-back hair.

And not from TV.

Abigail stabs a finger into his chest and says something I can't hear before stalking off.

It barely registers that the cameras are moving now, that Natalie is ushering the judges into their spots.

All I can look at is his face and pray that I'm wrong, that I'm not staring at Bryan Miller, the very man I'm supposed to deliver a pie to on my way home.

Chapter Seven

Natalie beams a smile at us. "Welcome, bakers, to your first ever challenge on *Bake My Day*. As usual, we'll begin with the mystery warm-up, where every baker will work off identical recipes to test their skills head-to-head. You'll have an hour and a half to complete this challenge, and I hope you'll find it a snap, as in gingersnap, because this week is cookie week!"

She pauses, and I know the cameras are getting reaction shots, so I make myself smile and share excited looks with the others. Vic looks genuinely thrilled to be starting with her specialty.

"Bakers, your recipe today comes straight out of the Big Apple, the iconic black-and-white cookies. Our judges, Juliet, Leland, and Bryan, will be looking for perfect textures, excellent flavor, and precise decorating, so bakers, do your thing!"

Bryan bloody Miller.

The very same Bryan Miller who has more than earned the mocha crunch pie sitting in Penny's freezer.

Fuck me.

Around the ballroom, bakers launch into action, and I shake myself out of my shock.

Later. I can deal with him later.

Right now, I have cookies to make.

Behind me, someone—I think Grant—says, "Are you serious?"

I flip the recipe card over and nearly echo him. Instead of a proper recipe card, it's a list of ingredients with three lines of instructions: *Make cookies. Prepare icings. Decorate cookies half black and half white.*

That's it. No oven temp, no bake time, no method.

I pull the black cloth off the ingredients and consider my plan of attack. I've seen black-and-white cookies before, so I know what they are, but I've never eaten one.

I crank the oven to 350, because that's always a safe cookie bet, and chuck the butter and sugar into the stand mixer to cream.

While it whips, I measure out my dry ingredients and sour cream, and right when I'm starting to feel comfortable, Natalie arrives at my bench with a camera. "Good morning, Daisy," she chirps. "Tell me, are you feeling good about this, or are your inner cookies crumbling?"

"A little of both," I say with a laugh. I'm mostly relieved that the judges have gone off with a camera operator to film whatever judge-y bits they need, but I don't say that. I'm rattled, not stupid.

"This isn't a cookie I've ever had before, so there's a certain element of winging it," I admit as I crack the first of my eggs into the bowl.

"Always an auspicious way to start things off! I wish you luck," Natalie says, moving on to her next contestant.

I hesitate with my sour cream, unsure if it goes in with the eggs or with the dry. I opt to alternate it with the dry and immediately panic when I realize how thick the batter is. I turn the mixer off as soon as it's combined, not wanting to make them tough.

The recipe doesn't indicate how many cookies we're supposed to end up with, so again, I wing it, making ten big ones. I mean, if I'm eating a cookie, I want it to be the size of my head.

"Going in," I say, popping the trays into the oven and setting a timer for a completely arbitrary ten minutes. I'd rather have it go off too early and need to reset than risk having burnt bottoms.

While the cookies bake, I wipe my worktop down and focus on the glaze. Instead of milk or butter, the icing is made with corn syrup and water, although the water is only marked *as needed*.

I mix the sugar, vanilla, and corn syrup together, holding the cocoa back. I fill a measuring cup with hot water, since it will need to dissolve the corn syrup and drizzle some in. I turn the mixer on, accidentally knocking the knob a couple clicks too far, and an explosion of powdered sugar puffs up around me. I slam the knob back to off, hoping no one noticed, but of course, a camera caught the whole thing.

"I'm trying to make my icing while the cookies bake, but instead I seem to have created a sugar bomb," I say, trying to channel the quirky calm-under-pressure all the contestants on the British show seem to have. I'm not sure it works, given that the entire front of my black apron is now dusted with white.

I turn the mixer on—slower this time—and add enough water to get a thick paste. I give it a taste, add a touch more vanilla than the recipe called for, and then scoop half of it into a bowl that I set aside. I add the cocoa, dark chocolate, and a bit more water to the mixer bowl and give it a whirl. It's not as dark as I'd like, but a taste says adding more cocoa is going to end in bitterness. Rats. Maybe I needed to take more of the vanilla out first.

My timer pings and I check the cookies. They're golden brown and already firm to the touch, so I pull them out, praying they're not overbaked and knowing that they probably are.

Behind me, there's a clatter followed by a curse, and the cameras whirl to capture the source. One of the operators holds a thumb up, and the others turn back to the rest of us. I cringe when

I see Chloe blowing on her fingers, the tips an angry red even from here, and flash her a sympathetic look.

"You good?" Courchesne asks from the station behind her.

"Yeah, just a burn, it's fine," she says.

In front of her, Ainsley smirks but doesn't take her eyes from her mixing bowl.

It feels like it takes hours for the cookies to cool enough for me to ice them, even though I know it's less than ten minutes. The sweet chocolate and vanilla scents swirling around the room are comforting, but not so much that I'm able to completely forget my Bryan dilemma.

When I accepted the order, I knew he was a wealthy restaurateur who took advantage of the women in his employ. I knew he beat his wife and how trapped she felt. I knew finding out about his secret dealings with a high-profile sex trafficker who had enough powerful connections to avoid conviction had been the thing to push her over the edge and into my in-box.

I knew he deserved a pie.

I did not know he was going to be a judge and that I would have to spend two weeks in his company before delivering said pie.

"Bakers, you have five minutes on the clock!" Natalie shouts, "Five minutes!"

I switch to the chocolate icing, trying to keep the halves as even as possible. If this woman knows that I'm Pies Before Guys, she's either government-level good at stalking or Melly let something slip.

Again.

"One minute, bakers!"

I arrange the cookies in rows on a long white plate that's not quite wide enough.

"Okay, bakers," Natalie says. "Let's get those cookies on the judges' table, right behind your photos, and we'll see who gets crowned cookie king or queen."

As we line up our bakes, I can see my cookies are by far the biggest. Shit. At least they're iced the right way. My place is also at the end of the table, which means I won't even be put out of my misery quickly.

"All right, folks," Natalie says in an off-camera voice. "This part is going to take longer than you probably expect, so hold it together, yeah? The whole thing won't air, but there'll be reaction shots of all of you, so try not to look bored."

"I don't think I can look bored when I'm this panicked," Gemma says, holding out her hands. "Look. They're still shaking and the challenge is over."

Natalie switches back to her camera voice. "Nothing is over until the judges have spoken," she says as the three file in.

There's a long moment while they peruse the table, making comments aimed at the camera.

"Well," Juliet says, moving to the first tray. "We have quite a range here. Let's get started, shall we?"

They pick up a cookie from the first tray.

"The icing is all wrong. When we said frost half the cookie with white icing, we meant half of each one, not half the batch," Leland says.

"Then they should've said that," Grant mutters.

"Texture is good, though," Bryan says. "But the flavor is off. The lemon zest is missing."

They move to the next one. "This is a textbook example of a black-and-white," Leland says, holding it up. "The icing is thick, the cookie is soft, and the texture is beautiful. Very nice."

They continue down the row, commenting mostly on icing patterns and texture. Finally, they get to mine. "These are quite large," Juliet says. "But the icing looks and tastes lovely."

"Too dry," Bryan says. "They're overbaked."

I feel my lip twitch with the beginnings of rage, because even though I know it's true, hearing him criticize me makes me want to eat glass. I know too much about him to feel any other way. He shouldn't be in this room.

The judges confer privately, and I wonder if I should tell someone. The accusation would mean nothing coming from me out of the blue, and I can't out his wife as the source of my information, not given what she's contracted me to do.

Plus there are cameras everywhere and the show is already under way. It's not like they're going to replace him now. I know the judges are staying at the estate too, but they're in an entirely different wing, so he shouldn't have any interaction with cast members outside of filming.

"Okay, bakers," Juliet says. "In twelfth place, we have these ones. Whose are they?"

Grant raises a single finger in response, his face impassive.

She indicates another plate. "Eleventh?"

Chloe raises a burned hand, cheeks as scarlet as her fingertips.

"It came down to the icing, dear. It was simply too runny and the drizzle pattern wasn't what we were looking for."

Juliet continues through the placing, and I'm shocked to land in a solid seventh.

"Our third place goes to these," Juliet says, and Freddie punches a fist in the air.

"I'll take that," he says happily.

"And in second place," Juliet says, allowing for a dramatic pause that will no doubt feature close-ups of Derek and Vic, the only two who haven't placed yet. "These here."

Derek smiles that red-carpet smile and nods, mouthing *thank you*.

"Which leaves us with Vic," Juliet says. "These were the quintessential New York black-and-white. Very well done, dear."

Vic is whisked away for a reaction shot, and she's grinning as she says, "I mean, it would've been a disgrace if I didn't come in first with this, you know? Cookies are my thing, and New York is my home."

Another camera gets Grant, whose stovepipe arms are still folded across his chest. "Of course I wish it had gone better, but it's a bake I wasn't familiar with. It is what it is."

The rest of us mill around, giddy with the relief at having survived the very first challenge.

Kate comes into the room and claps to get our attention. "Okay, bakers, Abigail is pleased with the footage we're seeing so far. You have a half-hour break, then we're back for the next segment. Don't be late."

I break away from the group and hurry after her retreating form. "Kate? Is it possible to sneak a phone call before we go back in?"

She shakes her head. "Save it for lunch. This is your chance to have a pee, grab a drink, not get caught up in outside business."

I want to argue, but it's not like I can exactly explain why my outside business is relevant to *Bake My Day* business. Not until I have more information. "Okay, sorry," I say, and rejoin the group.

The stone patio off the ballroom has been set up as a sort of cast lounge area, with clusters of tables and chairs scattered around. A single camera operator is the only nonbaker present.

I see Nell leaning against the waist-high wall, looking out at the grounds, and head over.

"Nice job," I say.

"I'll take a fifth in the first challenge, for sure," she says, beaming. "I think the next round is gonna be worse, though. It's scary enough baking with the cameras all over you, but I think the judges stay for the next two. I don't know if I can take Leland breathing down my neck. He makes Gordon Ramsay look like Tom Hanks."

I laugh, because she's not wrong, but I know he's not the real one to watch out for.

Not by a long shot.

Chapter Eight

The judges rove in a pack like culinary hyenas, zigzagging between contestants.

Our craft challenge is to present a cookie of our choosing, utilizing at least three flavor elements.

I can't help eavesdropping as they do their bit with Tony at the station in front of me.

He has a soft voice, but deep, and it carries more authority than I thought his slight frame could muster. "My cookies today are inspired by tea with my grandmother. They feature cardamom, cinnamon, and ginger biscuits with a lemon cream filling and will be served with a cup of sweet chai for dunking."

"You think you need the chai spices in both the cookies and the drink?"

"I think cookies are best served with tea, and the milkiness of the chai is complementary, not repetitive."

Leland nods. "We'll see."

"Good luck," Juliet says, before they move across the aisle to Nell. I try to beam as many good vibes to her as possible as Juliet asks her about her bake.

I busy myself with my prep work so I look well and truly busy when they get to me.

"Daisy, tell us about your cookie," Bryan says.

"I'm doing a cherry pie–inspired cookie with white chocolate and a twist of lime." I direct this more to Juliet and Leland than to him. I can't help it. I know it's something I'm going to have to get a lid on, but the realization of who he is is too fresh.

"I can't wait to try it," Juliet says, and they move off, leaving me to get to it.

It's a cookie I've practiced plenty, and I've had enough feedback from Noel, Juan, and the diner staff to feel confident about it. Even Frank liked them, and for a man who thinks putting nuts in chocolate chip cookies is too fancy, that's saying something.

Natalie breezes by as she banters with the bakers and steals nibbles of dough wherever she can. When I see she's doing it, I set aside a spoonful, amuse-bouche style, before traying up my cookies. I point to it when she arrives, and she gives a mock swoon for the camera. "Oh, this one knows how to get brownie points. Or should we say cookie points?" She pops it in her mouth and moans. "Oh, that's worth the risk of raw eggs any day." She makes to steal the tray I'm portioning dough onto, and I swat her away with my scoop.

Once the cookies are in the oven and the timer is set, I take a minute to look around and really absorb that I'm here, in front of cameras, on what is poised to become one of FoodTV's top baking series.

Surreal is an understatement, and that's without even factoring in the unexpected drama.

After the first challenge, everyone is more familiar with their stations and more relaxed. With many timers already set, several bakers are leaning against their worktops, chatting with the people around them.

If you could ignore the cameras, it almost has the air of the diner between rushes.

Even the sudden explosion of cursing.

Contestants and cameras alike turn toward the sound and find a royally pissed-off Vic.

"Who took my dough out of the refrigerator?" she barks, tray in hand.

Several cameras spin away from her, panning the rest of us as we look at each other.

"Oh no," Gemma murmurs, and I know it wasn't her; she's been rattling away behind me the whole time. Tony hasn't left his station either.

But I also haven't been paying attention. The question is, was it deliberate or was it accidental?

"Time?" Vic calls.

"Bakers, you have fifteen minutes. Fifteen minutes remaining!" Natalie trills.

"Fuck!" Vic slams the tray of dough onto her worktop, and Natalie scurries over.

"What do you need?" she asks, a camera at her heels.

"People to keep their hands off my shit," Vic snaps. She prods one of the martini-glass-shaped cookies with a finger and curses again. She yanks her ponytail out and resets it, pulling the elastic tight. "It's fine. They've gone too soft, they're gonna spread, but I'll manage."

"I know you will," Natalie says, and moves off to give her room to work.

My timer dings and I pull my cookies out, not wanting to believe that someone deliberately sabotaged Vic's challenge. Not on the first day.

The judges are scattered along the edges of the stations, watching us finish up, and I wonder if any of them saw what happened and, if so, why they didn't interfere. Surely they wouldn't stand by if someone was deliberately messing with another baker's stuff.

"Five minutes," Natalie calls, and there's a scramble as everyone rushes to finish plating. "At the end of those minutes, cookies better be at the end of your benches!"

I set mine in their place, trying to scope out everyone else's as they do the same. Vic looks absolutely furious, and even from here, I can see why.

"That's it, bakers!" Natalie calls, in full on-camera mode. "It's time to see who's our smartest cookie!"

The judges work their way through the offerings, condemning Derek's pistachio, white chocolate, and cranberry shortbreads as pedestrian, praising Ainsley's orange brandy snaps as a delight, and admitting Tony's chai-on-chai pairing is quite pleasant, if a bit homey.

Juliet deems mine "a nice riff on classic flavors," and Bryan says Freddie's look better than they taste and that Grant's are ambitious, but that's it.

Leland takes the lead on Vic, turning one of the sandwich cookies over in his hands. "I thought you were going for raspberry mint martini, not vague lollipop."

"The dough needed more time to chill."

"Yes, obviously," Leland says, snapping off a piece to sample.

"Flavors are good," Juliet says. "The mint is nicely balanced, and the raspberry in the cookie is sharp. Shame about the bake."

Vic nods once, sharply, and they finish the rest. Craft challenges won't be ranked on air, so it's a bit anticlimactic to be dismissed straight to lunch with a reminder that our makeup techs will be around before the afternoon session begins.

Almost everyone mills around for a bit, sampling each other's bakes and commiserating, but Vic storms off the minute we're released. I can't blame her. Cookies are her thing and I'm sure she expected to coast through this challenge.

"If Vic finds out who screwed up her dough, she's gonna kill them," Courchesne says as we make our way to the dining room. It's set in a self-serve buffet with meat, vegetarian, and vegan options, and everything looks delicious. I opt for the grilled veggie couscous, but all I can focus on is the calls I have to make. As much I might want to stay with this group and rehash our first morning of filming, I excuse myself as quickly as I can and go in search of Kate.

And can't find her anywhere.

Fine.

I have other options.

Our morning bakes have been gathered and brought into the dining room to serve as dessert, and I slip back in and grab a few of the best-looking ones before retreating to my room, just in case. I try Kate's extension but get no answer, and I'm not about to risk the wrath of Abigail by calling there.

I don't have to wait long before there's a knock at the door, and I let Julian in to do his magic.

"You've survived so far, I take it?" he asks, sifting through his powders for the correct one.

"Definitely could've been worse," I say. "I have a favor to ask, though."

"Oh, darling, please tell me we're not playing makeover when I still have three more people to see."

"We're not," I assure him. "And I do have a cookie bribe, if it helps."

"I'm listening."

"Can I borrow your phone? Just until you're done your rounds? Ours are in phone jail, and I can't find Kate."

"Ooh, is there a special someone you're already missing?"

"Something like that."

"Well, I've already told you you can't bribe me with sugar," he says, "but you can bribe me with intel."

"I'm listening," I say, deliberately mimicking him, and he gives me an admonishing swat with the makeup brush.

"Freddie. He's not one of mine, but I'd like to know more."

"Oh, really?" I say, unable to keep the grin off my face. "So a little spy work in exchange for phone time?"

"You facilitate my crushes, I facilitate yours. Deal?"

"Deal."

"You're a peach," he says, gathering his kit. "You have twenty minutes max."

"That's plenty," I promise.

When he's gone, I hesitate, though. Noel or Melly first?

Melly.

She doesn't answer, and I send her a text that I immediately delete out of the history. *Call this number, it's Daisy.*

She does, and I answer before the first ring finishes.

"The last pie," I say without preamble. "The one scheduled for our trip back. Did you tell the client that I'm on the show?"

"Nice to hear from you too," she says dryly. "And no, I thought it was supposed to be a secret."

"It was. So explain how I have a pie order for one of the very judges of that secret show."

There's silence, not even a crackle of background noise. Finally she says, "That's a big coincidence."

"It's a big coincidence that you set up."

"Coincidentally!" she insists. "I just thought it was convenient timing. Why is this my fault? Shouldn't *you* have verified it?"

"I didn't think *Is the target judging the baking show I'm competing on?* was a question I needed to have in my intake," I say. "You're sure you didn't let anything slip?"

"Nothing. Look, I learned my lesson last time. I want to help, for real, and I know to do that, I have to follow your rules. All anonymous, nothing that can identify you. Hell, I thought maybe it would help, having another layer in the mix."

I sigh. "Okay. It's just wild that he's actually here."

"What are you going to do?"

"Figure it out."

Chapter Nine

I'm halfway back to the ballroom when I hear the scream.

I break into a run, instinct propelling me forward.

Derek and Freddie are at my heels.

Natalie and Kate are at the entrance to the ballroom, blocking our entrance, but past them is Nell, her face ashen. Leland and Bryan are with her, their expressions mirroring hers.

I try to get through to get to Nell, because she's obviously distraught and the judges are being useless, but Kate steps forward, hands up.

"There's been an accident," Kate says. "Filming is going to be delayed for a bit."

"What kind of accident?" Derek asks.

Natalie has the same look of shock as Nell, and my heart kicks up.

"Please go back to your rooms," Kate says, louder now as others are starting to arrive, including the camera crew. Her phone lights up in her hand. "We should be up in a half hour, hour at most. Please, return to your rooms."

"I would like to know what's going on," Derek says, his voice a rumble that I'm sure brooks no arguments when he's at work but here only serves to annoy Kate.

Which I use to my advantage. While she's trying to placate him, I slip by her, ignoring Natalie's plea to stop.

Nell collapses into me, and I wrap my arms around her automatically. Before I can ask what's the matter, I see it.

No, not it.

Her.

Chloe is sprawled lifeless across the floor behind her station, chestnut hair spilling out around her, dark with blood. "Oh god," I whisper, and it's enough to break Nell. Her sobs echo through the empty ballroom.

I back away, pulling Nell with me.

Abigail storms into the ballroom. "You two, out, now," she commands, pulling the black cloth off the judges' table as she passes and draping it over Chloe's body with a crisp snap. "She's had an accident. Return to your rooms. We'll be calling you shortly."

I sweep my eyes around the ballroom, looking for any indication of what happened, but Chloe's worktop is clean and nothing appears out of place.

"Now!" Abigail barks.

"Okay," I murmur, more to Nell than to her. "We're going."

Nell's entire body is shaking as I lead her out. I bring her to my room, sit her on the bed, and hand her a cookie. If nothing else, the sugar will help.

"Tell me what happened," I say gently, moving the desk chair so I can sit in front of her.

Her hands, still clutching the cookie, tremble in her lap. "I don't know. I came down right after makeup, I thought I'd get settled, you know? I thought I was the first one there. But I wasn't." She scrapes her thumbnail against the edge of the cookie, one of Derek's shortbreads, and crumbs fall to the floor. "She was already gone."

"You didn't see anyone else? Crew? Other cast?"

She shakes her head. "There was nothing I could do."

"I know," I say, my heart a twisted knot in my chest as I mentally replay what I saw.

We're still sitting on the bed when the phone rings.

It's Kate. "Cast meeting in the dining room in ten minutes."

I hang up and relay the message to Nell. She wipes her eyes with the hem of her apron, and we make our way downstairs.

Courchesne rushes to catch up with us at the stairs. "It's true? Someone's dead? You guys were there?"

"It's true," I say.

"Maybe Vic figured out who sabotaged her dough after all."

"That's not funny," Nell says, more steel in her voice than I would've thought her capable of.

Courchesne sighs. "I know, sorry. Gallows humor. It's my vice. Freddie said it was an accident?"

"I don't know. She was already dead when Nell found her," I say, but my mind is still on the comment about Vic.

The dining room fills quickly with the bakers and more production staff than I realized the show even had. Some of the camera operators I recognize, and I assume the two girls standing with Julian are the other makeup artists, but there's still several people I haven't seen yet.

When Abigail and Kate arrive, the few quiet conversations going on fall silent, and the room practically vibrates with unasked questions.

"As many of you will have already heard, an accident occurred on set during lunch," Abigail said. Unlike the first time she addressed us, she's standing stock-still. "It appears that Chloe Moore slipped and hit her head on the edge of her worktop. It is a terrible tragedy, and I know many of you are going to need a chance to process it. A counselor will be available later tonight for anyone who wants to talk."

She pauses, and something about her energy shifts.

"You are still bound by your NDAs, so this is not something you can discuss with anyone outside of the production until after we air."

"So the show must go on?" Freddie asks, somewhat incredulously.

"Indeed. I understand it's difficult, but we are on a rigid timeline and we don't have the flexibility with either time or money to reschedule. We will be proceeding with filming as planned, minus the double elimination day. The best way to honor your fellow baker is to get back in the kitchen. Filming begins in one hour."

The film staff take this in stride, but several of the competitors erupt into pockets of heated conversation.

Nell looks aghast that she's expected to go back into the room where she just found a body, but Ainsley is saying, "It's sad, yeah, but it's not like we knew her, not really. It's no different than someone getting eliminated."

"Of course it's fucking different," Courchesne snaps. "She's dead. How would her family feel if they heard you say that?"

"I'm just being realistic," Ainsley says. "Like it or not, this show is a business, and we all signed up to be part of it. If the show must go on, then the best thing we can do is get back in the game."

"She's right," Derek says. "I mean, she sounds callous as fuck saying it that way, but really, dwelling on it isn't going to help."

"How are we supposed to go on camera and pretend like everything's normal?" Gemma asks, eyes wide, and it's suddenly clear how young she is, barely out of high school.

"The camera can't tell the difference. Stress about Chloe is going to look the same as stress about baking," Matt says. "Throw in a voice-over to really sell it, and no one's the wiser."

"That's cold," Vic says.

Matt shrugs. "That's show biz."

* * *

It turns out he's right. Once we're back in the kitchen with Natalie and the judges keeping everyone focused on the challenge at hand—four dozen decorated cookies, iced in four distinct patterns—the baking really does start to block out everything else.

It shouldn't surprise me, not really, not when I've often used baking to escape from the rest of the world before. I'm sure everyone in this room has done the same thing. There's a reason why stress-baking is a term that exists.

For this challenge we're allowed to use any base cookie we like, provided they're cut into shapes and decorated with royal icing. Nearly everyone is doing sugar cookies, although Freddie and Courchesne are both doing gingerbread.

The base of the challenge is producing a cookie that holds its shape, but the real test is in our decorating skills. I'm sticking with my pie theme, and while my pie-slice cookies are in the oven, I mix up a big batch of royal icing to divide and color. I leave each batch stiff to start, since I'll need it for outlines and can thin it down for flooding after, but a glance around the room makes me wonder if that's the right choice, given the amount of bowls Vic has lined up on her station.

I'm the first to admit that my piping skills are passable at best. I can do big stuff, swirls and rosettes, whipped cream borders on pies, but I rarely have a reason to practice the precise and delicate stuff.

Lucky for me, decorating sugar cookies is mostly a matter of tracing things in a logical order, and I've already mapped out the order I need to go in for each of the designs. That preplanning is the only thing saving me from disaster, because even as I focus on laying down the thin lines of border icing, part of my mind keeps straying back to Chloe and that wound on her head.

I know Abigail said it was an accident, a fall, but something about the sight of her is bothering me. Her hair was matted with blood, which would be consistent with hitting her head, but it was on the back of her head. Surely if she slipped she would've pitched forward, tried to steady herself on the bench, and if she couldn't right herself, she would've continued forward, striking the front of her head—her forehead or her temple, maybe.

Not the back.

I'm so caught up in possible scenarios that I don't even notice Leland and Natalie standing at my station until she stage-whispers, "The picture of focus here. Perhaps we shouldn't disturb her."

"Given how it's going, I would say not." Leland sniffs and they move off, Natalie offering a sympathetic *yikes* face.

"That was rude," I mutter, not caring if the camera catches it. I survey my cookies, and okay, maybe they're not going into the museum of fine cookie art, but they definitely could be worse.

I'm able to start plating with time to spare and already have them at the end of the bench when Natalie trills, "And that's time, bakers! Step away from your cookies!"

There's a brief lull while the cameras get close-ups of each bake, then the judges begin making their rounds.

Courchesne's pride cookies are simple and effective, while Derek's bookish sugar cookies can only be complimented on flavor. They may be messy, but it's a design choice that makes me doubt Vic's casting of him as villain.

Despite Leland's earlier snark, I'm let go with a *nice texture and decently executed icing*, and Gemma is told her design work is beautiful but her cookies are overbaked. Ainsley has the opposite problem, with underbaked cookies and runny icing, and Matt blames his lack of legible piping on being a doctor.

Nell gets praised for her fruit basket entry, each of her four shapes flavored to match their decoration, but it's Vic and Freddie who are clearly in a league of their own. Freddie went with gingerbread people decorated in the Funko Pop style, and even the judges can't help but appreciate the resemblance to themselves and Natalie. Natalie is particularly delighted with them, naturally.

Vic's butterfly cookies are equally elaborate, but unlike those of us who went with the typical outline-and-flood technique, she painted her designs on top of a base of crisp white royal icing.

The judges disappear to deliberate, and we're released to the patio to wait while set prep does their thing.

There's a web of wired tension connecting all of us that is equal parts about Chloe and the impending judging.

"God, I'm so nervous," Gemma says, and it's like she's given everyone else permission to speak.

"It feels wrong to even care about the outcome of this," Nell says, "but I still do somehow?"

"It's normal," Matt says. "There's room in your mind for multiple experiences, so dealing with one doesn't negate the need to deal with another."

And that's the thing I'm struggling with. Is Chloe's death actually being dealt with? Properly? I mean, obviously it's been reported to the proper authorities—the medical examiner was called in—but is it really being chalked up to *silly girl hit her head*?

Maybe it's all my work with Pies Before Guys, but I can't help feeling there's more to it than that.

I don't have a chance to dwell on it for long, though, because we're called back in for judging.

Nell grabs my hand as we walk, squeezing tightly, and I return the gesture.

We're lined up in front the judges as we were for the warm-up challenge, and Natalie steps forward.

"Bakers, in this first week you have shown us your finest cookie work, and we have had the privilege of tasting many amazing bakes. But this is a competition, so of course we must announce who is being crowned Top Baker and who we will have to say a very sad good-bye to." She pauses for an impossible beat before saying, "First, it is my absolute pleasure to announce this week's Top Baker is Vic. Congratulations.

"And now, I must ask Matt and Ainsley to please step forward."

They do, and she says, "Your performances in the warm-up and craft challenges were uneven, and both of you struggled during the creative, so it has come down to you."

Again, there is an interminable pause while the cameras get close-ups of both their faces.

"Unfortunately and with a very heavy heart, I must ask Matt to hand in your apron."

Ainsley sags with relief as he pulls the apron over his head and gives it to Natalie. She says something softly to him as the rest of the cameras capture our reactions to surviving day one, as if the only thing we survived was the baking.

Chapter Ten

The next morning, I'm ready for Julian before he even knocks on my door.

"Can you believe we're still doing this?" he says. "After what happened to that poor girl? She was one of mine too, the sweetest little thing."

"I know." I hardly slept last night, turning the scene in the ballroom over in my mind again and again. Something felt off about it, but I could be seeing murder where there's simply an accident. One of the hazards of my line of work. "Have you heard anything else about it since the meeting yesterday?"

"Not a peep," he says, hustling me into my chair.

I tilt my face up while he does his magic, wishing there were a way for my own magic to undo the events of the day before. "Did you see her for makeup after morning filming yesterday?"

"She wasn't in her room when I came by. I wasn't worried, though; I figured she decided she didn't need a touch-up. I had no idea she was—" He waves a hand to encompass the truth he doesn't want to say.

"None of us did."

That feels wrong, though. How did no one, in the midst of a televised baking show, not know Chloe was in danger until after the fact?

"All right, cupcake, you're done," he says, packing his brushes away. "Go be brilliant."

I give myself a final glance in the full-length mirror. I went with the cupcake dress today in an attempt to bring cheer through kitschy clothing, but I worry it appears garish now.

"You look lovely," Julian says, as if reading my mind.

"Thank you." I slip the apron over my head and tie the waist straps. "I have some of your intel, by the way, in exchange for the phone time? Freddie is single and most definitely into guys. Exclusively."

"That part's not intel, love, that part's obvious," he says with a laugh. "But the single part is good to know."

* * *

The meeting at the top of the stairs is subdued, but where yesterday that was due to nerves, today it's a combination of nerves and the knowledge that we're down not one, but two contestants already.

Natalie greets us with every bit as much cheer as she did yesterday, as if nothing in the world is wrong, and I hope they're paying her what she's worth for that acting.

"Bakers, welcome to cake week! Your warm-up challenge today takes us back to the Big Apple with a breakfast classic: a New York–style coffee cake. The judges are looking for moist cake, a perfectly spiced topping, and the correct ratio of crumb to cake, so bakers, do your thing!"

It's the perfect warm-up bake: easy enough to get lost in but enough steps to keep us busy. When Natalie comes around to get individual shots, her mood is infectious enough that we all rise to meet it.

Today I'm at the back, with Nell on my right and Vic in front of me, and as I mix my crumb topping—with my hands, like I always do—my eye keeps drifting toward Chloe's station.

There is no evidence she was ever there, not a drop of blood, not a dent on the bench. It might not even be the same bench anymore, since two have been removed.

Grant is at that station today, and if he's at all bothered by it, it doesn't show.

The instructions for the crumb are where the judges are trying to catch us, because where the cake has precise measurements, the topping ingredients are listed simply as *butter, flour, brown sugar, granulated sugar, salt, spice.*

I opt for cinnamon with a dash of cardamom and shoot for a solid fifty-fifty split of cake and crumb.

"Is there a such thing as too much crumb?" Natalie asks as I sprinkle the topping across the batter.

"Not in my book. I mean, the whole point of a coffee cake is to have a vehicle for the streusel, right?"

"Well, hopefully the judges agree," she says with a wink before moving over to Nell.

Luckily, the judges do. Like yesterday, the warm-up is judged blind, and when they get to mine, they compliment the ratio, and Leland even calls the topping well spiced. It's enough to get me all the way to the top two, and I can't even be mad when it's Gemma who beats me.

"It's my dad's favorite," she tells the camera for her reaction. "So I had an unfair advantage because I make it all the time."

"So it's teacher's pet *and* protégé," Vic says, giving her a gentle shoulder nudge as we make our way to the patio while set prep readies the next challenge.

Gemma grins widely and bounces on her toes, giddy with her win. "I can't believe I placed first!"

We all congratulate her, and even Grant holds out a taciturn fist for a bump.

"It's only the warm-up," Ainsley reminds her. "There are still two challenges to go."

"Don't be salty just because your crumbs were," Vic says, a note of iron in the singsong.

Ainsley's coffee cake ranked dead last because she mixed up her salt and sugar canisters before mixing her topping. To be fair, it's an easy enough mistake to make, given the tiny labels, but still, ouch.

Leland spit his bite out like it was poisoned, and even Natalie was so shocked she couldn't muster a cheery word to smooth it over.

When Ainsley stalks off without a word, Vic rolls her eyes. "The diva," she declares. "Definitely the diva."

"She's just embarrassed," Nell says.

"Still no reason to pee on Gemma's parade," Vic says, and I have to agree.

"Ignore her," I tell Gemma. "You did great, and of course you should be proud."

"Oh, I know," Gemma says, an unexpected glint in her eye. "She doesn't bother me."

"That's the spirit," Vic says.

* * *

"Bakers, for the craft challenge, the judges would like you to create a perfectly spiraled, perfectly textured Swiss roll," Natalie announces when we're back in the ballroom. "Your bakes may be made with any sponge, provided it rolls, and should be filled with at least two components. You have two and a half hours to complete this challenge, so bakers, do your thing!"

There is a flurry of activity as everyone gets started, because we all know there's not a moment to waste if we want our sponge layer to cool completely.

As I've learned from the many practice rolls I've foisted on the diner staff, filling a warm roll is a recipe for melty disaster.

Being in the back means I have plenty of time to rehearse what I'm going to say about my roll when the judges get to me for establishing shots, but when they arrive, I'm cracking eggs and end up ignoring them, lest I lose count.

Leland's head is cocked dramatically when I look up, and I already know how this is going to play on TV. Rats.

"Daisy, do tell us about your bake—if you have a moment, that is," he says.

"Yes," I say, wiping eggy fingers on my apron. I tell myself he's no worse than Frank on a bad day, he's just famous for it. "My Swiss roll is inspired by one of my favorite pies to make in the summer, the mango mint mojito. It's a vanilla sponge flavored with lime zest and fresh mint, filled with mango curd and rum-spiked cream, and finished with a buttery graham crumb."

"So yellow cake and yellow filling," Leland muses. "You're not concerned about highlighting the swirl better?"

"I wasn't until now," I chirp. "But the cream is a sharp white and the mango is brighter than the sponge, so I think it'll work."

"Well, I think it sounds mango-nificent," Natalie says, and they leave me to it.

I start the curd as soon as the cake goes in, knowing both will need as much cooling time as possible. As I whisk, I shoot a glance over at Nell, who's busy crushing cookies for her cookies-and-cream chocolate roll. The repeated *thwack, thwack* of the rolling pin on the bench is enough to draw the judges back, and I busy myself, hoping they stay away. I really don't need an audience for the fiddliest bit of this challenge.

Which, of course, means I get one, in the very unwanted form of Bryan himself.

He says nothing as he watches me pull my tray from the oven, the camera catching every move.

I send a silent prayer to the cake gods and flip the tray over in one fluid move, dumping the sponge, intact, onto the clean tea towel lining my worktop. I peel the parchment off the bottom and immediately begin to roll, using the edge of the towel to help get it started.

This is perhaps the most vital part of the challenge, because the initial roll will help set the structure for the final roll. If anything goes wrong here, I'm screwed.

But it doesn't. Cake gods for the win!

I carefully move the roll to a clean tray, scrawl my name on a scrap of parchment, and pop it in the nearest refrigerator to chill. I can't let it get too cold, or else it will crack when I try to unroll it, because this cake is nothing if not fickle.

I whip the cream while I wait, strengthening it with a bit of powdered sugar and adding a dash of rum at the end.

My mixer is going at top speed, but even that doesn't drown out Vic's growled, "Oh fuck me," from the station in front of me. "My cake split. Dammit!"

She momentarily becomes the center of attention as I pull my roll from the fridge. I place it on my bench and smile in the general direction of the camera assigned to me. "Here goes nothing."

I gently unroll the cake, praying with each rotation that it holds. Luckily it's still ever-so-slightly warm and unrolls easily. I'm sure the relief is all over my face when I make it to the end unscathed.

I spread a layer of the cooled mango curd over the whole surface and top it with dollops of cream. I spread it as evenly as I can while the camera operator moves around to capture various angles, and then I steel myself.

Using the edge of the tea towel to assist again, I begin the final roll. I go slowly, carefully, and I have never been so invested in a slab of cake as I am in this one. But it rolls beautifully and I settle it seam side down and trim the ends, revealing a perfect, if somewhat monochromatic, spiral.

"Bakers, you have five minutes remaining!" Natalie calls.

Plenty.

I pipe two long ropes of cream along the top and fill the space between them with a mix of graham cracker crumbs and toasted coconut. It gets a sprinkle of candied lime zest on top for a bit of color before I hit it all with a drizzle of rum icing.

I have it on the end of my bench, ready for judging, before Natalie even gives the signal.

While I wait for the judges to get to me, I nibble on the trimmed end scraps. It might not be the prettiest of all the rolls, but it is tasty.

Even Leland has to admit that. "I'm trying to find something to criticize," he admits. "But the swirl is even, the texture is nice, and the flavor is spot-on. Well done."

"Indeed," Juliet echoes. "Very nice."

Vic gets high marks for flavor but knocked for the split, and Gemma's lemon poppy fairs well, but it's Tony who knocks it out of the park, receiving a coveted recipe request from Leland for his blueberry basil cream roll. He's held back for a one-on-one while the rest of us are dismissed for lunch, and as much as I hate to admit it, for a few minutes there at the end, it was almost like nothing terrible had ever happened in that ballroom.

Chapter Eleven

"It was awful," Courchesne moans. "Real ace of cakes, my ass. You know what kind of cake I like? Layer cakes. You know what kind of cakes are overrated? Spiral cakes. Stupid, stupid spirals."

"I'm sure it's not that bad," I say.

"Nope, wait till they bring them in. It's like the goddamn Sahara in your mouth. I don't know how a filling with that much heavy cream in it can be dry, but Leland said it was and made me try it, on camera, and you know what? It was weirdly fucking dry. I think I put too much peanut butter in. I'm a cake fraud."

"You're not a cake fraud. It was one bake, in an unfamiliar place, under stressful conditions that didn't work out. You still have the creative."

"I know," she says. "But still. Ugh!"

"The creative is going to kill me," Derek announces as he sits down. "It's not even a baking challenge, it's an art challenge. And I am art challenged."

"I totally agree," Ainsley says from across the table. "And isn't fondant passe now anyway?"

"It doesn't have to be fondant," I remind her.

"I wish it didn't have to be sculpted either," Derek says. "I'm just glad I was high-middle of the pack in the first two. I figure as long as it doesn't end up on the floor, I should be able to hang."

At that comment Ainsley stiffens, no doubt recalling her disastrous warm-up. She smiles tightly and gets up without a word.

"That girl is wound too tight," Vic says.

"You're not wrong," I say, as Freddie arrives with two plates heaped with swirly cake slices.

"I brought tasting flights," he announces.

"Are you having any actual lunch?" Vic asks.

"Cake is a valid lunch," he says, stabbing a fork into a slice of Grant's chocolate raspberry.

Nell takes a small piece of Tony's blueberry basil roll. "When I was little, it was tradition to eat leftover birthday cake for breakfast the next day."

I nod approvingly. "Nice. I have pie for breakfast more often than I should probably admit."

"It's fruit and pastry," she says. "There are plenty of proper breakfast foods with that combination."

"Like Pop-Tarts?" Vic asks, eyebrow raised.

"And Danish."

"That's a breakfast pastry, though," Vic counters. "Not a random pastry you're having for breakfast."

"I think your definition of breakfast pastry is unnecessarily rigid," I say.

"Pie and cake are post-meal foods. Not meal replacement foods."

"Depends on your sense of whimsy," I say, pushing myself away from the table. "I'm going to see if I can find Kate for a peek at my phone before round two."

I wave a group good-bye and go in search of Kate, but when I stick my head into the ballroom, I only see set prep busy arranging the stations for the next round. I do hear voices, though, and continue through to the atrium and freeze.

Ainsley is there, along with Leland, and that's strictly against protocol. Contestants and judges aren't supposed to have any interaction outside of filming.

Her face is flushed, and anger radiates off her in waves.

They're so focused on each other that they don't see me, and I duck back outside, but I don't leave.

"Look, I got you a spot, but I can't save you from yourself," he says, the flippancy in his voice at odds with her rancor. "You gave me nothing to work with!"

"You spit it out," she hisses. "On camera. The look on your face, god."

"It was like eating a salt lick. I wasn't remotely prepared for that."

"Neither was I," she counters. "I think someone switched my ingredients."

He snorts. "Is that right? I think it's more likely you got them mixed up. It's fine. You're still safe."

"I better be." There's a wheedle in her voice and then silence. I'm painfully tempted to sneak a look to make sure they're still there, but I'm worried about being caught so obviously eavesdropping.

"Oh, you are," he says, a huskiness to his voice that wasn't there are a moment ago.

No.

It can't be.

This time I do risk a look, and holy shit. They're not fighting anymore. Nope. Their lips are far too occupied locking on each other's to waste time sniping.

After a moment Leland says, "We can't do this here. Lunch is over soon. I'll see you later."

"You better," she says.

I hustle myself back past the ballroom and toward the elevator, not wanting either of them to catch me anywhere in the vicinity of their scandal.

Still, the skulking cost me valuable time, and I'm only able to send Noel a *Miss you both, talk soon* text before I have to meet Julian for makeup and get back to the ballroom.

Now that I know what I know about Ainsley and Leland, it's impossible not to watch them for clues, but damn if they aren't slick. There's not even a hint of flirty eye contact as we wait for Natalie to give her spiel. In fact, Leland's eyes hardly stray to Ainsley's side of the room at all.

Maybe the evidence is the lack of evidence.

"Bakers, welcome to your creative challenge," Natalie trills. "This is cake week, and so far we've had snacking cake, we've had swirly cake, but now it is time for celebration cake! The judges would like you all to create a three-dimensional party cake, any theme, any flavor, so long as it is sculpted into something other than a layer cake. The judges are looking for originality, professional decorations, and of course, outstanding flavors. You have six hours to work your magic, so bakers, do your thing!"

I wish my magic extended to this arena. Sure, I could infuse my batter with joy and my buttercream with nostalgia, but I can't conjure fondant skills out of thin air.

Unfortunately.

But I have a plan.

I'm making a murder pie.

The cake is one hundred percent Juan's recipe, or at least, it's the recipe he pilfered from a culinary school buddy for me. I had to list high-ratio shortening as a special-purchase ingredient, but the rest of the components are pantry staples and I have a half-sheet pan full of batter into the oven in less than a half hour. I set the timer for eighteen minutes and begin melting white chocolate in a double boiler when all three judges arrive for their establishing shot.

"And what do we have going here?" Juliet asks.

"Prepping my modeling chocolate," I say, stirring it with a rubber spatula. "I'm using a mix of chocolate and corn syrup that I can color and use for the design elements."

"Not fondant?" Leland asks.

"Not fondant." I pull the pan off the heat and stir in my corn syrup. It seizes at first, but that's expected, despite the skeptical look Leland and Bryan exchange. "I find modeling chocolate is more forgiving than fondant, and it tastes better."

"Well, we're interested to see what you do with it," Juliet says as they move off.

I gather the modeling chocolate into a ball and knead it until it's smooth. This is the step the internet fought about the most, with some swearing you had to "milk" the oil out for it to set and others saying to just let it rest. Kneading worked well with my practice batch, so I stick with it.

Natalie sidles up to my bench with a camera in tow as my oven timer goes off. I drop the ball of modeling chocolate onto a piece of plastic wrap, and she pinches off a tiny piece to sample.

"That is tasty," she says. "So, Daisy, what could go wrong with your challenge today?"

"Everything, if you jinx it like that," I say, opening the oven to check the cake. It's golden and springs back when I poke the center.

Perfect.

"Well, at least that's not wrong," I say.

"And what are you turning this slab of fluffy deliciousness into?"

I grin. "A pie, of course."

* * *

Five hours later, it is, indeed, a pie.

Or, to be precise, a slice of pie.

"Well, I think it's delightful," Juliet says.

"I'm not sure it represents six hours of work," Leland says, pinning me with a withering stare.

The urge to squirm comes not from the criticism but from what I know about him now. Even if I hadn't known, I might've suspected based on how easily he let Ainsley's flower pot cake—a barely tapered three-layer base topped with basic buttercream flowers—slide.

"You have to admit it has character," Juliet counters, with obvious delight.

It's a reaction I'm used to my proper pies getting, but this particular slice is three layers of cherry-filled vanilla cake, frosted with bright red ganache and set into a modeling chocolate crust. It's topped with a little sculpted swirl of whipped cream, and the side of the pie sports a cute little happy face.

But the real charm is in the arm.

A modeling chocolate arm ends in a mitten-shaped hand wrapped around the waving hilt of a modeling chocolate chef's knife. It's held upright mostly by pure luck, but it's holding, and that's what matters.

"Well, let's see how it tastes," Bryan says, unceremoniously slicing it in half.

The knife topples, and Natalie groans dramatically.

It was fun while it lasted.

"That's a nice cake," Leland grudgingly admits. "Very nice texture."

"And I really like the cherry pie filling," Juliet says. "It may not be the most elaborate we've seen, but it's certainly one of the most fun."

"I'll take that."

The most elaborate are, unsurprisingly, Freddie's and Courchesne's, shocking exactly no one, given their backgrounds. Freddie has a gravity-defying hot air balloon, and Courchesne's elegant fox is almost too realistic to cut.

Grant also makes an impressive showing with his undulating snake, even if Leland dismisses it as more armature than cake, but it's Derek who gets the biggest reaction.

"Why does it look so scared?" Bryan asks, hardly able to hold back laughter as Derek places his cat cake on the table.

Leland's eyes narrow. "It's an accurate visual representation of my feelings on it."

Derek turns to throw us all that trademark grin before adopting a haughty air. "I prefer to consider it an examination of existential millennial dread. The horror in its eyes reflects our horror of the impending climate crisis."

Leland raises an eyebrow. "Dread is, again, the salient point."

"Well, let's give it a taste before we condemn it," Juliet says.

The inside is red velvet, and though it's tasty, the visual does nothing in the poor cat's defense.

"Okay, bakers," Natalie says, after we're assembled and the judges have had their deliberation. "The time has come to announce this week's Top Baker. We have been dazzled with all things sugar and sweet, but one baker has truly outfoxed the rest. It is my pleasure to announce that this week's best baker is Courchesne."

She whoops, and Freddie gives her a good-natured shove. There's a beat while the cameras get their reaction shots, and then Natalie adopts a somber face. "Which means we now face the unhappy task of deciding who will be going home."

The pause is longer this time, and Nell grabs my hand. Her first two challenges were solid, but the judges were not wowed by her baby whale cake.

"If Ainsley and Derek could please step forward."

Natalie looks at them both, sympathy in her green eyes. "It's only our second day and this part is already getting harder. Ainsley, the judges were very disappointed with your coffee cake and felt your Swiss roll could've been better. And Derek." She pauses, and he shakes his head. I can only imagine the look on his face. "You performed well in the first two challenges, but the creative was—"

"A *cat*-astrophe," he says in the slight pause she leaves.

"Yes." Natalie purses her lips. "Unfortunately, that cat has cost you your apron. We're so sorry to see you go, Derek."

Nell shoots me a surprised look as the cameras move to capture closing shots. Sure, Derek's cake was rather Picasso-like in its abstraction, but was it really worse than Ainsley's inedible coffee cake? Maybe the creative is weighted more heavily than I realized, or maybe it's just one of the perks of snogging the judges.

Like anyone with a functioning brain, I know reality TV isn't remotely based in reality, but I never realized how much more drama there is behind the scenes than on camera.

And we're only on day two.

Chapter Twelve

"Well, these stairs are lacking serious eye candy now," Freddie says, pushing his way between me and Courchesne as we wait for our signal to head down.

"I'm sure you'll survive," she says.

"Yes, but I won't enjoy it."

"I don't think I'm going to enjoy much about this day," I admit. "I feel good about my craft bake, but yeast? I don't trust temperamental microorganisms."

"If you're kind to the yeast, the yeast will be kind to you."

We all turn, wondering who turned into bread Yoda.

It's Tony.

Quiet, slightly standoffish Tony is suddenly offering bread platitudes.

"I brought starter from home," he says softly, but there's the kind of pride in his eyes usually reserved for new parents. "I've been cultivating it for over two years."

"I can't even keep a succulent alive," Courchesne says. "I'm impressed, my man."

Natalie appears at the bottom of the stairs. "Good morning, bakers! Make two groups and let's get this show *rolling.*" She leans on the last word to drive the pun home, and on her mark, we converge on the stairs and make our way to the ballroom.

Today I have Chloe's station, and I take a moment to let myself see her not as she was here but in the dining room that last morning, so full of excitement and joy.

It seems impossible that it was only two days ago that she died.

Or was killed.

I run my hand along the edge of the worktop like it's a Ouija board that can tell me the truth of what happened that day, but of course it can't.

There's a commotion up front as Juliet comes in, and it's enough to snap me out of my thoughts. Kate is right behind her, saying, "Well, we need them here now."

"I am neither their mother nor their babysitter," Juliet says with imperious calm. "I'm sure they'll be along."

"Abigail will be furious if we start late."

"Again, that is not in my control."

I exchange a look with Grant, who's across from me today, but he looks as unconcerned as Juliet sounds. Freddie, however, immediately turns around and whispers in a singsong, "Someone's in trouble."

"At least it's not us."

"Yet."

Bryan and Leland arrive moments later, still embroiled in whatever conversation kept them.

Kate claps twice and barks, "Places, now!"

The conversation is clearly not over, but they take their positions on either side of Juliet, and Natalie steps slightly forward, a wide smile on her face. "Welcome, bakers, to bread week! For your warm-up challenge, the judges would like you to make four perfectly identical French baguettes. They should have an open, irregular crumb, a crisp golden crust, and a uniform shape, so bakers, do your thing!"

The instructions are, as ever, extremely not helpful.

Make the dough. Proof the dough. Shape baguettes. Rest. Bake.

"Oh look," Courchesne says from the back station. "We have a rest scheduled right into the recipe. That was nice of them."

"Surely you don't *knead* to rest already," Natalie says, beginning her rounds to each station.

But it turns out Courchesne is sort of right, because the thing about bread, at least yeasted bread, is there's a lot of waiting around, and there's only so much watching dough we can do.

Once the cameras have shots of all of us doing just that, most of us head to the patio to wait for our doughs to rise in a bit of comfort.

I make a cup of mint tea and join the fringes of Vic, Courchesne, and Freddie's conversation. Nearby, Nell and Gemma are grilling Tony about the secrets of bread whispering, but I notice Gemma keeps sneaking glances back inside, and I can't help following her gaze.

Ainsley is leaning against Grant's station, saying something I can't make out, but he looks completely absorbed in setting up the folds in his couche, the stiff canvas cloth that helps baguettes hold their shape on their second rise.

I wonder if we're all supposed to be doing that now.

Ainsley leans over to touch his arm, but he pulls away before she can make contact. She huffs and flounces back to her station, ducking out of sight to presumably check her proving drawer.

Grant shakes his head, a small, tight movement, as if clearing it. He flicks a dusting of flour over the couche and brushes his hands off, joining us on the patio before she can corner him again.

Although joining may be too strong a word.

He comes out, pours a cup of black coffee from the urn, and leans against the railing as far from everyone as possible. The gardens he looks out over are gorgeous, no doubt, but something tells me he isn't even seeing them.

Vic notices me noticing and tilts her head in his direction. "Between him and Tony, it's like battle of the brooders. We can't have two mysterious ones."

"I think Tony's just an introvert," I say. "Who's only willing to discuss bread."

True to his nature, Tony is the first to abandon the patio to check his dough, and everyone follows like a pack. Natalie and the camera crew jump into action as we return, getting close-ups of our dough as we shape the baguettes.

Once the loaves are resting, we're back to doing the same, and I find myself wondering how Matt and Derek are faring elsewhere on the estate. There's something to be said for lounging around a heated pool and not being stressed about bread.

I'm channeling my stress into tea drinking, which is a tried-and-true coping mechanism. Gemma is also giving it a shot, rifling through the selection of bags.

"I don't even like tea," she admits. "I just feel like I need to do something with my hands. It's weird not having my phone all the time."

"I know. I'm not even on mine all that often, and I still feel naked without it."

She settles on an herbal berry blend and drops the bag into a mug, then sets the whole thing aside. "I figure we have at least a half hour before we have to start babysitting our bread, right? Do you think we're allowed to walk around the gardens?"

There's a manic intensity to the way she's asking that makes me a little worried she's on the verge of a panic attack.

"I don't see why we couldn't," I say. "You want company?"

"Yes."

It's emphatic enough that I don't hesitate. "Then let's take a walk."

Nell is sitting on the top step with Grant, talking quietly, and they both look up as we pass.

"Having a wander," I say in explanation. Neither makes a move to join us, and judging by the way Gemma is barreling down the steps, I think it's for the best.

We walk in silence for a few moments, putting some distance between us and the estate. Gemma is practically vibrating with unspoken words, but I don't want to scare them away by asking to hear them.

Eventually, she decides to just blurt it out. "I think something's going on with Ainsley. Something bad." I keep walking, trying to decide how much to reveal about what I know, but she rushes to fill the silence as people so often do. "I saw her. In the ballroom when we weren't supposed to be there. She wasn't alone."

So I'm not the only one who knows.

Man, that girl works fast.

I sigh. "I know. I saw her too."

Gemma stops walking and grabs my arm, forcing me to do the same. "You did? And you didn't say anything?"

She sounds so betrayed that I can't help remembering how young she is. Fresh out of high school and hoping for a win to fund her dream of pastry school in France.

"I only just found out," I say. I don't know how to explain that in the aftermath of Chloe's death, complaining about Ainsley and Leland's affair feels somehow petty.

She looks at me like we're speaking separate languages. "How did you only just find out, if you saw them too?"

"Because it was just yesterday? During lunch?" Something about her expression has my words coming out like questions even though I know they're statements. "I know it feels like we've been here forever already, but we practically just got here."

"Who did you see exactly?" she asks.

"Ainsley and Leland."

Her eyes widen and she shakes her head.

"That's not what I'm talking about," she says, and something in my stomach twists. "I didn't see her with Leland. I saw her with Chloe. And they were fighting."

Chapter Thirteen

Ainsley has one of the front stations today, and if I'm not looking at what I'm baking, I find myself staring at the back of her head.

We're knee-deep in the day's quick bread craft challenge, but my brain is so busy turning over thoughts of Ainsley and Chloe that I can hardly focus on the block of chocolate I'm chopping.

After her confession, Gemma seemed relieved, like she was passing the problem off to a responsible adult to handle. At her station, she's explaining her Mexican-inspired soda bread to the judges as if she hasn't just handed me a live grenade.

It's fine.

It's not like this is the first time I've baked with murder on my mind.

Using the edge of the knife, I scrape the shards of chocolate off the cutting board and into my bowl as Natalie and the judges arrive. Natalie, true to form, darts a hand into the bowl and plucks out a sliver of chocolate to pop in her mouth.

"Daisy, what is your bake today?"

"I'm doing a figgy dark chocolate and cardamom loaf," I say, piling the figs onto my board for chopping.

"Are you expecting to need a lot of cardamom to counter the dark chocolate?" Leland asks.

"The cardamom should come through in the background. The fig is the real star."

"I'm not a huge fan of cardamom," Bryan says, and I know it's just to be contrary. He had no complaints when I used it in my coffee cake.

"No one likes it when it's overpowering, but I'm not planning for it to be," I say, more to Juliet than anyone. With what I now know about Bryan and Leland, I'm finding it hard to look at either.

"I think it sounds lovely," Juliet says, and as she leaves, a small part of me wonders if I'm about to uncover some scandal about her too, just to round out the trifecta of terrible.

But as I chop my figs, I remember she already had her scandal, back when I was a kid, for insider trading. It was all my mom's clients wanted to talk about during their hair appointments, so I knew more about it than any eight-year-old wanted to. Juliet served a short sentence at a minimum-security prison and managed to emerge with all the dignity she entered with. Along with returning to her culinary empire, she immediately spearheaded several programs to improve the lives of incarcerated women, both during and after their time behind bars.

If anyone could put a positive spin on their time in prison, it's Juliet Barnes.

Once the figs are in, I give the dough a final mix, being careful not to overwork it. In quick breads, unlike yeasted dough, gluten development is the enemy.

I pop it in the oven, set my timer, and straighten my station, piling the dirty bowls and utensils on the end for set prep to whisk away.

It's a fun part of the filming to see, because as soon as the set staff move on a station, the cameras collectively turn to avoid capturing their work. The whole thing is like a strange ballet.

Because quick breads are, as their name suggests, quick to cook, there's no decamping to the patio this round, and soon the ballroom is filled with a plethora of rich scents and the soft rattle of oven doors opening and closing as people check their bakes.

"Ugh, why is it spreading?" Freddie moans from the front.

Natalie goes over to investigate while the judges watch from their places along the edge. It's easy to forget they're there until things go wrong.

At least it's not me under their scrutiny.

For now.

In the downtime, I consider my station—Chloe's station—through new eyes, visualizing what Gemma told me. Ainsley and Chloe. A confrontation.

Sure, Ainsley had been snippy at breakfast that morning, but was it enough for a full-blown fight?

She may be a diva, but as I watch her lean down to check her loaf, I can't picture her physically attacking Chloe, never mind killing her. I can't even fathom a motive for such an interaction.

Except for the obvious, which would be eliminating the competition. But surely that wouldn't be worth the risk. Killing one of us doesn't help her chances all that much, and it's not like she can kill us all.

My timer dings and I pull my loaf. The crust is dark gold, and when I tap it I get the telltale hollow knock. Perfect. Around me, other timers go off like out-of-sync alarm clocks.

"Bakers, you have ten minutes," Natalie calls. "Ten minutes to get those buns out of the oven!"

With my remaining time, I bang some heavy cream into my mixer and whip it on high until it turns to butter, then drizzle a stream of Noel's honey into the bowl. I finish it with a sprinkle of sea salt, scoop it into a ramekin, and have it set out with my loaf at the end of my bench just as Natalie calls time.

Freddie is first for judging, and it's not good.

"This is practically a cookie, it's so flat," Leland says, holding the whole loaf up for the camera. "The measurements are all off. The only thing I can even taste is baking soda. It may be soda bread, but that doesn't mean I want to taste the soda. Even the olives can't hide it."

"Disappointing," Juliet agrees.

Courchesne's muffin-style quick bread fares better, getting high marks for the sharpness of her citrus and the balance of the herbs. Gemma and Tony are both praised for their savory breads, but it's Nell who knocks it out of the park with her French onion–inspired cheese loaf.

"This is absolutely incredible," Juliet says.

Natalie picks up the loaf and mimes sneaking off with it. "I'll just be going with this."

Nell beams, cheeks flushed from the compliment, and I'm so thrilled for her that it doesn't even bother me when Bryan harps on the cardamom in my loaf.

"The honey butter is a nice accompaniment," Leland says. "Perfectly salted."

I don't want to accept the compliment from the unethical weasel, but I do, because he's right.

* * *

There's hardly a point to serving lunch, because all anyone wants to do is sample the breads.

Derek and Matt arrive moments after our group hits the dining room, and Derek immediately swoops in to congratulate everyone on their bakes.

"Nell! I knew you had a star in you," he says, pulling her into a hug. I laugh at her shocked expression, but he releases her quickly and turns to Gemma. "And fajita bread? You better have saved me a slice."

He does this for everyone, greeting them with a specific comment about their bakes.

When he starts singing *bring me a figgy bread*, it slides into place. "You've been spying."

He grins that Hollywood grin and elbows Matt. "We've been exploring."

"I've been chaperoning," Matt clarifies.

Derek's eyes shine with the excitement of a kid at Christmas. "Did you know there are secret passages in here? Seriously. I read about them before we came, but I didn't think we'd find them. I mean, fine, I hoped I wouldn't have time to find them because I'd be too busy winning, but here we are."

Derek and Matt clearly have the spotlight as we all sit down, and Derek needs no encouragement. "They're everywhere, not just where the servants would've been. I read the guy who built this place wanted to be able to slip between rooms during parties so he could escape conversations that were boring him, and let me tell you, my man was onto something."

"And one of them goes to the ballroom, I take it?" Vic asks.

"Two. That we found."

Even Matt looks pretty pleased with this. "We watched the whole challenge. I kept thinking we were gonna get caught, but everyone was so focused on what they were doing that no one even noticed the wall panels weren't lined up right."

"Where does it connect to?" I ask.

"One probably is a servant passage, because it goes along the hall to the kitchen, but the one we were watching from links to the library."

Courchesne's brown eyes go wide. "Please tell me there's a secret door in the bookshelves."

"There's a secret door in the bookshelves!" Derek crows. "It's so awesome."

"You have to show us," she says.

"Nope. Not unless you get eliminated," he says.

"What? How is that fair?"

"If you know where it opens, you're going to want to look there while you're filming," Matt explains. "Your brain won't be able to help it."

"And we're not about to have you give away our front-row seats," Derek says. "Just think of it as a consolation prize if you get the boot."

"I'm hoping to stick around long enough to have a chance at the actual prize," Nell says, but as soon as the words are out of her mouth, her cheeks flush scarlet, like she can't believe she said it out loud.

Derek points at her with the last bite of her French onion bread. "Keep making things this good and you will be," he says, and this time the wattage of that charming smile is directed one way and one way only.

Vic shoots me a knowing look, and I bite back a grin.

Who'd've thought Hollywood was into the shy girl?

"Well, you might as well show me," Freddie says, oblivious to the moment he's interrupting. "Because after that round, I'm probably toast."

"Leave the food puns to the professionals," Courchesne says and then whirls on me, waving a hand. "Speaking of. Pie girl. We need to talk."

"We do?"

"Yes. I told you I could come up with a better name than Pie Girl for you. And I have." She pauses in a way that's straight out of the Natalie school of dramatics, and everyone, even Grant from his seat at the end, turns to hear. "I would very much like to know why your bi ass is not calling your business Pie-Curious."

There's a range of groans and giggles from around the table, and Courchesne looks proud of herself, and all I can think is how much Melly would love that name.

"I definitely should've had that on the list," I concede.

"Rebranding is a thing, you know," she says. "I'm pretty good at it."

"And I already have more Pie Girl labels than I know what to do with."

She waves that off. "Details. You should think about it."

"I will."

But even though I actually might, at least for a social media promo or something, what I'm really thinking about is Derek's discovery of the passages. I need to talk to Ainsley, of course, but if I'm right, if she's not the kind of person capable of murder, that means any number of people could've slipped in and out of the ballroom unnoticed while Chloe was there.

If I'm right and she really was killed, it could've been anyone from *Bake My Day*.

Chapter Fourteen

Matt was right. Even though I know I shouldn't, I find myself searching the perimeter of the ballroom, looking for the spot that might conceal a hidden door, as Natalie sets us on our creative challenge.

"Bakers, for this final challenge, the judges would like you to create a filled yeast bread. It can be sweet, it can be savory, but most importantly, it must be spectacular. You have four hours to complete the challenge, so bakers, do your thing!"

In the initial flurry of activity that has come to mark the start of each challenge, I try to convince myself that a filled bread is basically a fluffy pie and something I can absolutely handle. After all, I've made pies for some of the worst men imaginable. A little yeast shouldn't scare me.

And yet, even with my heavily annotated recipe on hand, I find myself willing the bread gods to be kind.

I start by scalding my milk, because supposedly cold milk is the one thing the yeast itself is scared of, and start weighing out my flour while it cools to a non-yeast-scorching temperature.

This is exactly why I don't like yeast. No ingredient should be allowed to be so picky.

I'm doing a brioche-style dough, which is a risk given the time frame, but if I can get it in the fridge in time to set the butter, I should be fine.

I think.

Around me, mixers begin to whir, and I combine the flour, salt, and remaining sugar in my bowl and add mine to the cacophony. In the background, there's a rhythmic thwacking as Tony kneads his dough by hand. He has the entire cadre of judges watching each throw, but he's as cool as can be, never breaking the thwack-stretch-gather routine.

I feel like a bit of a cheater letting the mixer do the work for me, but that dough throwing is not a skill I have.

As I add the softened cubes of butter to the mixer, I think it's one I might like to acquire, though. I can see the appeal in the physicality of it, and I bet it would be as easy to trap magic in all those folds as it is to work it into pie dough.

Including magic in my show bakes was something I considered for half a second before dismissing it outright. For one thing, even though the process isn't obvious from the outside, the thought of doing it on TV felt a bit like competing naked.

Also, and this is the part I haven't even admitted to Noel, I kind of want to see how far I can get without it. My magic is so intrinsically linked to my pie making that I couldn't separate it if I wanted to, but this is an opportunity to go cold turkey. It's a chance to see if I'm really any good, or if it's just the magic that makes it seem so.

When Natalie arrives and asks, "Daisy dear, what kind of magic are you cooking up for us with this challenge?" the timing is so uncanny that for a tiny second it feels like she knows the truth about me.

Which is impossible, but still.

"I'm making a caramelized white chocolate and hazelnut praline swirly wreath thing," I say, instantly fighting the urge to groan. "And yes, I'm realizing now that I should've figured out a better name for it before I started talking about it."

As it is, I've cobbled it together from a couple of recipes, so it's not quite a babka, not quite a couronne. But when it works, it's tasty, so I'm okay with it not being a real thing.

Hopefully the judges are too.

As the dough comes together, I scan the perimeter of the room, trying to look casual enough that the cameras don't take an interest. I don't want to ruin things for Derek and Matt's entertainment, but I do want to know where the access point is.

I try to remember what I know of the layout of the estate and what Derek said about the discovery. It's obviously not on the patio wall, since that's all exterior, and it doesn't make sense that it would be on the wall where the main doors are either, so I focus on the two sides. They're both paneled in gleaming dark wood and from this distance it's hard to make out the seams, but I think I see something in the gap between two of the refrigerators, one section with a slightly thicker border along the right edge.

That's the mistake, I realize. I'd been looking for a proper door, one that swings open, instead of one that slides into the wall itself. From here the gap looks minuscule and there's no way to tell if the guys are there watching or if I'm making the whole thing up, but either way, I'm so tempted to wave that I pull my caramelizing chocolate from the oven, just to have something to do.

I stir it until it's an even gold and spread it into a thin layer so it will cool faster.

Then I realize I have the perfect excuse to get a closer look at that panel. Sure, it makes more sense to use the refrigerator on my side of the room, but if I take the tray on the pretense of having a peek at Nell's progress, well, I'm already halfway there.

Most of the bakers are starting to hit a lull as they finish prepping fillings and begin the wait for their dough, so I'm able to mingle easily. Nell is arranging paper-thin slices of heirloom tomatoes on sheets of paper towel for her caprese pinwheel.

"All good?" I ask.

"If you count a lecture on the danger of adding too many wet ingredients to the dough as good, then I'm grand," she says, but she's cheerful as she gives the tomatoes a sprinkle of pink salt before covering them with another layer of paper towel.

"Leland?"

"Naturally."

"I got one on the dangers of kneading chocolate into dough, so I'm living on the edge right along with you."

She laughs. "I've spent long enough living safely in the middle. The edge was looking exciting."

"I don't think tomatoes and mozz exactly counts as the edge," Vic says from behind us, but it's a good-natured jab.

"This whole show is the edge," Nell clarifies.

"Fair enough." Vic gives the contents of her pan a brisk stir with a pair of tongs, and we're hit with a wave of spicy scents. She pulls it from the burner and covers it with foil. "Patio break?"

"Sure," I say, hefting my tray. "Let me pop this in the freezer."

I give a quick glance to make sure I'm not being watched, but the lull in action has even the judges looking bored. As I put the tray in the freezer, I search the wall and sure enough, there's a small gap between two of the panels.

Bingo.

Chapter Fifteen

When we return from our break, it's almost impossible not to watch the gap in the wall for signs of spying, but I know better than to be obvious while the judges are prowling. With Bryan looking on silently, I run a knife down the top in one long slice, involuntarily imagining the tail end of a Y incision, because my brain is, on occasion, a creepy place to be.

I separate the halves so the delicate rows of filling are exposed and then twist them together. It may not be pie dough, but it still looks pretty good. I loop the ends together to form a circle and manage to transfer it onto the baking tray. It's a bit like handling a sleeping snake, all long and loose, but I rearrange it on the pan and am pleased.

When it comes out of the oven, I'm even more pleased. The filling is bubbling happily, and the layers are still clearly defined. More importantly, it smells divine.

The yeast gods have been kind.

"Bakers, you have five minutes," Natalie trills, and I shoot an involuntary glance to the maybe-door/maybe-panel, wondering if Matt and Derek are watching this part and wondering who's about to join them.

I give the loaf a light dusting of powdered sugar and set it on the end of my bench.

All three judges are lined up at the front, looking serious as the time ticks down.

"Bakers, I know you're on a roll, but time is up. Please step away from your breads."

A long moment passes as we stand behind our stations, trying not to look at the cameras getting their anticipation shots.

Finally, the judges step forward, calling Ainsley up first.

Juliet takes the lead, sectioning off a portion of her loaf for them to sample. "The bake looks good," she says. "There's a good shine to the crust, and it would look lovely on a brunch display."

"It's quite bland," Leland declares after sampling it. "There's a lot of spices in here, but not enough of any of them. There's no punch, no single flavor to anchor to."

"The glaze is nice," Bryan says.

"And if it was glaze week, that would count for something," Leland retorts.

Up next, Tony's smoky chipotle loaf for its complex flavors and intricate star design, and I don't need magic to see Top Baker written in his future.

Nell is next in the line of fire, and Leland doesn't hold back. "This is a bit too Pinterest for my tastes. I think it's reasonable, at this level, to expect more than potluck fair."

Still, they all sample and Juliet nods. "It may not be elaborate, but it is yummy. If that was on offer, I would absolutely go back for seconds. The pesto is particularly nice."

"It's cheesy bread," Bryan says. "Who doesn't like cheesy bread?"

Leland bristles, but they move on, and when I'm called, I'm prepared for Leland's wretched mood. I'm not prepared for Juliet to be the one to take me out.

"It's underbaked," she says. "See how it goes back to dough when you press here?"

I nod, because I have no choice but to acknowledge the truth of her statement. Dammit.

"I bet you were judging doneness based on the color of the top, where the filling is showing, rather than the bottom. The sugar content makes that brown faster than the dough. Covering it and letting it bake for another ten minutes would've made all the difference."

"The flavor is good, though," Bryan says. "It has a fancy Nutella vibe."

Leland puts his unfinished piece down. "We're not in the business of judging vibes."

There's a very slight flexing of Juliet's jaw that I would've missed if I weren't so close to her, and I can see she's completely over Leland's attitude. He may have made abrasive his brand, but there's a sharp undercurrent that was missing the first two days. Maybe Ainsley and Vic are rubbing off on him too.

When the judges retreat for their deliberations, the tension lingers, and most of us retreat to the patio to escape it.

"I don't know about the rest of you, but I'm ready for the drinks portion of the evening," Courchesne says.

No one disagrees.

"Is anyone else getting weird vibes from Leland and Bryan?" Gemma asks.

"I think they're having a lovers' spat," Freddie says.

"I think Juliet is ready to kill the both of them," I say, and instantly regret it. The uncomfortable quiet that follows doesn't help, and I know everyone is thinking of Chloe. It's impossible not to.

It's Vic, unsurprisingly, who comes to the rescue. "They might think they're badasses, but Juliet is the queen. That woman ran a culinary empire from prison and never even broke a sweat. She can squash a couple of fragile male egos like bugs."

"Wait, what?" Gemma asks. "Prison?"

"Oh, you sweet innocent child," Freddie says. "Let us tell you the tale."

He launches into an enthusiastic, if slightly exaggerated, telling of Juliet's misdeeds, and the whole time Gemma looks half convinced he's messing with her, but the easy, unprompted input from Vic convinces her.

Nearly everyone is at least half listening to Freddie, mostly because it's impossible not to, but Ainsley, unsurprisingly, has stationed herself at the far end of the railing, and Tony, even though he's within earshot, seems to have closed in on himself somehow. It's nothing overt—not a turning away or an unfriendly expression—but a certain stillness, like he's shuttered himself off from the rest of us without even moving.

Or like he's trying to hide himself in plain sight.

I watch him discreetly, wondering if it's prejudgment nerves or something else. Maybe I missed a side comment, something that offended him. Out of the whole group, he's the one I've had the least interaction with, but I found his quiet passion for bread endearing and thought it might be a sign he was coming out of his shell.

The stony look on his face says otherwise.

I realize with a jolt that it was probably me who did it, by bringing Chloe's specter back into the mix, and I curse myself again.

Before I can formulate an apology, Natalie's voice cuts through the air. "Bakers, assemble!"

Freddie groans and heaves himself off his chair. "And so begins my death march. It's been nice baking with you all."

Grant claps him on the shoulder. "Don't count on it. Got a feeling I'm on that chopping block with you."

"We'll see."

The judges are already waiting with Natalie when we come in, and we line up before them. Nell is holding my hand, and on my other side, Freddie is starting to sweat.

"Bakers," Natalie says in her camera voice. "This week has been a labor of loaf, but one of you has risen above the rest. This person has dazzled us with technique, tantalized us with flavors, and never even broke out the mixer. It is a pleasure to award this week's Top Baker to Tony."

We all congratulate him, and I'm relieved to see his smile goes right up to his eyes, chasing away any residual stress from the patio.

"And now," Natalie says, "We must sadly bid farewell to one of our own. This only gets harder with each challenge, but I must ask Ainsley and Freddie to please step forward."

Freddie sags and I reach out to squeeze his shoulder, just a small touch to acknowledge that I see his angst.

Natalie makes them stand in silence for an impossibly long moment while the cameras get their close-ups, then says, "This is our first challenge where the judges had trouble agreeing on the outcome, but they all felt you both struggled more than the rest with technique and flavor. Therefore, one of you won't be continuing. I'm sorry to say that this week, that person is . . ." She pauses for far longer than is kind, and my heart hurts for Freddie. "Ainsley. I'm sorry. Please hand in your apron."

Chapter Sixteen

Dinner is late and Ainsley doesn't join us.

There's a certain shocked air that follows us through the meal, and Freddie's frequent exclamations of disbelief at his luck do nothing to dispel it.

Every so often Gemma meets my eye and I wish I hadn't mentioned Leland to her. Surely she's questioning the same things I am, and it's not a good road to be going down.

On the one hand, I would've expected Leland to protect her to the bitter end, but objectively, she deserved to be in the bottom two with Freddie.

"Freddie, mate," Derek says, "I thought for sure you'd be joining the rejects tonight. No offense."

"None taken. I still don't know how I made it through."

"Well, I'm in favor of the ruling," Vic says, surprising no one.

There's an uncomfortable shifting as it becomes clear everyone agrees but doesn't want to say so.

Courchesne raises a pointed eyebrow at Matt and Derek. "So are you inviting her to spy with you?"

They look at each other, each too polite to stick their foot in it.

"Who wants to take bets on whether she's sulking or fighting the ruling?" Vic asks.

Nell tuts. "That's not fair. It would be awful to be eliminated. Being awful yourself doesn't make that part less awful." Her cheeks flare red even before she finishes speaking, and Vic and Courchesne dissolve into laughter.

"See, even Nell gets it," Vic says. "She was the diva and she got what was coming. Just a bit earlier than I would've expected for that arc."

"They're not really judging us as characters," I protest.

"Not exclusively," Vic says, "but I bet it contributes."

"Well, I for one am glad to have landed the role of charming one and live to bake another day," Freddie announces. "Drinks on me if anyone wants to partake. Virgin or boozy," he adds, for Gemma's benefit.

There's a chorus of affirmatives from everyone but Tony, who only manages to extricate himself after another round of congratulations on winning Top Baker.

"I'm gonna sneak a phone call first," I say. "Then I'll be along."

I know my chances of finding Kate for my phone are slim, but that's not really what I'm after.

I jog to catch up with Tony before he reaches the stairs and regret not just calling for him, because now I have to catch my breath before I can speak without sounding like a dying fish.

He at least has the grace not to comment.

"I wanted to apologize," I say, "if I made you uncomfortable on the patio with the—" I make a vague gesture, realizing I'm about to repeat my original crime. "With the killing comment. It was insensitive, given what happened, and it slipped out before I could stop it."

He cocks his head ever so slightly, and the hint of a smile plays at his lips. Behind that quiet demeanor, he has a very kind face. "It was just a turn of phrase. I know."

"Still. It seemed to upset you, and it wasn't my intention. I wanted you to know that."

"Honestly, it's fine," he says, but there's something in his dark eyes again, something closed off, and I know that even if he wants it to be, on some level it's not okay.

I just don't quite know why.

But I want to.

"Well, I wanted to apologize either way. I know this hasn't exactly gone off the way any of us were expecting so far."

"You're not wrong," he says. "I'm starting to wonder if signing up was the right thing."

"But you got Top Baker. And a recipe request! If anyone should be feeling secure about this, it's you." I mean for it to sound reassuring, but he shakes his head, just a bit.

"I didn't expect it would all get so out of hand."

I want to ask him what he means by that, but he begins the climb up the stairs, turning only to say over his shoulder, "Have a good night, Daisy."

I'm left standing at the foot of the stairs feeling strangely out of sorts in a way I can't quite place but know I don't like.

I shake myself out of it and head off in search of Kate, feeling a sudden need for the reassuring familiarity of Noel and Zoe.

If there's one thing Tony was right about, it's that things have gotten out of hand.

Way out of hand.

Not only are there contest nerves to contend with, but Chloe's death has taken up so much of my mental space that I've almost forgotten my own problem—how am I going to pie Bryan?

I can't do it here, not with so many witnesses and not when his wife Matilda already requested delivery to their home. I sometimes have clients who want me to deliver directly to the target, but this isn't one of those cases. Matilda wants to be the one to serve it, and from what she's told me, she's earned that privilege.

But still, if anyone saw me showing up at his house, especially before the show even aired, it could be bad. Really bad. There would be questions I wouldn't have answers for, and it would make whatever scandal Leland and Ainsley are flirting with look like *Sesame Street*.

This is what I get for thinking I could go on a baking show like a normal person.

If Tony had any idea how out of hand things are in my world, he might feel a little better about his.

It's a thought that instantly brings back the memory of Chloe comparing her nervousness to Freddie's at breakfast, and I feel a pang. We can compare all we want, but at the end of the day, everyone is carrying their own load, and sometimes it's bearable and sometimes it's not.

Chapter Seventeen

Chocolate day starts with truffles in a two-ingredient warm-up challenge that ends with Grant in first and Gemma fighting tears after a disastrous attempt at tempering lands her in last place. Even though I end up in the upper half of the pack, Bryan's and Leland's commentary is consistently scathing enough to put me on edge, and when they arrive at my bench during the craft challenge, I brace myself.

"Daisy, tell us about your brownie," Juliet says, taking an exaggerated interest in the ingredients arrayed on my bench.

"As usual, I'm taking inspiration from my favorite pies and will be incorporating banoffee flavors."

Juliet nods and Leland adopts his trademark skepti-stare. "Remember the key part of the challenge is the brownie. Aside from a bad bake, the biggest risk is overwhelming it with too many components."

"I like an excessive brownie," Bryan says, and I have a feeling it's simply to spite Leland.

I don't know what it is about men that can make them act like such toddlers. "I hope it will hit the sweet spot between classic fudge brownie and decadent dessert."

"We'll see," Leland says as they move off.

"Well, I'm excited," Natalie stage-whispers as she trots after them.

Of course she is. I have to hand it to whoever hired her; she's the perfect mix of high energy and genuine enthusiasm, unlike Kate, who is watching the proceedings with a pinched expression from the main entrance.

My base brownie recipe is a simple one-bowl cocoa concoction that uses a high percentage of sugar to get the signature crackly crust that marks a good brownie. The diner went through an obscene amount of brownie sundaes while I was working out the recipe, although no one seemed to mind.

I've just started mixing when a clatter behind me stops everything. A metal bowl is skittering across Grant's bench and he's storming up to Gemma's station, who's red-faced and doing her bake explanation to Juliet, Leland, and Natalie, while Bryan hovers close to her shoulder.

Too close.

"Get away from her," Grant barks.

Every baker in the room stills at the tone of his voice, whisks and spatulas paused midstir.

Cameras turn to their assigned bakers for reaction shots, and the extras zero in on the confrontation.

"Excuse me?" Bryan looks as though there's no way in the world Grant is addressing him with such hostility.

"Get your hand off her. Stop invading her space. You're making her uncomfortable, and you're old enough to be her fucking father."

"Cut cameras!" Kate barks, storming up the aisle between stations. "Clock is paused."

Gemma is frozen, face stricken, and Bryan raises his hands with something dangerously close to a smirk on his face. "I think you're overreacting, mate."

"I'm not your mate, and she's not your entertainment."

A look sweeps over Bryan's face, just for an instant, that confirms everything his wife told me about his capabilities, but it disappears as quickly as it appeared, smothered by manufactured charm.

"I was simply observing her technique," he says. "I don't know what you thought you saw, but it's all good, right, Gemma?"

Gemma looks like she's about to cry for the second time today, and Kate stabs a finger at Bryan. "You, outside, now." She turns to the other judges and Natalie. "Do the rest, then come back to her. Refilm from scratch; we'll sort it in post. Gemma, pull yourself together. You're still in this."

She nods and swipes under her eyes.

Kate turns to Grant and doesn't even seem to notice she's staring down the human equivalent of a rabid bear. "And you, worry about your own station. This morning was the first time you performed in a way that's going to endear you to audiences—let's not ruin that yet, yeah?"

She stalks off before he can answer, and there's a low whistle that can only be from Vic.

For a moment, even Natalie looks off-balance.

"Are you okay?" Grant asks Gemma.

She nods and pastes on a brave smile. She turns to face Vic's station and inclines her head to Grant. "Tough big brother."

Vic snorts a laugh. "Hell yeah. Sure you're good?"

Gemma nods again, and Natalie claps her hands together. "Okay, bakers," she says in her normal voice. "On three, the clock restarts with fifty minutes remaining. We'll get Tony and Courchesne done next, then back to Gemma. Ready?" When no one objects, she counts to three and trills, "Rolling!"

Bryan returns for the remaining twenty minutes, roaming the ballroom and pausing often so the cameras can capture him in a variety of locations. It's going to be interesting to see how this episode looks when it airs.

When it comes time for judging, Bryan acts like nothing happened. He praises Tony's star anise brownies, tells Freddie he's focusing too much on style instead of substance, and dubs my banoffee brownies upscale-homey.

Leland goes a step further, complimenting the consistency of the dulce de leche and the texture contrast with the banana chips. He even takes a second bite, which I take as proper praise indeed.

When the trio arrives at Gemma's bench, everyone stills. It's normal to watch each other being judged, but as Gemma recaps her bake, the air feels electric.

Juliet is the first to remark, complimenting the Fluffernutter combo as delightfully nostalgic, while Leland says, "They're almost a bit too fudgy, though, like perhaps they needed another five minutes in the oven."

It's a restrained criticism from him, with none of the usual zing, and I think even he is aware of the charged air.

Bryan says nothing, merely nods along with his colleagues' assessments.

I would admire his restraint, except that it flies right out the window when they get to Grant.

"They're dry and bland," he declares. "Store-brand box mix would perform better."

Juliet and Leland exchange glances, and Natalie dramatically pops a second bite in her mouth to lighten the mood. "Well, more for me, then!"

"I do think they're a touch dry," Juliet says, "but I don't find them bland at all. That gingerbread stout flavor comes through nicely, and if I had a glass of milk or a scoop of ice cream to go with this, it'd be quite a treat."

"Thank you," Grant says, pointedly ignoring Bryan.

Yup, it's definitely going to be interesting to see how this episode gets edited together.

* * *

Matt and Derek are waiting when we arrive for lunch, and they both immediately check in with Gemma. Once satisfied that she really has emerged unscathed from the drama, Derek claps Grant on the shoulder. "It's a good thing you stepped in, because we were about to come through the wall. Who knew Bryan had a creeper side?"

Me, I think, but don't say.

"Honest, it's fine," Gemma says. "I'm mostly embarrassed. He was only touching my back. It's not like he grabbed my butt or anything."

"He had no business touching you at all," Vic says as we make our way to the buffet table. "But he assumed you wouldn't say anything, so he took it as permission. There's a reason he doesn't try that shit with me."

"It's not because you're scary," Freddie says, waving the salad tongs at her. "It's because you're very obviously not playing for the right team."

"It's because I'd skin him with a vegetable peeler and make him eat the strips. Straight men need to learn boundaries. Even famous ones."

"Especially famous ones," Courchesne says.

Derek looks like he's about to protest on behalf of his gender but seems to realize there's nothing he can say. "Well, I don't think he's going to be breathing down anyone's neck after all that."

If only they knew how close he is to never breathing anywhere ever again.

Chapter Eighteen

"Bakers, for your creative challenge, the judges would like you to tackle the most *temper*amental of the chocolates—white chocolate. Your task is to create an elegant celebration cake incorporating at least two white chocolate elements. You have three hours, so bakers, do your thing!"

Cake is not my strong suit, but because this is creative and one where we had preplan, at least I know what I'm doing and I'm ready when the judges descend on me.

"I'm doing a white chocolate cake layered with alternating lemon and raspberry curds, topped with a whipped white chocolate ganache and finished with fresh raspberries and candied lemon peel," I say, turning the heat up under pans of milk and cream.

"Raspberry and white chocolate isn't particularly creative," Bryan says.

I paste my cheeriest Pie Girl smile in place and say, "It's a classic for a reason."

Juliet nods and Leland asks, "How are you flavoring the cake layers?"

"I'm melting the chocolate right into my milk."

"Clever," he concedes. "And you expect the flavor to come through?"

"It has when I practiced," I answer. It was an honest question, so I'm not defensive, but what I don't admit is that none of my practice runs have been done on the clock.

No need to set myself up for that kind of extra scrutiny.

They move off and I get to it, dumping white chocolate shards into the simmering milk. This entire challenge is going to be a symphony of cooking and cooling, and I can only hope it doesn't get messed up.

I opt to bake five thin layers instead of three thick ones so they'll cool faster, because I've learned the hard way there's nothing worse than trying to torte warm cake.

With the layers in the oven, it's time to make the curd. I'm vaguely aware of the other bakers talking to their cameras and rattling around, but it all fades to background noise as I crack my eggs and measure out my sugar.

The raspberries they've provided are shockingly good, tiny and pungent, and nothing like the grocery store berries I was expecting. They look wild, and I wonder if there are bushes on the property somewhere.

I hold a handful back to add in whole at the end and dump the rest into the top of my double boiler with the rest of the ingredients and start whisking. That's all curd really is: fruit, sugar, eggs, butter, and motion. When it's nice and thick, I pour it through a strainer to catch the seeds and set it in the fridge to cool with my ganache.

I'm halfway through juicing my lemons from the next batch when my timer catches my eye. The timer that's supposed to be for my cakes. The timer that isn't set. "Shit."

"Problems?" Natalie asks, appearing as if on cue and popping one of my reserved raspberries into her mouth.

"Let's hope not." I pull the door open and sigh.

They're fine. Not burnt. Not even fully baked.

I can work with that. During practice, the thin layers took thirteen minutes to bake, but because time loses all meaning in this artificial environment, I have no idea how long they've been in for.

I set my timer for a slightly arbitrary five minutes, knowing that if this were a pie I could figure it out down to the second based on sight alone.

The lemon curd is barely over the heat before the timer beeps. The color on the cakes looks good, and when I tap the middle of one, it springs up nicely.

Crisis averted.

"Coming out!" I have a camera on my oven almost instantly, and the first three layers come out looking perfect, just like the one I tested, but the rest, the two that were toward the back, have officially crossed the line from golden to bronze.

I groan. "It's fine," I tell myself and the camera. "They're not burnt, just caramelized."

I let them rest in their pans while I finish the lemon curd, then turn them out onto parchment-lined sheet pans. Juan told me the secret to a clean release is to show no fear. I take each pan in turn, flip it, and slam it onto the tray. The noise draws more attention than I strictly care for, but each cake drops out like it's meant to.

Until the last one.

I don't know if it's the pressure of doing this under scrutiny or if I just didn't grease it well enough, but the entire center of the last round sticks to the pan. "Ooh," Natalie says. "That's not good, is it?"

"It's not ideal."

"Can it be saved?"

I'm aware of Bryan lurking beyond my bench, but I refuse to acknowledge him. I figure I can either try to salvage this layer or just act like it never existed.

Using an offset spatula, I gently pry the stuck cake away from the pan and settle it into the hole in the layer. Maybe as it cools, it will meld itself back together.

I wish.

While the layers cool, I pop my ganache bowl onto the mixer and let it whip until it goes from thick and creamy to light and fluffy.

At least I know that part will be good.

"Bakers, you have thirty minutes on the clock, thirty minutes!" Natalie calls.

Now or never.

I decide to use the messy layer to keep the correct ratio of fillings and move it to the slate square I'll be presenting the cake on. I pipe a ring of ganache around the perimeter and fill it with curd, repeating this process until everything is used up.

I've opted for a rustic take on elegance, since it means I won't have to rely on intricate piping, and when it's finished, I have to admit I'm quite pleased with it. You'd never know from the outside that there's a wonky layer holding the whole thing up.

Of course, since I'm the first one to be judged, it doesn't stay secret for long.

"It looks like there was a problem with the bake," Leland says, prodding the bottom layer with his fork.

"It's a fair attempt at salvage, though," Juliet says. "Which I think was worth it to keep the ratio even."

"I am getting the white chocolate coming through in the layers," he concedes.

"I would've rather seen jam than curd for the raspberry layer," Bryan says.

"I quite like the curd," Juliet says, and even Leland gives a grudging nod of agreement. "The fresh berries give it a little textural interest, but really, I like how the entire thing just melts in your mouth. It's lovely."

"Overall, very nice," Leland says. "The design is perhaps a bit too simple, but it's not offensive."

"I'll take that," I say with a grin.

In a way it's a relief to have gone first, because now I get to sit back and watch the rest without worrying. Tony also has a simple design, with white chocolate meringue buttercream frosted naked-style and topped with dried-pineapple flowers, but his passion fruit and lime flavor combo gets high marks. Similarly, Nell's white chocolate and matcha gets through without criticism, the flavor and design meeting the challenge if not completely wowing anyone.

Vic's white chocolate mocha doesn't fair as well. Leland calls the coffee overpowering, and all are unimpressed by the temper on her white chocolate decoration.

Courchesne's cake is gorgeous, tall and slim with subtle gold accents. When the judges slice into it, they reveal a cascading ombré of cake and ganache, which she explains goes from pure white chocolate to caramelized white chocolate to milk to dark.

"This is exquisite," Juliet says.

"Superb," Leland agrees. "The flavors are perfectly balanced."

Bryan shovels another forkful into his mouth and says, "This is the kind of cake you can charge entirely too much money for."

"Thank you," she says, unable to temper the little victory dance she does on the way back to her station.

I mouth *nice job* at her as she goes by, and she grins.

"Grant, would you bring your cake up?"

He does and places it on the table. He went for a monochrome look, with smooth white sides and a crisp edge. A half-moon of white macarons and meringue kisses decorate the one side, and I marvel that he found the time to make them and the cake.

Juliet gives him an indulgent smile. “If you plaster walls as neatly as you frost cakes, I’m sure you’ll have no trouble staying in business. This is a very nice-looking cake.”

“But what really matters is if it tastes good,” Bryan says, and even though his face is the picture of neutrality, it’s hard to interpret it any way other than overtly hostile. Whoever edits this episode together is going to deserve all the cake.

The interior is as snowy as the outside, with white peppermint filling sandwiched between white cake.

“The filling ratio is all wrong,” Bryan declares. “The cake is too thick, and it’s overbaked. There’s not enough filling to counteract the dryness.”

I wish I could see Grant’s face, but his body language gives nothing way.

“It does need a bit more moisture,” Juliet agrees.

Leland takes one of the macarons off the top and bites into it. “These are very good, though. If you had used this filling in your cake, this would be an entirely different conversation. Shame.”

Grant nods and returns to his station, face impassive.

Freddie goes next with a spectacular sculpted swan.

“The neck and head are made entirely of white chocolate,” he explains, setting it on the judges’ table. “And the feathers are piped ganache.”

“It’s stunning,” Juliet says, clearly delighted. “I almost don’t want to cut it.”

Leland prods the head. “Is it freestanding?”

Freddie shakes his head. “I made an armature. If I could’ve allowed it more time to set, I might’ve skipped it, but honestly, probably not. I prefer not having heads fall off if I can help it.”

"I see. Still, it would've been nice to have it completely edible."

Freddie doesn't say anything and Leland cuts into the body, revealing white layers separated with more ganache.

"Good distribution of filling," Juliet remarks, taking a sample.

"Nice bake," Bryan says.

Leland chews slowly, a thoughtful look on his face that seems patently designed to make Freddie and the viewers squirm. Finally, he sets his fork down and declares, "It's boring."

"Excuse me?" Freddie blurts, as if he can't imagine a bigger insult.

"This isn't lemon cake. At best it's a cake that once sat in the same room as a lemon and sort of remembers what it smelled like. This is essentially white cake with white chocolate ganache. It's well executed, but it's uninspired."

"But—" Freddie gestures at the swan's head.

"Visually, it's absolutely stunning," Juliet says. "But when you make that kind of promise, it's important for your flavors to follow through, especially at this level."

"I—" Freddie starts, then stops. "Okay. Yeah. Fair enough."

He gathers up his swan and returns to his station. I try to give him a sympathetic look as he passes, but he's too busy looking at his swan to notice.

"Gemma?" Leland calls.

She picks up her cake, a white chocolate and macadamia creation she filled with her own version of white Nutella, and makes her way up the aisle, a look of panic on her face.

At first I think it's from having to face Bryan again, but when she passes me, quickening her pace, I see the issue. Her layers must not have been cooled when she filled them, because the whole thing is shifting inexorably to the left.

I say a silent prayer to the cake gods that it holds together, and she's almost there, almost placing it on the table, when the cake gods abandon her. I don't know if she jostled it or if it was simply its time, but the layers slide in a wave down the side of her base, landing on the floor with a splat.

There are gasps throughout the room and murmured words of concern, but there's nothing we can do but watch in horror as cameras fly into action to capture the mess.

Chapter Nineteen

"Well, bakers," Natalie says, "This challenge has certainly been choco-full of ups and downs, but I am pleased to announce that this week's Top Baker is Courchesne."

She steps forward and gives a dramatic bow, eliciting laughs from more than a few of us. At least from those of us who are content in the safety of our middle-of-the-pack placing.

Natalie's expression turns solemn when Courchesne is done accepting her congratulations. "Unfortunately, we must also bid good-bye to someone, and I have to say, this has been the most difficult decision yet." There's a long pause as she looks us over, and Nell grabs my hand. I see her do the same with Gemma on her other side. Beyond them, Grant is rigid. "Grant and Gemma, could you please step forward?"

Gemma's eyes shine with tears when she hears her name, but she walks with her head up, and Grant follows a pace behind. They take their positions in front of Natalie, and Gemma clasps her hands behind her back, fingers twisting together like snakes.

"Grant. Gemma," Natalie says, looking at them each in turn. "Both of you have displayed amazing talent so far, but you've also been plagued by trouble this week. From chocolate that didn't set to cakes that set too much, it hasn't been an easy week. Grant, while your truffles wowed the judges, they felt it wasn't enough to counter the problems with your final cake. And Gemma, the judges expected to see a better mastery of chocolate skills than you displayed and were disappointed that your creative never made it to the table." Again that brutal pause, and Nell squeezes my hand. Natalie looks genuinely sorry when she says, "Therefore, Gemma, I must ask you to hand in your apron."

Those of us who are safe exchange shocked looks. After the blowup with Grant, I think we all expected him to be the one to go, not poor Gemma.

As she pulls the apron off, Juliet steps forward to accept it before Natalie can. It's the first time the routine has been broken, and even Natalie looks unsure of how to respond.

"Gemma, dear," Juliet says, "I know this challenge hasn't been kind to you, but I don't want you to think it's a reflection of your inherent skill. Sometimes in the kitchen, things don't go according to plan, and that's just life."

Gemma nods, but I can't imagine the speech is helping.

Juliet continues. "I know you came here hoping to win so that you could pay to attend pastry school." Again Gemma nods, and I wish Juliet would just give her the dignity of a clean exit, but she doesn't.

"I think it's a travesty that we live in a country where a young person, especially one as naturally talented as you, is forced to participate in a TV show in order to afford an education. So even though I need to keep this apron today, I want you to know you'll be putting on a new one very soon, because I am personally going to finance your program for you."

There's an audible slap as Gemma's hands fly to her face, and I find tears are stinging my own eyes. A quick look around shows I'm not alone. The cameras move around, getting their shots, and

Gemma throws her arms around Juliet in an expression of such pure gratitude that we break into applause.

* * *

"Okay, I'm just saying, if random prizes are a thing now, I should get a prize for being the first kicked off," Matt says, gesturing with his drink for emphasis.

"You can fund your own education, *Doctor*," Gemma says. Even though she's been eliminated, it somehow feels like she also won, and there's a general air of merriment around us. "But I do expect to be shown the tunnels now. I intend to spend the rest of my time here lounging in the pool and spying on the rest of you."

Derek raises his pint glass to toast her. "There are worse gigs to have."

"Well, I for one would like to avoid it as long as possible," Vic says. "I'm in it to win it."

"Same," Freddie says, "but that doesn't mean I wouldn't take a cash consolation prize."

"I think that might've been a one-off," I say, realizing that the possibility of extra prizes could change the entire vibe of the show.

"Let me dream," Freddie says.

"Am I the only one who thinks it wasn't planned?" Courchesne asks. "Natalie looked confused as hell when Juliet interrupted her."

Vic nods. "And Bryan looked like a constipated bullfrog. If it was planned, it wasn't shared. I think the boys finally realized Juliet runs this shit."

The door swings open and I turn, glad Grant and Tony changed their minds and decided to join us after all. I understand Grant wanting a chance to decompress on his own, but I worried Tony was avoiding us and really hoped it wasn't because of my slipup yesterday. Thanks to the strange reality of filming, that already feels like ages ago, but I thought my apology might've made things worse by drawing attention to his discomfort.

But it's neither of the guys. Instead, it's Ainsley, joining the group for the first time since her elimination.

"Ainsley!" Derek greets her with that movie star grin. "Pull up a chair! What are you drinking?"

In that moment, she may be the only person alive who's immune to his cheerful charm. She approaches the bar and asks for the oakiest Chardonnay they have and doesn't acknowledge us until she has it in her hand.

"Do you want to sit here?" Nell offers, nudging an empty chair away from her table.

Ainsley, naturally, ignores it, and the effect is like dumping ice water on the festivities.

"It's true, then," she says in a way that's not quite a question. She's looking at Gemma, who's perched on her barstool, her joy rapidly fading beneath the scrutiny. "You got paid to leave. Why is that?"

"It's great, right?" I say, trying to infuse my voice with levity the same way I infuse pies with magic. "What a kind thing for Juliet to do."

"Kind?" Ainsley scoffs. "I think you mean unfair."

"Nah, I think she means kind," Vic says.

"Everyone on this show was meant to have the same shot at the same prize. At no point was there any mention of pity prizes being up for grabs."

"Ainsley, reel it in," Derek says, his deep voice edged with iron. "Sit, have a drink, hang out. We're all here to have a good time."

"No," she says. "We're all here for a reason. To win. That prize money matters to all of us."

"Didn't matter to me," Derek says.

"Or me." Matt shrugs.

"Right, the banker and the doctor. You're the exceptions. You two just wanted to play at peasanthood for a while. But for the rest of you? That money matters, same as it did for me. It's why we're here. And it's not right that bonuses are getting handed out for what? Being young and innocent?"

"Whoa, okay," I say, hopping off my barstool. Next to me, Matt does that same. "Yes, we all want to win because we want the prize money, but we also love baking and want to have fun. Gemma getting a scholarship in no way affects any of that."

Ainsley looks like she's about to protest, but it's Gemma who cuts her off. "Maybe it's not me we should be talking about. Maybe it's you. At least the only thing the judges noticed about me was my potential in the kitchen. Should we talk about what they noticed in you?" Even though her words are calm, there's a wild recklessness in Gemma's eyes, and I know things are about to get very ugly. "Should we talk about that? Should we talk about Chloe?"

"Chloe?" Nell asks.

Ainsley glowers at Gemma, but her anger is now tinged with something very close to fear. "You have no idea what you're talking about."

"Don't I?"

Freddie glances between them, interest lighting his face. "It's no fun if you don't share with the class."

The glare Ainsley shoots him would send lesser men cowering, but Freddie just waits expectantly.

Everyone does.

Ainsley breaks first. "I don't need this," she says, more to herself than us as she turns and stalks out. "This whole thing was a mistake."

"Was killing Chloe a mistake?" Gemma asks, off her stool now and any trace of frivolity gone.

There's a hitch in Ainsley's step, but she keeps walking, and Matt puts himself in front of Gemma before she can go after her. She doesn't try to get around him. The fight leaves her as quickly as it hit, like the adrenaline from the day stopped being able to differentiate between good excitement and bad excitement.

Vic lets out a low whistle and Freddie says, "More drinks? This round's on me," in a voice that's desperately trying to salvage the evening. I hesitate for a fraction of a second, torn between joining them and going after Ainsley, but in the end, curiosity gets the better of me and I slip out the door, ignoring the questions thrown at my back.

She doesn't have enough of a head start to get away, and I find her on the stairs.

"Ainsley, wait."

When she turns, the sneer on her face doesn't surprise me, but the tears do. "What do you want?"

"Just to talk. Really."

She doesn't consent, not verbally, but she pauses long enough for me to catch up. She's still carrying the wineglass from the bar and takes a long sip before continuing the climb.

I expect her to go back to her room, but she bypasses our hall and leads me to a plush sitting room with a pair of wingback chairs tucked in an alcove. Leaded floor-to-ceiling windows frame the night outside, and as we settle in, I realize I'm not sure how this conversation should go.

"It's not true," Ainsley says, before the silence can stretch. "I didn't kill Chloe."

"Okay."

"I didn't," she insists, taking another sip of wine.

"Why do you think Gemma would say that you did?"

"She fell, okay? It was an accident. Kate said so and the police said so."

"Did you see her fall?"

She shakes her head, raising her glass to her lips with a trembling hand and not even noticing it's empty until she tries to drink.

"You weren't with her in the ballroom?"

"I didn't kill her," she insists, fresh tears welling again.

"But you were there? When she . . . fell?"

Ainsley shakes her head again, but it morphs into a nod, and her breath catches in a sob. "I was. Before."

I don't say anything right away, giving her room to explain. In the face of silence, most people will.

"We were fighting."

"What about?" I ask gently, like the answer might not even matter, but all I can see is Chloe's body on the floor and the fury that twisted Ainsley's face back in the bar. I could easily imagine an argument turning into a shove, into something more than either of them bargained for.

"She was trying to blackmail me," Ainsley says, and it's so far from what I was expecting that I almost laugh in disbelief.

"She was what?"

Ainsley hesitates, twisting the stem of her glass in her fingers. "Our rooms were next to each other, and she . . . overheard some things and thought she could use them against me."

I consider this. I would bet my KitchenAid that what Chloe heard was Leland, and she threatened to expose them. Chloe was an elementary school teacher, after all. Following rules would've mattered to her.

I take a gamble, knowing it could backfire but also that putting all the cards on the table could get her to stop dancing around the truth. "Did she find out about Leland?"

The shock on Ainsley's face is almost comical. "She told you?"

I shake my head. "You guys aren't as stealthy as you think."

"Damn it," she mutters. "I guess it doesn't matter anyway. I'm eliminated, so it's not like I'm benefiting from it. Yes, Leland and I slept together, and I would strongly prefer you don't mention it to anyone else. Married men aren't usually my type. They're definitely not anymore."

"That's what you and Chloe fought about?"

"She wanted to go to Kate and Abigail with it, said it wasn't a 'fair playing field.'" Ainsley hooks dramatic air quotes around the last words like she can't see the truth in them.

"And what happened?"

"I told her not to. Told her if I won, I'd give her a cut if she kept her mouth closed."

Something tells me it won't help to point out that Chloe wanting to tell the truth wasn't blackmail, but that paying her not to was definitely bribery. "Did she agree?"

Ainsley shakes her head. "No. She said either I could tell the truth or she would, but either way it was coming out. Then she died."

"And you weren't there?"

"I swear, I wasn't. I was pissed and I yelled at her, but I didn't touch her." Her face clouds with embarrassment, and she says, "When I left, I was planning how to sabotage her bake. I wanted to get her eliminated."

"And then she died."

"Then she died," Ainsley echoed. "And I feel like I'm being punished, like I manifested it and I'm the one who got eliminated."

She starts to cry in earnest, and as much as I think she's a selfish, entitled princess, I can't help feeling bad. Even if she didn't kill Chloe, it can't feel good knowing her final words to her were filled with such anger.

Chapter Twenty

I'm awoken before dawn by the unfamiliar ring of the desktop phone.

It takes me long enough to place the sound that I'm surprised the person on the other end doesn't hang up before I get to it, but when I answer, Kate is there, sounding far more awake than I feel.

"Filming is canceled for the day, and we ask that you remain in your rooms. Breakfast will be delivered shortly."

"What? Why? What's going on?"

"Please remain in your room," she repeats, and hangs up without offering more explanation.

I check the bedside clock. Barely past five. Christ on a crumpet.

In the stillness of the morning, I think I hear the muffled ring of Nell's phone next door, but perhaps I only imagine it.

I check the phone list, wondering if there's a code for the other rooms, but no. I can reach Kate, housekeeping, after-hours room service, and an emergency line, but not the other bakers.

I look at my lush, rumpled bed, but I know there's no chance of getting back to sleep now, not after that wake-up. Surely it would've made more sense to gather us at breakfast to tell us we weren't filming rather than wake us like this?

Being told to stay put has made me want to leave my room more than I ever have, but since I don't relish the idea of incurring Kate and Abigail's wrath this early in the morning, I opt for the balcony rather than the hall.

"So you got it too," Nell says, already leaning against the railing. Her hair is a halo of pale tangles against the velvet blue of the predawn sky.

"Kate's cryptic wake-up call? Yup. I think we all did. Did you get anything more than a *stay in your room, breakfast is coming*?"

"No. It's weird, though, right? I mean, we didn't even stop filming when Chloe died."

"Maybe it has something to do with that?"

A swath of light spills onto the balcony beyond Nell, and Freddie steps out. "How can they do this to us and not even give us coffee? I'm too nosy to go back to sleep but too undercaffeinated to be awake this early."

"Right there with you," I say.

"Would it be wrong to call the emergency number and report cruel and unusual punishment?" he asks.

"Or you could do the reasonable thing and try room service," I suggest. He's far enough away that we're practically shouting, but I figure if everyone got wake-up calls, it doesn't matter.

"Where did reasonable ever get anyone?"

"Uh, guys?" Nell interrupts. "Is that an ambulance?"

She's right. In the distance, there's a swirl of red and white lights, eerily ghostlike in the silence.

"There's no siren," I say, more to myself than either of them. Goose bumps prickle my arms despite the warm morning air.

"Maybe it's not an emergency?" Nell says hopefully.

I don't tell her that's not necessarily a good sign, that they don't bother with sirens if someone's already dead.

I wish that weren't something I know.

"We should go see," I say, the urge overwhelming.

"What? We can't," she protests. "They told us to stay."

"I'm down," Freddie says. "Bang on doors, get everyone. They can't do anything if we all go."

He's right. One of us might be kicked off for disobeying a directive, but they wouldn't get rid of all of us.

I take only enough time to trade my pajamas for a dress—the simple navy one, because something tells me this isn't the day for the festive ice cream sandwich print.

When I get to the hall, Freddie's already banging on doors, shouting, "Come on, we're going in search of coffee!"

"And information," I remind him.

"And also coffee."

In the end, Nell does join us, along with Vic, Courchesne, and surprisingly, Tony, who looks less like he's just been roused from sleep and more like he's been awake all night.

It's not quite the complete army I was hoping for, but still, six of us would be a lot to eliminate at once, so we set off down the hall in varying stages of dress.

Vic, naturally, takes the lead, but I'm right at her side. We descend the grand stairs in a parody of our normal filming routine. Tony and I are the closest to presentable, but the others seem completely unbothered to be making the trek in pajamas.

"I hear voices," Vic says, raising her chin in the direction of the dining room.

"Might want to get that checked out," Courchesne quips.

"Shush," I say, hoping to overhear whoever it is we're approaching.

"Ten buck says it's just the catering staff," Freddie stage-whispers. "Making coffee."

I shoot him a look that I don't entirely mean but can't quite help. In a way, I envy his lack of Spidey sense, the blissful denial that has him treating this like a snow day from school instead of an unprecedented interruption to what was supposed to be an unbreakable schedule.

If the show went on without Chloe, I can only imagine what it took to bring it to a halt.

Before we can investigate, Abigail storms into the hall with fury, and something more than a little like panic, playing across her features. "What part of stay in your goddamned rooms don't you people understand?" She advances on us with her arms wide, like she's trying to herd a group of unruly ducklings toward a pond. "Upstairs. Now."

"We're just wondering what's going on," I say, trying to meet her rage with concern rather than naked curiosity.

"When I'm ready for you to know, you'll know," she says. "Rooms. Now."

Thwarted, we turn, our retreat punctuated by the sharp sound of Abigail's heels moving in the other direction.

"Cop," Vic murmurs as we approach the staircase.

Courchesne sucks her teeth, and I feel Tony stiffen beside me. Vic's right. Down the hall where the main entrance is, a uniformed officer is talking to someone we can't see, saying something we can't hear.

Dammit.

"Go," I say, checking over my shoulder to make sure Abigail is gone.

"What? No," Nell says, grabbing my arm. "C'mon."

I shake her off, all my attention on the cop down the hall. "Go," I repeat. "I'll report back."

"Good hunting," Vic says, lips quirked in a smile that is pure Melly.

Tony hesitates at the base of the stairs like he's not sure if he should follow me or the group, and it's enough to snag in my brain but not enough to keep me there. I know the elevator alcove is just ahead, and if I can duck into it, maybe I can hear something.

I make it there undetected and press myself against the wall, knowing it will take next to nothing to be found. What I wouldn't give for a pie right now, filled to the brim with honesty and candor, but I'll have to settle for good old-fashioned eavesdropping.

"It's vital that this is handled discreetly," Kate insists.

The cop snorts. "Yeah, we'll try, but this is the second one this week. There's only so much we can do."

Another death then. Part of me knew, based on the silent ambulance, but having it confirmed is a whole different story. I do a rundown of who I saw or heard this morning. Matt called that he was staying put when I knocked, but Derek, Grant, and Gemma didn't join us either, and I make a note to ask the others if they got a response from them. I don't know if anyone tried getting Ainsley, but I doubt it. I'll have to check on her too.

A man in a suit joins Kate and the cop, and even though he's out of uniform, everything about him screams official. Detective, then.

"We'll send a unit to notify his wife at a more reasonable hour. Better to wait until we have a clearer picture of what happened."

"Surely it was an accident," Kate says indignantly, but I'm fixated on *his wife*.

"The second this week?" the detective asks, echoing his subordinate's earlier comment.

His. Wife.

I know Matt is married, but Derek and Grant aren't, so it's not them, which I'm grateful for. I have no idea about Tony's relationship status—he has given nothing private away—but since he was with us and is very much alive, it doesn't matter.

"Well," Kate says brusquely, "we can close off the west wing library if you need somewhere near the scene to gather, and the dining hall will have refreshments available."

"Very hospitable," the detective says, an edge in his voice that makes me wonder if he already has a theory about what's going on.

I hear the machine-gun click of high heels on polished floors and bite back a curse. That can only be Abigail.

Time to go.

Chapter Twenty-One

Back in my room, I pull my hair into a bun and sit on the bed. I'm not ready to share my theory yet, so I don't risk the balcony, where someone might be waiting.

If Kate said the west wing library was the most convenient spot for the cops to gather, that can only mean the crime scene is on that side of the building.

Which is the production side.

And as much as I hate to say this, if the show wouldn't stop for Chloe's death, it wouldn't stop for a camera operator's or set hand's either.

But it might for a judge.

There's a knock at my door, and a voice calls, "Room service."

I open the door, and a woman hands me a covered tray with a folded note tucked into the lid's handle. I thank her and set the tray on the desk, unfolding the note before I sit. *Full Cast and Crew Meeting at 11, Dining Room.*

I check the clock. It's barely past seven, and I already feel like it's lunchtime. This is going to be a long day.

The tray contains an array of offerings—pastries, eggs, and fruit along with covered cups of coffee and juice.

I eat quickly because I'm not dumb enough to continue the day on an empty stomach. Adrenaline already has me jittery enough; I don't need low blood sugar on top of it.

Then I slide my shoes on and set out.

My first stop is Derek's. I knock lightly, not wanting to draw attention from any of the other rooms.

He opens, looking wary, then relieved that it's only me. "What's up?"

"Can I come in?"

He raises an eyebrow, and I notice then that he's barefoot, dressed in only a pair of sweatpants that sit low on bare hips.

The man has abs like an anatomy drawing.

"Shirt and shoes required," I say, pushing past him.

He chuckles, and it's warm and low and the kind of sound that could do things to a different kind of woman. The kind of woman not focused solely on murder, for instance.

"What's the adventure?" he asks, leaning against the desk and crossing his arms across his broad chest.

"I need you to show me the tunnels."

"Now?" He's still not making a move to get dressed, and I want to throw something at him. Mostly clothes.

"Yes, now. Aren't you the least bit curious what's going on?"

"I'm curious about why you're so curious." He picks up the note, identical to the one I had on my tray, and waves it at me. "Looks like we're getting the full scoop at eleven."

"We're getting the version they want us to hear," I say. "Which, as I'm saying it, sounds more conspiracy theory than I want it to. But you know what I mean. When Chloe died, they sent us right back in to film, but now we're losing the entire day? And the cops—"

"Wait, what cops?"

"Do you not pay attention to anything but your own reflection? Yes, the cops. There's been another death."

All the casual pretense drops away. He pulls on a black T-shirt and sits on the edge of the bed.

"Who? Why didn't anyone tell me?"

"You didn't answer your door. And if you weren't on your balcony right after Kate's call, I guess you could've missed the lights."

"I figured we were off for a technical issue or something," he says, rubbing a hand over his head. "Shit. I feel like a jackass."

"Not your fault," I say. "And it's not a baker, and I don't think it's crew either." I give him the rundown of my deductions so far.

"So Leland or Bryan, then," he says. "Christ. Everyone else knows?"

I shake my head. "I don't know for sure yet either, which is why I'm here. I overheard Kate say the cops could set up in the library, and I figure that's my best chance at getting some answers."

"You don't think they'll tell us at the meeting?"

"I think I'd like to hear for myself."

* * *

The tunnels are amazing.

If I were exploring them under any other circumstances, I would feel like a kid in a playscape, and okay, yeah, I still kind of do.

I mean, no one ever outgrows the appeal of secret passages behind bookshelves, not if they have a molecule of whimsy left in them.

They're not what I envisioned at all, not grubby, cold hallways meant for servants or scandals but sly little openings where you'd least expect them. They're efficient more than anything, and soon we're camped out behind a library wall with no one the wiser. Derek shows me the latch, and we ease it open just a crack, enough to let in a sliver of light and a scrap of sound but not enough to draw attention. He's tall enough to see over my head no problem, and his presence is enough to make the dark confines of the space seem cozy rather than claustrophobic.

The narrow gap is enough to give us a view of the cop seated in one of the plush reading chairs but not who he's talking to.

The unknown woman's voice carries clearly despite its tremble. "Yes, it was just before five. I was walking in—"

"You don't live here?" the cop interrupts.

"Oh no," the woman says, "Very few of the staff are residential. I start at five, and I saw . . . him when I was on my way in. I was upset, because at first I thought someone had thrown laundry out the window—guests do all sorts of things—but when I saw Mr. Miller—" She breaks off and inhales a ragged breath. "He must've fallen."

I snap my head around to Derek, and even in the dark, I can see his eyes reflecting my shock.

Bryan.

Bryan, whose pie is no longer needed. It's a realization that rocks me. This has never happened. Sure, women have killed their own husbands before—once a woman at one of the domestic support groups I donate strength pies to up and beat her abusive husband to death with a frying pan, but that was all her. I've never had a PBG target die *before* they ate their pie.

It's unheard of.

"And you didn't move him?" the cop asks his interviewee.

She sniffles. "I mean, it was obvious he was already gone, so I left him there. I didn't think it would hurt anything."

"And you didn't think to call the police?"

She hesitates, then says, “I ran to tell Kate first, because she’s the point person for the production. We were told that while they’re filming, they’re the ones in charge. But I did call Mr. Galston too, because I thought he should know right away, since it’s his property. He wasn’t pleased to be woken up so early, but he was glad I told him.”

“You didn’t think the police would’ve been glad for a phone call too?”

“I assumed Kate would take care of that part, which she did,” the woman says, starting to sound offended. “I don’t appreciate you talking to me like I did something wrong. This has all been a terrible shock, and I’m not sorry for bringing it to the people on premises first. They needed to know what was going on.”

The cop shifts gears. “Is there a problem with your status we should know about? Is that why you held back the information?”

I bristle on the unseen woman’s behalf and feel Derek lean forward like he’s ready to step in. I press back into him, just slightly, stilling him.

“Asshole,” he mutters into my ear, and I nod.

“Let it play out,” I whisper.

“I didn’t hold back information,” the woman says. “I brought it to my employers, and they handled it appropriately. And I resent the implication that because I have brown skin and work in hospitality, I can’t be a legal citizen. I was born and raised in this country, thank you very much.”

By the time she finishes the last sentence, the meekness we heard on our arrival is gone, the shock at being part of a death inquiry replaced by outrage at yet another cop’s casual racism.

“We should make sure our bakes start getting shared with the estate staff,” I whisper, knowing pastry won’t solve the world’s wrongs, but if they can brighten a moment of someone's day, that's not nothing.

"I wouldn't mind sharing a poisoned one with that guy," Derek murmurs, and I stiffen, reminding myself it's impossible that he knows about what I do. "I've heard eye drops can do wonders."

I stifle a snort of laughter, relieved that he's thinking high school prank rather than murder-pie levels of punishment.

"Right. Well, I think that'll be all for now," the cop says curtly. "Please have a coffeepot delivered to this room. I still have a long line of interviews."

"I'll see what I can do," the woman says, and when she rises I catch a flash of white shirt tucked into black pants, the same uniform the room service attendants wear.

I watch the cop type something into his phone while I give the woman enough time to get down the hall, then nudge Derek. "Let's go," I whisper.

"Already?"

"If they're interviewing everyone, we shouldn't be missing from our rooms. What if we're next?"

"Good point."

He leads the way back through the tunnels, and I commit them to memory. There's one dicey passage near the atrium where we have to wait for a trio of housekeeping staff to move on, but we make it back to our floor undetected.

Derek looks exhilarated by the cloak-and-dagger of it all, and I know sending him back to his room alone would be cruel at this point, so I tip my head to my door. "Debrief?"

He follows me, and I'm glad I made the bed and don't have clothes strewn around. Living in the confines of my pie van has made neatness second nature.

"Okay, so this is wild, right?" Derek says, propping himself on the desk. "First Chloe, now Bryan. Maybe this place is cursed."

"I don't think the place has anything to do with it," I say.

He eyes me and I wonder if it's wise, talking to him like this. I needed him for his tunnel knowledge, but I'm not sure he's the Watson I'm looking for. Still, my gut tells me he doesn't have anything to do with it. He's been nothing but charming to everyone, and while he was eliminated early, it wasn't necessarily Bryan's ruling that did it. Even if it was, Derek doesn't seem like the grudge-holding type.

"You going to tell me what you're thinking, or are we gonna dance around it some more?" he asks, full lips quirking into a challenge.

"I think," I say slowly, walking to the glass door that leads to the balcony, "that there's no way you fall over that railing accidentally."

He joins me and considers it. "You think he jumped?"

"Or got pushed."

"Okay," he says, sliding the door open. "Let's test it. I'm about Bryan's height, right?" He bellies up to the railing and leans out. "I mean, it's not impossible, but even if I was drunk or screwing around, this is a little high to accidently topple over."

"Could you climb it?"

He raises an eyebrow and shrugs, gripping the railing and leaning back like he's winding up to jump.

I grab his shoulder. "Hypothetically, you idiot," I say. "I'd rather not have another body if we can help it."

"Nice to know you care," he says with that wicked sparkle in his deep-brown eyes. "But for the record, hypothetically, yes, I could vault over this, but I'm also a lot fitter than Bryan."

"Thank you, Mr. Humble. That was never in question."

"It's relevant," he protests. "What I'm saying is you'd have to be committed to getting over it. It would take coordination and some effort."

I nod. It's what I thought. "It would also take effort to throw someone over," I muse, considering who has the strength. Grant immediately jumps to mind, but really, any of the guys could probably do it if they were sufficiently motivated. Vic too.

"Not necessarily." Derek braces with his arms and hops up so his hips are level with the railing. He lands lightly and was in no danger of going over, but I see his point immediately. He turns and arches like he's trying to backbend over the railing. "Harder this way," he says, "but possible."

"Like a fulcrum."

"Or judo," he confirms. "By using the natural weight and momentum of their opponent, smaller fighters can take down larger guys all the time." He leans back over the railing, and I catch a movement behind him as Freddie steps onto his balcony. He freezes when he sees us and gives me an exaggerated shocked face before covering his eyes in a pantomime of *see no evil* and heads back inside.

Great.

Just what I need, Freddie thinking there's something going on with me and Derek that most definitely is not.

"Hell, it'd probably be easier for you to get me over than me to get you over," he says, oblivious to Freddie's quick retreat but not the implication of his words, because he rushes to clarify, "Not because of weight, but distribution."

"You're top-heavy," I say, not offended.

He smirks. "I think the proper term is *higher center of gravity*."

I wave away the distinction. "Point is, it's not about getting the body all the way over, just to the natural tipping point."

He nods. "Work smarter, not harder."

Chapter Twenty-Two

By 10:50 I'm going stir-crazy and decide it's close enough to eleven to head downstairs, but I almost have a heart attack when I find Nell sitting on the hall floor.

"Oh thank god," she says, getting to her feet. "I didn't want to go down alone."

"You could've knocked," I say.

She shrugs. "I didn't know if you wanted to be bothered."

I stop and look at her. "Why would you say that?"

She doesn't meet my eyes, but her cheeks flush red, and I'm already thinking about making Freddie the next body that turns up. I sigh. "Let me guess. You had a balcony talk with Freddie." It's not a question and I'm already marching to his door, hand raised to knock.

Nell grabs it before I can. "It's okay. I was just surprised. I thought you already had someone."

"I do," I say, pounding on Freddie's door. I hear movement inside and knock again. Of all the things I don't have time for right now, nonsense rumors are high on the list.

"Christ, I thought you were the police," he says. "We heading downstairs?"

I don't miss the obvious look he takes over my shoulder, and I shake my head. "No. First we're having a chat. Us three, right now."

He raises his hands in mock surrender. "Hey, what you get up to is your business, but you can't fault me for jealousy."

"There is nothing going on," I hiss.

"So you're just canoodling on your balcony with Derek as what, friends?"

"Yes. No. It's not even like that."

"It sounds like that, doesn't it?" he asks Nell, who is still red and not looking at either of us.

"Christ, I don't want Derek," I say, then stab a finger at Freddie. "And he doesn't want you, so can cool it with the jealousy. You have better options anyway. He was helping me spy. That's it. Nothing scandalous."

Nell looks up at that. "Spying? On who?"

"Wait, what?" Freddie asks. "What options?"

I roll my eyes. "My makeup guy, Julian. It's a whole thing. But what's important is that we know who died."

That's enough to get even Freddie's undivided attention, and I'm aware enough of the time to not pull a Natalie-style dramatic pause before telling them who.

"And you didn't tell us immediately?" Freddie says, with a dramatic hand to his chest. "Did our morning sleuthing mean nothing to you?"

"I was kind of occupied," I say, starting toward the stairs.

"With Derek! I knew it," Freddie cries, trotting after me.

And for once, the timing gods are smiling on me, because at that moment Derek's door opens and he slips out, having traded the sweatpants for well-fitting jeans but keeping the high-wattage smirk firmly intact. "What'd you know?" he asks Freddie, bumping his shoulder playfully before falling back a pace to walk with Nell.

Freddie groans. "I hate you all."

"No you don't," I say, spotting Vic, Courchesne, and Gemma talking on the stairs ahead of us. Tony sits a few steps above them, looking tired.

"Felt weird walking down without the pack," Vic says.

"Feels weirder walking down without cameras," Courchesne says when we reach the bottom. Instead of taking our usual path, we veer off for the dining room, where Matt and Ainsley are already seated. Others are filled with production staff, and I don't miss Freddie's less-than-subtle search for Julian.

"Nice of you to join us," Abigail says as we take seats around the center table.

"We're not late," Vic says, loud enough for Abigail to hear, and the fact that she doesn't react shocks me more than Vic's sass.

"We're going to get started right away," Abigail says. "First, thank you all for your patience this morning. I know it hasn't been easy being kept in the dark. It is with deepest sadness that I must inform you that Bryan Miller passed away in the early hours of the morning."

Gasps and murmurs ripple through the room, and Derek catches my eye from across the table, but we're not the only ones who aren't surprised. I try to watch for out-of-place reactions, but there are enough pockets of people who clearly already knew that it's hard to gauge.

So the information wasn't withheld from everyone this morning.

Interesting.

"As you know, this isn't the first tragedy of the week, and I would like to take a moment of silence to remember both Bryan and Chloe."

I tip my head in respect, but my eyes are still scanning the room. Most people have their eyes closed, but not everyone. Not the cops standing behind Abigail and not Tony. His gaze is flicking between the table and the cops until he feels me watching him. He meets my gaze briefly, then bows his head.

Right or wrong, my Spidey sense stirs.

"Thank you," Abigail murmurs. "Now, I wanted to gather everyone together this morning to make sure everyone is on the same page, to answer questions, and to shut down rumors."

Kate steps forward and begins handing out sheaves of paper and pens.

"What you're being handed is an updated copy of the NDAs you signed at the start of filming. The altered portion is flagged in red; please review it and sign. Also note the penalty for violation." She pauses while papers shuffle, and someone—Derek, I think—lets out a low whistle. "As you can see, it is imperative that you do not discuss what has happened here today with anyone until after the show airs."

One of the cops clears his throat, and Abigail cedes the floor. "The exception to that is, of course, us," he says. "We will be talking to everyone over the course of the day and would appreciate full cooperation."

Freddie shoots a hand up like he's still in high school but doesn't wait to be called on—probably also like in high school. "Is this a murder investigation?"

My Spidey sense pulls my attention back to Tony, who's rigid in his seat. But it's not just him. Grant, Ainsley, even Nell and Gemma have sat up at this.

The cop is clearly annoyed by the question, but he makes a valiant effort to hide it. "Right now it is simply an open investigation into the manner of death. When someone dies under unknown circumstances, this is what we do."

"But not for Chloe, right?" Vic's voice is harsh. "Only for the rich white guy."

"That's enough," Abigail snaps. "Chloe's death was a terrible accident, and I'm sure we'll find that Bryan's was too, but in the meantime, we will assist these officers however we can."

"I appreciate the stress this is causing," the cop says, "but the fact is, we do need answers in this case. Answers that weren't in question with the previous death. You may feel like you have nothing to tell us, but often people don't know what they know, so we ask that you cooperate fully with the questioning."

"Lunch will be served shortly," Abigail says, "but the police have asked that you refrain from discussing details of the morning with each other. As you can see, we have extra tables set, so please spread out, and then we'll ask you to return to your rooms until you're summoned."

"So we're prisoners?" Vic asks.

"You're helping with an investigation during an extremely difficult time," Abigail says, and each word is delivered like a warning.

There's a powder-keg moment where it feels like Vic might keep pushing, but in the end, she nods once, a sharp, upward jerk of her chin, and settles back in her chair.

Abigail's shoulders drop a fraction, but she purses her lips in a way that makes me think she's not ready to be relieved just yet. "Now, as you all know," she says, sweeping her gaze around cast and crew alike, "Sunday was meant to be a day off from filming, but due to the circumstances, we must shift the schedule to accommodate things." She holds up a hand to silence a ripple of murmurs. "I do not mean to be crass, but time is money and the show must go on. The police have assured us they will have their initial interviews completed today, and barring any surprises, we should be free to commence filming tomorrow."

Beside her, the cop nods in confirmation.

"We're just supposed to keep going like nothing happened?" Nell whispers, but not softly enough for Abigail to miss.

"If anyone has a problem with this," she says crisply, "you are free to withdraw from the competition, but I must remind you that such a decision would put you in breach of contract."

Nell flushes pink and shakes her head. I reach over and squeeze her hand.

"So?" Abigail looks around impatiently. "Is anyone availing themselves of that option?"

She knows we're not.

Even if we wanted to, the only ones who could afford the penalties would be Matt and Derek, and that kind of fine wouldn't be comfortable even for them.

"Very good," Abigail says. "A counselor will be available throughout the afternoon and evening in the east second-floor sitting room should anyone wish to talk, although the police have asked that you wait until after your interviews to make use of those services. If there are no other questions, I suggest we have lunch and get started."

Chapter Twenty-Three

In the end, two officers announce they'll be splitting the interviews, one keeping his spot in the library and the other setting up in one of the many first-floor meeting rooms.

It's not ideal.

The rooms aren't adjacent, and there are too many people out and about now for me to be roaming back and forth.

Shit.

The cops are on us the instant the lunch plates start being cleared, and Nell and a camera operator are the first summoned. Nell's face goes ashen and panicky, and for a second I'm worried she might faint.

"Are you okay, miss?" the cop asks.

"Sit," I tell her, and she does. Courchesne sees us and raises worried eyebrows. "Get her tea? Lots of sugar?"

Courchesne nods and hurries over to the buffet.

"Sorry," Nell says shakily. "I think it's the stress."

"Understandable," the cop says. "Take a minute."

I see my opportunity, and as concerned as I am about Nell, I can't pass it up. "I can go first," I say, more to Nell than the cop, and she nods gratefully. Only then do I look at the cop, sweetly, like we're in on helping her together. "I think she could a use a few minutes."

The cop hesitates, and Courchesne brushes past him with a steaming mug that she presses into Nell's hands, which are shaking enough that I'm worried she's going to spill hot tea all over her legs. Courchesne sees it too and drops to a crouch in front of the chair, wrapping her own hands around Nell's and the mug both. "No fainting allowed," she says, with mock sternness. "We're already at max drama for the day."

Nell nods, but Courchesne continues to hold her hands steady around the mug.

"Okay," the cops relents. "Just relax. I'll come back for you."

I touch Courchesne's shoulder and murmur, "Thanks."

"Not my first panic rodeo," she says easily.

I follow the cop out of the dining room on knees that have gone weak. Yes, I wanted to go first so I could be freed up to monitor the rest of the interviews, but as we make our way to the library, I realize that being first also means having no idea what's coming.

If I had waited and watched a few, I could've prepared my answers, because it's one thing to know I had nothing to do with Bryan's death and another thing to know I fully intended to cause it later.

It's the kind of muddy gray area cops aren't known for handling well.

While the cop pours himself a coffee from the urn on one of the reading tables, I pull the arm of the wingback to shift it out slightly, then settle in, trying to look more relaxed than I feel.

The cop lays his phone on the table, opens a voice recorder app, and recites his name—Tom Rensler—and badge number along with the date and location of the interview.

"Can you state for the record your full name and address?" he asks, and I do, reminding myself not to underestimate him.

After a few softball questions about my background and how I came to be on the show, he asks, "Have you had any interactions with Bryan Miller outside of filming?"

"No. We only see the judges during segments. They don't even eat with us."

"What about prior to filming?"

My first instinct is to say they didn't eat with us then either, but something tells me joking isn't going to help anything. Still, it's hard to bite back the snark, because to a degree, Vic was right. They care about Bryan because he was famous, powerful in his own way, but more importantly, the fact remains that if the cops actually did their jobs, I wouldn't have to do mine.

Protect and serve, my ass.

I keep all of that off my face, though. I have to. "The only interactions I've had with Bryan have been on set," I say honestly.

"And what about his wife Matilda?"

"I don't think she's been on set," I say, aware of the ice I'm on. "Or if she has, I haven't seen her."

"Have you had any interactions with her?"

"No."

He waits, and I'm not stupid enough to fill the silence. That trick only works on people who don't use it themselves. Still, the question concerns me. If the police suspect Matilda of wanting her husband dead, I could be in danger. It's not like I know for sure how carefully Melly covered our tracks.

"Did anything about Bryan Miller's demeanor seem off while you were filming?" Rensler asks, shifting gears. "Excessive stress? Anger? Depression?"

I pause, recalibrating. "I mean, angry was part of his brand. Him and Leland were the critics, and Juliet was the nicer one.

Which is kind of sexist, now that I'm thinking about it," I say, recalling Vic's typecasting theory. "Why does the woman have to be the nice one?"

"Ms. Ellery," Rensler says pointedly. "I believe there are bigger issues here."

"Right, fair. Because I don't know Bryan personally, I don't know if he was acting off during filming."

"Did he have any run-ins with anyone that you noticed? Conflicts with any cast or crew?"

I hesitate, not wanting to throw anyone under any buses, but because it's all on film, it's not like it can stay a secret. "Yeah, actually. He and Grant got into it on set. Bryan was harassing Gemma, and Grant stepped in."

"Harassing how?"

I explain what happened, hating that Gemma's going to have to go through this with the police, but it's not like she killed Bryan. Even if she used his bodyweight against him, she's so small that there's no way she could've gotten him over that balcony.

"So Grant and Gemma," Rensler says. "Anyone else?"

"Not really," I say, trying to remember if anything seemed beyond the normal competition drama. "He definitely wanted to eliminate Grant and seemed salty that it had to be Gemma—she dropped her cake—but it's not like he got in a fistfight about it."

"How did Grant handle that?"

I want to say he should ask Grant himself, but I don't, because I know he will. "He felt bad for Gemma, of course, but he deserved to stay and was gracious."

"Did he seek Bryan out after filming? Maybe to have words?"

"No, of course not. He— " I break off, realizing what I was about to say isn't true. Grant didn't join us in the bar last night. I shake my head. "I'm sure he didn't."

Rensler notices the hesitation. "Did you see Grant after filming yesterday?"

"No."

"Then how can you be sure he didn't?"

"Because he wouldn't," I say. "He's still in the running. He has no reason to stir up trouble."

"Not even in defense of another castmate?"

I hesitate again, because I actually could see Grant wanting to put Bryan in his place after what happened on set. Gemma was right when she told Vic he was the protective big-brother type, but I'm afraid saying so will paint Grant in a guiltier shade than he deserves.

Still, Grant has the kind of physicality that wouldn't even need physics to help him get Bryan over the railing. With enough rage, he could just throw him.

I don't want to believe Grant would do such a thing, but I have to admit it's possible.

Chapter Twenty-Four

The problem with the tunnels is having to pee.

When they show stakeouts on TV, no one ever talks about this part. Sure, penis-having folk can theoretically pee in bottles, but me? I make it through two crew interviews and half of Matt's before I'm about to burst, and I have nothing to show for my efforts except boredom and bladder pain.

I ease back into the passage and wait, making sure the corridor is silent before I slip out and hustle down the hall. It would be so much easier if there were secret elevators too, because I'd feel a lot safer depositing myself onto my own floor than out in the open.

Such are the risks I take.

I duck into a bathroom unseen and am back in my library hideaway before anyone's the wiser.

Thanks to my earlier bit of furniture adjusting, I can see that Matt has been replaced by Tony. The new angle of the chair still doesn't let me see him fully, but it's better than what we were working with this morning. Tony's olive skin has taken on an unhealthy sallowness, and the hand he has draped over the arm of the chair would look causal if he weren't rhythmically pressing his thumb to the tip of each finger, one after another, in small, meditative movements.

"Were you present for the altercation between Mr. Miller and Grant Reed?"

"Yes."

"And?"

"You asked me if I was present, and I was."

"Can you elaborate on what happened?" Rensler sounds testy in a way he didn't with me, and I wonder if it's because he's been here for so long or if Tony said something to piss him off while I was in the bathroom.

"It happened behind me, so I didn't see what set him off, but Grant confronted Bryan about how he was treating Gemma's space. He was upset, but it seemed justified."

"You have a sister Gemma's age, is that right?"

Tony's finger tapping stills, and he draws his hand out of sight. "I don't see how that's relevant."

"Well, if someone treated her the way Bryan allegedly treated Gemma, you'd be upset too, right?"

"Again, I don't see how that's relevant." Tony is polite but unwavering. "I don't need shared DNA to be bothered on someone's behalf."

"So you were upset?"

Even though their tones are entirely civil, there's a coiled energy to the questioning that has me holding my breath.

"Yes, I was upset that a young girl was made to feel uncomfortable. Of course I was. We all were."

"But you all don't have a record of violent behavior, do you?" Rensler hooks verbal air quotes around the *all* in the sentence, and something about Tony becomes very contained, like he's put himself in a glass box, visible but shielded.

"I have no way of knowing everyone's background," Tony says.

"But you know yours," Rensler says. "And so do I."

Shit.

In a flash, it's easy to turn Tony's quiet introversion, his standoffishness, into something suspicious, dangerous even.

"Again, I must question the relevance," Tony says, his impeccable politeness at odds with the tension radiating from him.

"You don't see how it's relevant that on the one hand we have a pair of dead people and on the other you, our very own convicted killer?" Rensler snorts. "Right."

My hand flies to my mouth while the logical part of my brain tries to work out if I've misheard what I know I didn't.

Tony takes a steadying breath, which, in my shock, is something I can't seem to manage. In the silence there's a soft creak, the subtle shifting of floorboards, and I whirl, panic rising, before I make out the broad outline that can only be Derek. I gesture at him to be quiet and refocus on Tony.

"My past is not relevant," Tony insists, maintaining complete civility.

Derek gets in close behind me to peek through the crack. "Thought you'd be here," he whispers. "Hear anything interesting?"

"Shh," I hiss, refocusing on Tony.

"Where were you last night?" Rensler asks him.

"In my room."

"Alone?"

"Yes."

"So no one can confirm that?"

"I don't know what other people can confirm. I can only tell you what I know, and that's that I was in my room," Tony says. "I went up after dinner and didn't leave."

"You were out this morning," Rensler points out.

"Yes."

"Why?"

"I was curious what was going on."

"Curious what was going on or curious what we already knew?"

"Damn," Derek whispers. "My guy wasn't such a dick."

I don't tell him what he missed, the alluded-to criminal record that Tony didn't deny. I'm still processing it myself.

"Curious what was going on," Tony says. "Freddie knocked on my door, so I suppose he can confirm that I was there."

I think back to our morning trek, remembering Tony was the only one other than me not in pajamas. At the time I chalked it up to just wanting to be presentable, but could there have been more to it? He did seem tired, like maybe he'd been up all night.

I shake my head. It's not time to theorize, not yet. Right now it's about getting information, learning what the cops know, and hoping it all leads firmly away from Matilda and, by extension, me.

"This morning, anyway. The ME puts time of death somewhere between one and three."

"Dude thinks Tony killed Bryan? Seriously?" Derek asks, the words warm puffs of air against my ear. "Isn't he a librarian?"

"Shush." I file away the time of death. It's unlikely anyone was still in the bar that late, not when we have to be up so early for filming, but it's possible.

"Tell me," Rensler continues, "Have you ever been in contact with Matilda Miller?"

"I don't know a Matilda Miller," Tony says.

"Did they ask you too?" I whisper to Derek.

"Yup."

Shit.

If Matilda is under suspicion, that's not good. I need to find out if Melly's hacker friend is really as good as she claims.

Rensler escorts Tony out and I lean against the wall, knowing there will be a few minutes before he returns with the next person.

"What else did they ask you?" I'm still whispering, even though the chances of being overheard are slim. It seems wrong to talk normally while hiding in a wall.

Derek does the same, so it's not just me. "Just if I noticed anything off about Bryan's moods or if any of the eliminated bakers were holding grudges. Made a joke about Ainsley that didn't go over well, but he knew I didn't mean it."

I give him a look I know he probably can't see, but I can't help it. "When they grill her, it's going to be your fault, you know."

"She'll forgive me."

"Someday that charm is going to fail you, my friend."

"Hasn't yet."

There's a murmur of voices from the library, and we fall silent before I can ask him if he was questioned about Grant.

Rensler is noticeably softer in his speech now as he escorts his interviewee in. "Please, take a seat."

"Nell," Derek whispers, and my stomach knots in sympathy stress.

He walks her through what has become the standard opening, and after he has her basic info, he asks, "If you think back to yesterday, is there anything you can recall that seemed out of character with anyone? Either Bryan or the people around you?"

"Not really," Nell says, "but we've only been here for a few days, and there's nothing normal about any of this."

"I understand you were the one who found Chloe's body." It's a statement, not a question, and Nell tucks her hands between her knees and hunches forward, as if the memory is rain, pelting her back.

"Can you tell me about that?" Rensler prompts.

"I just found her. We were going to start filming, and I wanted a few minutes to get settled before the cameras came in, but she was there, on the floor, and it was too late." Her words are halting, and I want to go stop him from making her relive it, but I can't. "I couldn't help her."

"You didn't see anyone else in there?"

Nell shakes her head.

"Verbally, for the record," he says.

"No, just Chloe."

"Would've been nice if they'd asked about this when it happened," I whisper.

"Let's go back to Bryan," Rensler says, and even though he's gentler about it than he was with me and Tony, I recognize the abrupt shift in gears is a tactic of his. Perhaps his only one.

"I didn't find him," Nell says.

"I know. But can you tell me about the last time you saw him? How did he seem?"

"I don't know. Normal?"

Rensler seems unsatisfied with that. "Nell, these aren't the first deaths you've been involved with recently, are they?"

"What?"

Beside me, Derek goes rigid, and I put a hand on an arm that's all corded muscle, and I know I couldn't physically stop him if he decided to burst into the library right now. "Wait."

Derek's breathing is shallow and angry, but he doesn't blow our cover.

Rensler repeats his question, and I keep hold of Derek.

"You mean my mother?" Nell asks. "How do you know about my mother?"

"We have access to all the cast files," Rensler says. "Please, tell me about that."

"Fucking bastard." Derek's curse is barely more than an exhale, but the fury in it makes the tunnel feel too small.

"I know," I whisper, because I do. I want to rescue Nell as much as he does, but we can't.

"If you saw my file, you know she had cancer. It was slow right up until it wasn't," she says, speaking more to her lap than to him. "Then it was over."

"She died at home?"

"Yes."

"But not from cancer." Again it's not a question but a statement.

The air in our hidden nook changes, and before I can even articulate why, I pivot, putting myself squarely in front of Derek in the tight space and planting both hands on his broad chest. He towers above me, but while I'm used to that with Noel, I'm not used to staring down this much angry well-muscled mass.

Everything Derek said earlier about judo and using your opponent's body weight against them goes out the window, and I know if push comes to shove, I can't stop him, not physically, and right now every part of him wants to burst through the wall and put a stop to Rensler's questioning.

"It was terminal," Nell says.

"It would've been, eventually," Rensler agrees.

And I know. Nell didn't tell me this part, but it must've been in her application essay and my heart breaks for her, because I understand exactly what it's like to watch what she did.

Nell swipes her hands across her eyes. "She got confused in the end," she says, voice thick with tears. "And yes, she took too many pills."

"Took too many or was given too many?" It's somehow worse that his demeanor is still gentle, like he's on her side even as he drags her through her worst memories.

"Took too many," Nell says. "She was palliative and had plenty available."

"I see," Rensler says. "That must've been very traumatic for you."

"Of course it was."

"Tell me, did you keep any of the pills after she was gone? Sedatives, perhaps?"

Something like a growl rumbles through Derek's chest, a low sound I feel as much as hear. I rise on tiptoes, leaning into him, against him. "Don't," I breathe. "Be there for her when it's done."

For a moment I think he's going to push through me and throw our hidden door wide open, but he shifts his weight off the balls of his feet and takes a silent step back. I match it, guiding him gently away.

"He has no right—"

"I know," I whisper. "Just go. I'll make sure she's okay from here. You be ready to check on her when she gets back."

"Fucking cops," he murmurs.

"I know." I watch him go, making sure he doesn't double back to the library before I return to the gap in the wall. The objective part of my brain, the part that's not absolutely aching for my new friend, files away the fact that Rensler questioned her about a potential overdose, and I can't help wondering what he knows about Bryan's death that makes that specifically relevant.

Chapter Twenty-Five

On Sunday morning, it feels wrong to gather at the top of the stairs for our entrance shots, and not just because this was supposed to be our day off.

Abigail addressed us all at dinner last night with a less-than-rousing speech about how the best way to honor Bryan's memory was to get back in the kitchen. No one commented that it was the same line she used after Chloe died, but if I noticed it, I bet others did too.

Now there's a somberness to our dwindled group that keeps us quiet, worse than the uneasy air that followed the loss of Chloe on that first day. It's not that Bryan's death matters more; it's that circumstances are so irrevocably different now.

Aside from Nell and me, none of the other bakers saw Chloe, so it was easy to believe she really did succumb to a tragic accident. Even I could almost convince myself it was true, but with two deaths and a police presence, that's no longer an option.

As we wait for Natalie to arrive with the cameras, the interviews swirl around my head, just as they did all night. Tony sits on an upper step by himself, eyes fixed at a point between his knees, fingers tapping the same rhythm I witnessed yesterday, each finger touching his thumb in a fluid cascade.

He's the first one I would've been digging into last night had I been home with my laptop. If the cop was right and Tony really has been convicted of something, a simple Google search would probably give me an answer, but if not, the PI databases I subscribe to would.

The accusation feels off, though, because surely FoodTV wouldn't cast convicted felons on a baking show. It has to violate some kind of liability or insurance thing.

I silently curse myself, realizing I'm jumping from convicted felon straight to irredeemable psychopath, and I know better. I know because for all intents and purposes, I'm a serial killer and I'm still here, and I know because Frank has hired several ex-cons, including one of his last dishwashers, who was able to use the experience and glowing reference to move into a higher-paying position.

Next to me, Nell picks at the edge of her apron, and I lean into her, just to let her know I'm there.

"This is not the fun time I signed up for," Freddie announces from his spot on the landing. "I still think we should've had a proper Irish wake last night and got tanked."

"You're not even Irish," Courchesne points out.

"I can be in spirit."

"I feel hungover and didn't even drink anything," Nell says quietly. "I hardly slept."

"It's the stress," I say, because I feel it too. I spent most of the night staring at the ceiling, trying to sort through everything I had heard and everything I still needed to learn.

Poor Julian definitely had his work cut out for him this morning.

Footsteps sound above me, and I turn to see Grant settle himself against the wall, the last to arrive. His was the interview I most wanted to see yesterday, but he must've been on the other cop's list, because Rensler never brought him in. His face is stony, but then again, he always has resting murder face, so it's hard to read anything into it.

Below us, Vic rises and nudges Freddie with her foot. "Showtime."

This morning it's Abigail herself leading the charge of cameras, and literally anyone would've been a better pick.

She stops at the bottom of the sweeping staircase and claps her hands. "Before we roll, I shouldn't have to remind you that you are to proceed as normal. You are not to mention Bryan's absence or give any indication that things are amiss. We will be sorting the narrative around this in post, so please just carry on."

She doesn't ask if there are questions, only steps to the side, looks at the pair of camera operators for a moment, and with a sharp nod says, "Roll!"

We descend the stairs as usual, converging from the respective wings in the center, and make our way to the ballroom.

Natalie is standing with Leland and Juliet when we enter, and even she looks tired.

At least she does right up until she steps into position; then it's like magic. "Welcome back, bakers," she says with a flourish. "This week we're focusing on the most important meal of the day, and that is, of course, breakfast!

"Now, Leland and Juliet would like you to begin with a breakfast classic. For the warm-up challenge, you are to create six identical bagels. These should be well risen, with a golden crust and a chewy interior, so bakers, do your thing!"

As usual, the recipe is woefully short on detail. *Make dough. Shape bagels. Poach bagels. Bake bagels.*

Thank you, judges.

I set about scaling my ingredients and immediately have to start over when I realize I didn't tare my scale after putting the bowl on.

Fuck.

"Off to a rough start, then?" Natalie asks, voice chirpy but sympathetic.

"Caught it early," I say, tipping the bowl of flour, salt, and diastatic malt into the bin.

"That's all that matters," Natalie says as they move off.

I reweigh my ingredients and tell myself to focus, that while the cameras are rolling there's nothing I can do about the deaths anyway, so there's no point wasting energy thinking on it.

I set my bowl on the mixer and almost drop the dough hook when a harsh *thwack* makes me jump. It's Grant, working his dough by hand, throwing it against his bench in big sweeping arcs that are somehow graceful and aggressive all at once.

I set mine to mix mechanically, and soon the stiff dough is slapping the sides of the bowl and making the mixer skitter.

Even through the noise, the steady slamming of Grant's dough is audible, every thud a reminder that I'm not the only one capable of violence.

* * *

Outside, the sky is ominous and the occasional fat raindrop darkens the patio stones, promising more to come. Off camera, Kate warned us that getting wet would not look good on camera and she would not be pausing production for us to dry off, so most people have opted to stay close to their stations while the bagels rise.

But not Grant, so not me either.

He's leaning against the railing, looking out over the grounds, and if he hears me come out, he doesn't show it.

"Nice day, huh?" I say.

"Always liked storms," he answers, eyes toward the sky.

"You wouldn't if you lived in a camper," I say, huffing out a laugh as I remember the tropical storm that managed to make its way up to Massachusetts last year and how it felt like Penny might get blown clear away.

Zoe was not impressed.

The memory of her curled up and shaking in the bed is enough to make me miss her in a way that physically hurts, but I bury it, because that's not why I'm out here risking water damage.

Realizing there's no great way to be subtle about it, I lead with the question I want to ask. "How'd your interview go yesterday?"

He turns to me then, the look on his face guarded and mistrusting. I don't blame him, but I don't retract the question either.

"Less than pleasant," he finally says, looking back out across the gardens.

"Same."

He snorts. "I doubt that."

"Maybe not the same questions," I concede, "but less than pleasant is pretty accurate."

He shakes his head, just slightly. "They implied I had something to do with it because we got into it earlier."

"Did you?"

He whips around like I've electrocuted him, eyes narrowed. "Did you?"

"No." I don't tell him it's only true because Bryan died before I had the chance to kill him myself. "But I didn't get in a public fight with him either."

“I should’ve laid him out right there,” Grant says, shaking his head. “Fucking sleazebag.”

There’s a beat in which I have to admire the honesty. If Grant had something to do with Bryan’s death, he’s not going out of his way to hide his animosity. It’s either brilliant or batshit, and I’m not quite sure which. Normally I would consider that kind of guilelessness a clear indication of innocence, but the seething rage radiating off Grant’s big frame makes it clear he would’ve had no problem throwing Bryan off a balcony.

“They’re going to deify him now that he’s dead, you know that, right?” he says. “Even though he was a perv.”

I look at him sideways, wondering just how much he knows about Bryan. Or, perhaps, how little I know about what actually happened with Gemma the other day.

There’s a strong gust of wind, and with it, lashings of rain begin their assault across the far gardens. We have minutes at most before it reaches us.

“I’ve known guys like him,” Grant says, apparently unbothered by the weather. “They think they’re untouchable.”

“They’re not. Not always.” The words are out before I can stop them, and Grant looks at me in a way that makes me feel dangerously exposed.

“I know.”

Chapter Twenty-Six

When we return to the ballroom for the second challenge, I leave the morning's bagel baggage at the door. It's fine that Leland compared mine to rustic spaceships. Really. And so what if Tony's were the Platonic ideal of bagelhood?

I'm not out yet.

What's up next isn't pie, but it's pie-adjacent, and that puts me back in my element.

"Bakers," Natalie greets us. "For the craft challenge, Leland and Juliet would like to see eight turnovers. You may use full or blitz puff pastry, but it must of course be prepared from scratch, and your fillings must be delectable."

Blitz, or rough-puff, pastry is practically pie dough on flaky steroids, so it's an easy choice. Besides, the last thing I want to do is screw around with full lamination when I have three fillings to make.

I'm already up to my elbows in flour when the judges arrive for their establishing shot, and I'm ready for them.

But instead of asking for the overview of my recipe, Leland eyes my bowl of flour for a long moment before meeting my gaze. "So you're going blitz?"

"I am," I say, refusing to let him shake me. His pointed questions and unflinching eye contact might've rattled me on a different challenge, but not this one. This is a glorified hand pie, and I know how to make it work. "I'm doing a black currant turnover with lemon and frangipane, and I find full-puff to be a little too delicate for that much filling."

I don't tell him the only full-puff I've tested has come frozen courtesy of Juan's supply order at the diner. No need to look like a total amateur.

"The delicate flakes are part of what makes a good turnover," Leland says.

"Oh, there will be plenty of flake, I promise."

"Let's hope so."

I finish up the dough, resisting the urge to work any pie magic into it. It takes a conscious effort, and after the morning's bagel debacle, I wonder if I'm making a mistake leaving it out.

While the dough rests in the fridge, I get started on my trio of fillings, and with my black currants simmering in cassis and the bright aroma of lemon zest filling the air, it almost feels like baking in my own kitchen.

Or at least it does until the crashing clatter of metal spoils it. It's followed by a sharp, "Fuck me!" that has the cameras beelining for Grant. One makes a show of following the path of the bowl still spinning its way across the aisle toward Nell's station and the trail of hulled strawberries left in its wake.

Nell stops what she's doing to retrieve his wayward bowl and crouches down to help gather the berries. Because they're in the aisle, everyone sees him grab the bowl from her. "I've got it," he says shortly.

"It's okay—" she starts, but he interrupts.

"Worry about your own bake. I've got it."

She stands, looking embarrassed, and goes back to her bench.

"Chill," Vic says from the station behind Grant.

He ignores her, just keeps throwing berries into the bowl. In front of me, Tony's eyes are narrow as he watches the scene, but when he turns back to laminating his dough, his face is impassive.

Natalie approaches Grant, puts a hand on his back, and says something I can't hear, but he nods once.

"I'll have to start over," he says to the camera, and one of the set preppers sets a bowl of fresh berries at the end of his bench before scurrying away.

On my own station, the butter I added right before the interruption sits pooled on top of the warm curd. Dammit. I whisk hard, bringing it all together in a smooth emulsion, then pour it onto a half sheet pan to cool.

The rest of the challenge proceeds without catastrophe, although the calm I was enjoying doesn't return.

I'm still feeling wired when Natalie calls, "That's it, bakers! Move your turnovers to the end of your benches!"

I do, feeling good about what's on the tray if not what's in my head. The way Grant snapped at Nell keeps replaying in unfortunately high definition.

The judges start with Courchesne, whose banana foster turnovers earn high marks for flavor despite being overfilled. "I'm trying not to make sloppy-banana jokes," Natalie says as she swipes a finger through a pile of filling that oozed out.

"I'd thank you if you didn't," Juliet says primly.

At Tony's station, even Leland is obviously impressed. "This is what we're looking for with a good puff pastry," he says, holding it up for the camera. "You can see all the fine layers built up by the full lamination. Very nice."

"Lovely filling too," Juliet says. "Just the right amount of anise to set off those pears. Well done."

Shit. Of course Tony went full lamination. I hope that hasn't become the official bar we need to clear.

"Well, these certainly are cheerful," Juliet says, picking up one of Freddie's rainbow-sprinkled turnovers.

"Tell us again about this," Leland says, eyeing it skeptically.

"Birthday cake," he says. "The pastry is flavored with vanilla bean and has an almond-Funfetti filling and vanilla buttercream drizzle."

"And sprinkles," Leland says. "On a turnover."

"I think they're delightful," Juliet says, after sampling it. "It's very sweet, very out of the ordinary, but it's a lot of fun."

"The flavor profile is a bit too third-grade bake sale for me," Leland says. "And the pastry could be flakier. The problem with rough-puff is it's very easy to overwork it and lose that structure."

"I believe we'll have to agree to disagree on this one," Juliet says, and then it's my turn.

Leland breaks one in half, and Juliet nods approvingly. "Attractive filling. Nice shatter on the pastry."

"It's about more than nice looks," Leland says. "It's about how it tastes."

"We eat with our eyes first," Juliet replies with a wink.

It feels like an eternity while they chew. After he swallows, Leland stares at me in that disconcerting way of his, like he's waiting for you to read his mind.

He rubs his chin and shakes his head.

Shit.

No. Not shit. I know it's a good turnover. The filling is well balanced, and the rough-puff is plenty puffy. Fuck him if he doesn't like it.

"You know," he says, "I hate that there's not a single thing I can criticize about this. I would love your black currant jam recipe."

I'm so shocked, it takes me a moment to respond. "Yes, of course."

"They really are very good," Juliet agrees, and Natalie mimes stashing a pile of them in her pockets.

Behind them I see Freddie give me a thumbs-up, and I can't suppress a grin. This is definitely enough to make up for the morning's catastrophe.

Chapter Twenty-Seven

"I'm starting to feel like your phone company," Julian says.

"And you have no idea how much I appreciate it," I say, taking the phone from him.

He sighs. "The things I do to foster love."

That's so far off the mark it's not even funny, but I don't correct him. "You're the best."

"I'm aware. I can give you fifteen minutes max."

"Plenty."

He gathers his makeup kit and sets off for his next victim, and I tap out a text that I immediately delete after sending. *It's Daisy, pick up when I call.*

I give it a minute to go through and be seen, then I dial the same number.

Melly picks up on the first ring.

"Hey there," she purrs. "What happened to your own phone?"

"Are you somewhere you can talk privately?" I ask.

"Yeah, I'm home," she says, voice wary now. "What's wrong?"

"Is there any way for the message you posted on that board to be traced back to us? Any at all?"

"No, I told you, my contact was good. This is some top-level stealth shit. Why?"

"Because Bryan Miller is already dead. Pre-pie dead." I give her a rundown on what happened.

"Whoa. That's either a hell of a coincidence or . . . I don't even know. Whoa."

"Yeah," I say, knowing there's not a lot of time for her to process it before I have to give Julian his phone back. "The thing is, the police are implying Matilda might be involved, and I need to know if they go looking through her computer that they're not going to find me sitting there."

She hesitates, but not for long. "You watch too much TV. Podunk police forces don't have computer geniuses sitting around waiting to pull answers out of the deep web at a moment's notice."

"But if you could find her and she could find you, surely someone else can find that."

"Sure, if they were pointed in the right direction, maybe, but they won't be. This is layers and layers deep."

"Scrub it," I say, knowing the kind of information I can find with the databases I subscribe to. I have no doubt the law enforcement versions are even better. "If there's anything your friend can do to erase those conversations, do it."

She snorts. "It's already done. You think I'd leave incriminating evidence sitting around?"

"Melly, seriously. Just go back through and make sure. Please."

"Okay, sure," she says. "But you didn't even kill him, so you don't have anything to worry about."

"If it comes to light that his wife was looking to hire a hitman and that my services were the ones on offer, then yes, I do."

Again, the reminder of why I usually work alone hits me like a punch in the ribs. It's safer for everyone that way. Safer for the women who need me, safer for my friends, and safer for me.

Unexpected tears of frustration burn my eyes. I was so stupid to think I could play both sides, that I could be this avenging force of justice and still have friends. Friends. For fuck's sake. I kill bad men with good pies; of course I can't have friends.

But I do, and now they're in as much danger as I am if I don't get to the bottom of this soon.

* * *

The burst of happiness that came from the turnover challenge is gone when I return to the ballroom, replaced by the weight of, well, everything. I feel stupid for even being here, for acting like this show even matters when two people are dead and one of them should've been neatly dispatched at my hand without involving any of the people in this room or in my life.

Bryan deserved his end, but he deserved it without taking anyone else down with him. If he sent himself over that balcony, fine, that's one thing, but I should've handled this before anyone else felt they had to step in. I look around the room as we wait for the judges to arrive, aware now that everyone is hiding their own secrets. Tony, Grant, even sweet Nell. I can only imagine what was brought out in the others' interviews.

And here's the thing: at the end of the day, I don't want any of them going down for Bryan's murder. Even if they did it. Because right or wrong, he was a terrible person who deserved what was coming to him, and I don't believe for an instant that anyone in this room would've killed him for fun. If they did it, they had a reason.

Juliet and Leland arrive with Kate on their heels. She hovers in the doorway as they take their places, and Natalie steps forward. "Welcome, bakers, to your creative challenge. Today the judges would like you to make a spectacular themed donut display. Your creations should be comprised of at least two dozen donuts and include filled, cake, and yeast-raised offerings. Remember, do or do-nut, there is no try, so bakers, do your thing!"

I try to lose myself in the sounds of baking, the clatter of bowls and whir of mixers as everyone gets to work. By the time the judges get to my station, I've compartmentalized enough to get back in the zone.

"I'm doing a cornucopia of autumn pie–themed donuts," I say, gesturing toward the wicker horn at the end of my bench. The set prep people are wizards at sourcing some of this stuff. "One will be filled with a pumpkin pie pastry cream and topped with a spiced oat streusel, and I'll have a cider cake dipped in honey glaze, and a pecan pie frosted ring."

"Sounds very festive," Juliet says.

I don't tell them that while I'm confident in my flavors, I'm still less than thrilled to be facing my temperamental yeasty nemesis again. The dough I'm using is amazing when it comes out right, but it's also incredibly delicate, and moving delicate things into extremely hot oil isn't my favorite activity.

When the dough is ready for its first proof, I move right into my pastry cream. I catch snippets of Freddie describing his cocktail-inspired donuts as I whisk my eggs and sugar together and wonder if I've been too tame in my choice of theme.

Too late now.

With fillings and frostings to be made, the ballroom stays jumping despite the long rises the doughs need. I pop my pastry cream in one of the fridges to chill, pausing to listen as Juliet says, "Grant, you had an excellent showing in the warm-up challenge but a rocky ride with your strawberry balsamic turnovers. Tell us what you're making and if you think it's enough to overcome the craft challenge challenges."

"Well, obviously I hope it will be enough to make up for the turnovers," he says. "I'm sticking with the breakfast theme and doing a blueberry pancake–flavored cake donut, coffee-and-cream-filled rings, and orange juice–glazed donut holes."

That makes me feel better about my own selections as I get started on my apple dough. Not everything has to be big and flashy to be good.

* * *

"Okay, bakers, step away from the donuts," Natalie says. "Time is up. I repeat, time is up!"

Set staff descend on the stations, cleaning furiously while the cameras get close-ups of everyone's offerings.

Leland and Juliet take their places behind the judges' table, and Natalie calls up Courchesne.

Luckily, she only has a short walk, because her board is enormous. Unlike the rest of us, she opted to do four flavors to get the colors she needed for her ace flag display.

"Well, that is pretty," Juliet says when she sets it down.

Leland peruses the rows of donuts long enough to give the cameras time to capture Courchesne squirming. "It's a bit simple," he finally says, "but it is neat. Remind us of the flavors?"

She points to each row of her flag as she says, "Chocolate cake, vanilla frosted, coconut filled, and ube cake."

Leland selects one of the silver-frosted rings. "Just vanilla? What's the color from?"

"Silver luster spray."

"I like that you incorporated flavors into your other color choices, particularly the purple ube. I would've liked to have seen that carried all the way through."

Courchesne shrugs. "Not a lot of tasty gray things out there."

Juliet chuckles. "I suppose there's not," she says, slicing pieces from each donut.

"The ube is excellent," Leland says, but he goes back to the vanilla ring. "This is your problem. The flavor is boring, but not only that, it's absorbed too much oil. You needed to watch your temperature better."

She nods, and Natalie calls Tony up.

"This is a lovely little display," Juliet says. "Look at those garden stakes."

"The herb garden theme is very interesting," Leland says, breaking off a piece of one. "You know, I'm usually not a fan of lavender because it can taste like potpourri, but the balance with the lemon is spot-on. Very nice."

"Thank you," Tony says.

"I'm not done."

I sneak a glance across the aisle at Freddie, who cringes. No one wants to hear that tone this early in the judging.

"When we set the donut challenge, we expected an unparalleled sugar rush, so when you came out with a savory donut, we were skeptical," Leland continues. Juliet nods in agreement. "But the cheddar-and-rosemary is exquisite, and I would like that recipe very much."

"Twice, that lucky bastard," Freddie says, and I cover my face to hide a laugh.

"Thank you," Tony says again. "I'm glad you liked it."

He returns to his bench as calm as can be, but there's a lightness to his face that isn't quite a smile, though it's close.

"Daisy, bring up your donut horn," Natalie says.

"Not like that was a tough act to follow," I say with a grin, placing my cornucopia on the table.

"I think this is very festive," Juliet says, plucking a trio of donuts from the horn. They start with the cider. "Oh, I do think I could get in trouble with these."

"Pecan is overly sweet," Leland says. "Salting the nuts would've helped."

I hear a snort of laughter behind me, and it takes every ounce of willpower not to turn and acknowledge Freddie. Instead I nod, biting my lip to keep from laughing myself.

"Oh, this is unfortunate," Juliet says, cutting into the pumpkin donut. She sounds genuinely disappointed, and it's enough to dissolve the bubble of laughter in an instant. My heart hammers as Leland peers down to inspect it.

"Raw," he declares.

"Perhaps it was a one-off," Juliet says, selecting another one.

"Failure of technique," Leland says, holding one up for the camera. "They simply needed longer in the oil. The outside is done, but you can see there's a border of raw dough surrounding the filling. There are eggs in this, correct?"

I nod.

"Then we will not be risking that. Thank you."

My face is flaming as I return to my station, and I barely hear Freddie's or Grant's comments. I'm screwed. Between the rustic bagels and raw donuts, there's no way I'm not in danger.

"Nell," Natalie says, "please bring up your donuts."

Nell has a tray of mismatched vintage teacups, each with a donut in it.

"How charming," Juliet says. "This would be delightful at a baby shower or morning wedding."

Nell explains her matcha, Earl Grey, and Moroccan mint flavors, and I wonder if I'm better off eliminated. It would give me more time to investigate. I could have free run of the place. Hell,

I could maybe even find a way into Bryan's room and see if there are any clues there.

I shake my head and realize only after I do it that it'll be caught on camera and I will probably come off looking petty about the praise Nell is getting heaped on her donuts.

I try to refocus, to show that I'm happy for her, because I am, but as she returns to her bench and Vic goes by with her tower of Italian-inspired donuts, I'm back to rationalizing.

Even if I can get into Bryan's room, surely the police have already found and taken anything that would be relevant, right?

So that doesn't help.

"I think that's the one I left in too long when I got burned," Vic says, snapping my attention back to the judging. "They're not all like that."

"They are, I'm afraid," Juliet says, prodding the donuts around Vic's tower.

"Again, this comes down to technique," Leland says. "The oil temperature was too low."

"Tell that to my arm," Vic says, waving her bandaged wrist at them.

Leland addresses the camera, ignoring Vic. "When the temperature is too low, it's still possible to cook through all the way, but it comes at a cost. Extra time in the oil means extra oil in the dough."

Once Vic returns to her station, the judges leave to deliberate.

"Well, Tony's safe," Freddie announces.

"We'll see," he says.

"Oh, don't be modest. You're not only safe, you're on top," Vic snaps. "I, however, am fucked."

"I don't know," Courchesne says. "Your bagels were middle of the pack, and your turnover was fine."

"It wasn't great either."

"At least it wasn't third-grade bake sale," Freddie says, mimicking Leland's manner.

"At least your donuts were surprisingly elegant," she says, doing the same.

"At least yours weren't raw," I tell Vic.

"True."

"It feels harder now," Nell says. "Like at first there were enough of us that it was okay to hide in the middle of the pack, but not anymore."

"Again with the safe people having comments," Vic mutters.

"Well, I had bagel rolls instead of bagels and boring vanilla donuts, so I get to comment all I want," Courchesne says. "And I don't want to leave yet."

"None of us do," Freddie says.

Chapter Twenty-Eight

It surprises no one when Tony gets Top Baker, but it shocks all of us when the judges call three of us forward for the elimination decision.

I stand between Vic and Courchesne, not daring to breathe. Suddenly all the rationalizations I made earlier about being able to use the time to investigate seem foolish. I want to stay. I want to win.

Hell, I at least want to make it to pie day.

"This was one of the most difficult weeks to judge," Natalie says. "All of you performed well in at least two segments, but unfortunately, someone has to go, and this week it came down to the creative. The judges expect these final presentations to be truly spectacular, both in presentation and in taste, and unfortunately, they felt you all had issues with that."

There's a long pause to let that sink in.

"All of you presented excellent flavors that were marred by technique. However, for two of you, those issues only affected one of your donuts."

Vic goes rigid beside me, and my heart drops.

"But for one baker, it affected all of them, so unfortunately, this week we must sadly say good-bye to Vic." Natalie sounds truly sad to say it. "Please hand in your apron."

Vic steps forward, pulling it over her head, leaving Courchesne and I stunned.

"It was supposed to be one of us," she whispers, hand over her mouth. "After the bagels, I thought for sure it was us."

"I know."

I watch Juliet, wondering if there's another surprise here, something to make this better. But no, she merely watches as Vic hands her apron to Natalie and accepts a hug before she's whisked off with Tony for one-on-ones.

Vic stops in the doorway and jabs a finger at me and Courchesne. "Drinks are on you fuckers tonight," she calls as the camera crew ushers her out.

"Do you feel like you dodged a bullet?" Natalie asks, a camera at her side.

"Yeah," I admit. "Somehow that feels worse than if I got kicked off myself."

"Almost," Courchesne says with a wicked grin.

"Almost," I agree.

* * *

"I think my fryer was broken," Vic grumbles. "It was set to three-fifty; there's no reason I should've had soggy donuts."

"I think it's just shit luck," Courchesne says.

"Not for you," Vic says, holding out her empty glass.

Courchesne takes it, pours a measure of my leftover cassis in it, and slides it down the bar. "Prosecco me," she says.

"And me," Freddie says, holding out his glass.

The bartender tops them up with bubbles and checks in with the others. Nell and Derek are at a table by themselves, oblivious to the rest of us.

"So Vic, how are you planning to spend your brief retirement?" Matt asks.

"Not skulking around with you lot," she says. "I'm pretty sure there's a sauna with my name on it somewhere around here."

"We do not skulk," Gemma says, giggling.

"You skulk. It's all Derek talked about when he still talked to us." Vic says it loud enough to draw his attention, but he just waves her off.

"Don't be jealous," he says, not looking away from Nell.

"Of you? Hardly," Vic says, then tips her glass between me and Courchesne. "You two, however."

"I know," I say. "I feel awful!"

"I don't." Courchesne shrugs. "All's fair in love and baking."

"Fair my ass," Vic says.

"You know what's not fair?" Freddie says, "Flipping Tony. Twice. Twice that bastard gets Top Baker. I had sophisticated donuts!"

"And third-grade turnovers," Vic says.

"I thought they were good," Gemma says.

"Because you're still practically in third grade."

"With a scholarship," Gemma reminds her primly.

"Fine, you get a spot on my jealous list too."

"Why do you think he never joins us for drinks?" Freddie asks. "Tony, I mean."

"Maybe because you call him a bastard?" Courchesne suggests.

"He's shy," Vic says. "It's his role. Now that Grant's tough big brother, he's definitely the mysterious one."

She's only half right, though. After hearing Tony talk to the cops, I know he's not shy. He's steely.

But he is also absolutely mysterious, and mysterious means on my radar.

* * *

I excuse myself early, feigning a headache, and make my way to Tony's room. I wish I had a better plan than to ambush him, but the fact is, with cameras rolling for most of the day, this is my best opportunity to talk to him alone.

I knock softly, listening for movement, but only silence answers. It's possible he's already asleep, but I doubt it. I can't pinpoint why, but I get night owl vibes from him.

I knock again, harder, and call, "Tony? It's Daisy."

This time there's movement, but not from his room. The door next to his opens and Ainsley leans out, wrapped in a silky robe that stops midthigh. "He's on his balcony. I don't think he can hear you."

"Oh," I say, feeling oddly exposed despite being the one not half-naked.

She stares at me like I'm stupid, then says, "Do you want me to tell him to go in?"

"Yeah, thanks, that'd be good," I say. I feel like I should say something else, ask how she is at least, but she disappears back into her room before I get the words out.

I shift my weight, wondering how I'll explain my hovering in the hallway if the others come up from the bar. This would be so much easier if we all had our phones and each other's numbers.

Tony's door opens a crack, like he's not sure he wants to let in whoever is out here.

"Hi," I say. "It's just me."

He opens the door wider but still looks wary.

"Can we talk?" I ask.

"About?" It's not rude so much as guarded, and I figure my best bet is honesty.

"Everything. The stuff with Bryan and the cops. I think we talked to the same cop."

"Rensler?"

"Yeah."

"I'd prefer to put that behind me," he says, taking a step back like he's going to close the door.

Shit.

Before he can do it, I move forward, sticking my foot in the gap. "Please. Ten minutes of your time, that's all I ask."

He regards me for a moment, then nods, once. "Fine." He slips out into the hall, pulling the door closed behind him. "I could use some air anyway."

I cock my head, sure Ainsley said he'd been out on his balcony, but I let it go. He leads the way, farther down the hall and away from the main staircase.

"There's an exit down here," he says, opening a discreet door near the end of the hall.

Apparently Derek isn't the only one who knew about the secret passageways.

The stairs are steep and narrow, and these do feel like something meant for servants rather than the tunnels I've already explored.

"How'd you know this was here?" I ask.

"I have a thing about exits," he says. "Plus, Ainsley uses it, and she's not as stealthy as she thinks."

"I bet," I say, picturing her clomping down in her heels, then wondering why she would bother when there's a perfectly good elevator in the other direction.

"Here," Tony murmurs at the landing, holding open one of the doors. I step out onto grass still damp with rain, and above me, the sky is filled with stars. "This way."

I follow him around the building, and all at once I'm oriented to where we are. The gardens behind the ballroom spread out in the dark, small LED lights marking the walkways at regular intervals.

It's magical and almost otherworldly, with the crickets singing and the scent of rain lingering in the air.

"Nice, right?" Tony asks as we fall into step along the paths. In the distance, tiny lights flicker like stars. Fireflies.

"It's amazing."

I feel like I'm being let in on something secret, and there's a part of me that wishes I could ignore what I heard and simply enjoy this walk with a fellow baker.

But I can't.

"I wanted to ask you something," I say. "About your interview with Rensler."

"So you said."

"What did you talk about?"

He keeps walking at the same easy pace, but his silence feels thoughtful. "We talked about Bryan. And what happened with Grant and Gemma. I imagine that's what everyone talked about."

"Right." I inhale, wishing I had a better plan of attack here. "Okay, so I have a confession."

"About Bryan?" He sounds genuinely surprised, and I almost laugh.

"No. About the interviews." I'm glad we're walking, because I realize how awkward this could be if I had to admit this while looking him in the eye. "You know how Derek and Matt were talking about the passages they found? I was in one during the interviews. And I heard them."

Tony stops, and even the crickets seem to go silent as that sinks in. I'm suddenly aware of the distance between us and the estate and the fact that I've barely even started this conversation.

"Why?" he asks.

It's not the reaction I expected, but thinking back to what I saw with Rensler, it fits. Contained and giving nothing away. Setting off at the same steady pace, I say, "Because I needed to know the truth. Or as much truth as I could find out."

"About me?"

"About the situation. About Bryan."

"Why?"

"Because I think the wrong person could end up in trouble. I can't ignore that." It's not close to the whole truth, but it's also not a lie.

Tony is quiet for several paces, and I wait for him to fill the space, although he seems like he could stay comfortably in it for ages. Eventually he asks, "And you hoped to learn what exactly?"

"Anything that would help."

"And did you?"

"I don't know. Maybe." This time the silence is mine to fill, and it takes me a minute to jump into the heart of why we're out here. "You told Rensler you had nothing to do with Bryan's death."

"That's right."

"But he implied you might've because of your history."

"You know nothing about that." The words are firm, but they're not rude. A statement of fact.

"This is me asking."

"It's not relevant."

I ignore the warning in his tone. "That's what you told Rensler, but here's the thing. Bryan wasn't a good person. I know it's taboo to speak ill of the dead, but if anyone deserved to be killed, it was him, and I know someone here had something to do with it."

"Perhaps, but not me."

"You have a record, though?"

"A lot of people do. It doesn't always mean something."

"I know." I try to magic the words like I magic my pies, so that he feels the truth of them, but I know it doesn't work that way. "Was Rensler telling the truth?"

"It's not relevant," he repeats, but this time there's heat behind the words, a crack that wasn't there before.

"What isn't relevant?"

"Any of it. It was an accident. I'm not a murderer. I'm not."

The last line guts me in a way I'm not prepared for, and I can't stop my hand from covering the soft hollow below my sternum. He walks faster, like he can outrun the words, and I hurry to catch up. "What was an accident?"

"This was supposed to be a fresh start. Something new, something untouched by all that. I just wanted to start over."

"And Bryan got in the way of that?"

"Bryan's death did. And Chloe's. If they hadn't died, none of it would've come back up. It wasn't supposed to follow me here."

"Tony, what was an accident?"

"The death. The one Rensler was referring to. I didn't kill Bryan, but I did kill someone else."

* * *

We walk as he tells the story, like stopping will let it get too close. "I was drinking. It's not an excuse and it's not even an explanation, it's just a detail. But if I had been sober, it might have been different." He draws in a ragged breath before continuing. "He was worse than I was, though. I knew I was over, but he was so far gone he thought he was invincible. All I wanted was the keys, but he wouldn't listen, and when I tried to take them, he swung at me. So I shoved him."

I close my eyes, hating myself for not just taking him at his word in the beginning, for not believing him when he told Rensler he had nothing to do with Bryan's death and this wasn't relevant. Because it's not. It's just heartbreaking.

"He fell. His head hit the curb at just the right angle. It was instant. You always hear that on TV, that people die instantly, but he really did. One second he was there and the next he wasn't. Because I pushed him."

"Oh, Tony, you didn't mean—"

"I was charged with manslaughter. I did five years. I deserved it. I spent so long focused on punishing myself that I forgot to figure out a plan for when I got out. I couldn't go back home, not after what I put my family through. I thought coming here could make me a new person. Even if I didn't win, I could be that guy on the baking show instead of that guy who killed his brother."

Chapter Twenty-Nine

I don't sleep.

I can't, not with Tony's story playing on repeat in my brain.

I may have crossed him off my list of suspects, but at what cost?

When I slip into the dining room for breakfast the next morning, it's half-awake and bleary-eyed. This is going to be a long day, and the only hope I have is to caffeinate my way through it. I grab a pair of mugs and fill them both with coffee and more sugar than is probably advisable. I take them back to my room along with a blueberry oat muffin and wait for Julian.

I knock back the first coffee like it might actually quell the nerves coiling like snakes in my belly.

It definitely doesn't.

But it does start to fight against the lack of sleep, so there's that, and by the time Julian knocks, I'm halfway through the second and have eaten enough of the muffin to be reasonably confident that the coffee won't eat through my stomach.

"Well, you're a sight," Julian says, getting to work.

"Thank you."

"Long night?"

"Something like that."

"Well, you better get your game face on, kitten, because filming starts in twenty."

"Isn't that what you're here for?"

"I'm a genius, but I'm not a miracle worker."

"Try to be."

He does his best, and in the end, the circles under my eyes are reduced to mere shadows. Eye drops have banished the worst of the redness, and whatever magic he brushed over my cheeks is having a distinctly un-corpse-like effect.

"Miracle worker," I confirm.

I opt for my favorite lemon dress, the one I always say is for luck, and when I get to my station, luck does, indeed, seem to be on my side.

Sitting on the end of the bench is my favorite French rolling pin, the one I packed for pie day.

Perfect.

"Welcome, bakers, to pie week," Natalie announces from the front of the room. "For your first challenge, the judges would like you to decide whether what you're making is even a pie at all, because there seems to be some debate." She pauses, grinning, as the judges give her mock-stern looks for the camera. "Nope, okay, apparently we're going with it. For your warm-up challenge, Juliet and Leland would like you all to make a classic strawberry cheesecake. You have an hour and a half, so bakers, do your thing, and may the pies be ever in your flavor!"

As we start, Natalie switches to her off-camera voice. "Remember, everyone, because no one wants to eat hot cheesecake, there will be a gap between finishing and judging. In that time, it's vital that you don't change anything about your appearance. We need to keep the continuity."

"Got it," we chorus.

"Lovely," she says, switching back to camera mode as she and the judges begin making their rounds.

When they get to me, my filling is already in the mixer and I'm at work on the crust. It's killing me to follow the basic recipe and not add any embellishments, but this is the time for technique, not flair, so there's nothing special added into the graham cracker, sugar, and butter mixture I'm pressing into the base of my pan.

"So Daisy, tell us, pie or cake?" Natalie says, sticking an imaginary microphone in my face.

"Pie," I say, without hesitation. "And because I'm a heathen, I never make it in a springform pan. If I'm making cheesecake, it's going in a pie tin and it's definitely getting more than a drizzle of strawberry sauce for flavor, but if they want boring, I'll give them boring."

It's a bake I can do on autopilot, and even though it should be soothing, I can't stop my brain from straying back to Chloe and Bryan as it did all night, and by the time we hit the patio, I'm ready to drop.

"Worried about your cheesecake?" Nell asks, tucking herself in at my side.

I sigh. "Actually, no. I didn't sleep well, and I think my coffee is abandoning me in my hour of need."

"You sound like Freddie," she says with a giggle.

"What sounds like Freddie?" he says, hopping up on the patio railing next to Nell.

"Daisy's in caffeine withdrawal."

"Oh, don't get me started," he says. "I got you, though. Wait here."

He jumps down as quickly as he jumped up, and we watch him scurry off, bypassing the patio's tea-and-coffee station.

"Your guess is as good as mine," Nell says with a shrug.

He returns minutes later bearing two mugs. The one he hands me is half-full, with a frothy foam topping thick, dark espresso.

"Double shot," he says, clinking mugs. "Extra sweet."

I sip, and it's hot and strong and like a burst of pure adrenaline. And sugar.

"Too sweet?" Freddie asks, levering himself back up onto the patio railing.

I take another sip, considering. "It's like turbo coffee ice cream. I'm not complaining."

"Yeah, it occurred to me last night at the bar," he says. "Sure, there are urns of coffee all over the place, but the bar? The bar has an espresso machine. They've been holding out on us."

"The bar is staffed this early in the morning?" Nell asks.

Freddie swings his feet. "Not exactly."

I groan. "Tell me you didn't steal the espresso machine."

"Not the whole thing," he says. "Just access."

"Tunnel?"

"Tunnel," he confirms. "Gemma was feeling pretty smug about finding it. Matt and Derek aren't the only keepers of the tunnels."

At Derek's name, Nell smiles. I don't think she even realizes until she sees me notice, then she flushes. "They just want to keep something fun for the people who are kicked off," she says.

"You don't have to defend him to me," Freddie says. "But you saw. They weren't jazzed that she told, that's all."

Huh. I wonder what else I missed by leaving early last night.

"Probably because you're using it for crime," Nell says.

"If liberating espresso is a crime, then cuff me," Freddie says, throwing back the rest of his and hoisting his mug like a prize.

* * *

It shouldn't, but it nags at me, the thought of the tunnels being used for crime, and my attention keeps straying to the panel I know leads to one of the passageways as the cheesecakes are judged. Of course, it makes sense that Bryan's killer could've used them, same as Derek and I did, the same as all the ousted contestants have been. It's not the first time it's occurred to me, but the thought of Derek being proprietary about it nags me as Grant's cracked cheesecake places last.

The tunnels are common knowledge, to a degree. Their existence is mentioned in writings about the estate, but their specific locations aren't, and I know from experience they're not easy to spot.

I assume that the estate staff probably know about most of them, and obviously we've figured out a few on our own, but I wonder if they're fully documented somewhere. While it doesn't make sense that any would lead directly to guest rooms, having a map of the tunnels could still be helpful in figuring out how Bryan's killer got away without being seen. I'm so fixated on the idea that I don't even notice my cheesecake hasn't been placed until Nell squeezes my hand, hard.

"So that brings us to the top two, which are very, very close," Juliet says, indicating mine and Nell's. There's a beat for dramatic effect, and then she points to mine. "Whose is this?"

I raise my hand, the one Nell isn't holding.

"Very nice," Juliet says. "Excellent texture and lovely sauce. So that leaves us with Nell in first. Congratulations."

I'm not bothered by the second place. For one thing, I'm happy for Nell.

For another, we still have two real pies to go.

Chapter Thirty

"Bakers," Natalie says, "for your craft challenge, the judges would like to see a bounty of fruit pies. It can be any flavor that you like, but it must have a flour-based crust—no crumb crusts allowed—and be primarily composed of fruit. Remember to pie your best and do your thing!"

I start with my dough, and it's like being home.

I work the butter into my flour with my hands, same as always, as around me food processors whir. I glance beside me and see Grant is working his with a pastry cutter, and given his violent bread-kneading technique, it's probably for the best.

I stir in my water and a dash of cider vinegar and bring it together into a ball as Courchesne finishes explaining her coconut raspberry pie to the judges in front of me.

"Tell us about your fruit pie," Juliet says. "If I'm correct, this is a spin on your award-winning honey crunch apple pie?"

"It is," I say, cutting my dough in half and flattening each piece into a disk as I talk. "It's going to be filled with cider-caramel apples, but because we already had a cheesecake challenge, I thought I'd leave out the cream layer and do something a little different."

"Well, I can't wait to try it," Juliet says as they move off.

I pop my dough in the refrigerator to chill and start peeling apples, aware that at home this could just as easily become a murder pie. I shake the thought from my head. The last thing I need to be thinking about is murder while I'm making pie on national TV.

No.

That's not true.

The realization is enough to make my knife slip, and I curse as blood pools at my knuckle. "Dammit. Band-Aid!" I call, and the set medic appears at my side, blue-gloved hands holding a first-aid kit. "It's minor, really."

She nods in agreement, working quickly as she wipes a cold alcohol pad across the cut and wraps it in a bandage. She's finished and gone in less than two minutes, leaving me to my apples.

And my plan.

Because I was wrong.

Of course I should be thinking about murder while I'm making pie.

That's what I do.

It's who I am.

So when I dump the apples into the sauté pan with cinnamon, sugar, and cider, I don't stop there.

I heap in magic too, crafting a blend that won't affect the judging but will, with any luck, start getting me the answers I need.

Once the apples start to soften, I turn the burner to low and retrieve my dough. I'm aware of the camera capturing every move as I unwrap it. It's had a shorter rest than I would usually give it and is still pliable, but that's not a bad thing right now. Taking a pinch of flour, I hold it for a moment, setting my intention, and flick it across my bench like a spell. Another pinch goes over the top of the dough, settling like snow before I begin rolling, letting the flour sink into the surface of the dough. I brush my hand over it as if checking the thickness, then fold it in thirds, like a letter, then in half so it forms a square.

"The folds are just to add some extra flakiness," I tell the camera, but it's a lie. They don't need to know the magic I've folded in, which will infuse the whole crust as I roll it out. It's not the best way to do it—which would've been working the magic in at the butter stage—but it will do.

I feel reckless and a little wild, doing this while the camera records it all, even though I know that to anyone watching, it only looks like baking.

I arrange the crust in the pan and crimp the edges, further sealing the magic in. When it's filled, I'll alternate rows of braided sugar-sprinkled pie dough and honey crunch streusel, but for now, I line it with parchment and pie weights and pop it in the oven to parbake. I almost explain to the camera that at home I would weight it with sugar, but I don't. Sometimes more than the magic should be kept secret.

* * *

When it's time for judging, I'm practically buzzing. I blame it on Freddie's espresso as much as the fact that the pie at the end of my bench is magicked within an inch of its flaky life.

But it's mostly the pie.

The ballroom smells as good as it ever has, the rich aroma of buttery pastry and pungent fruit more than masking the leftover donut oil from yesterday.

The judges start with Tony, who presents a double-crusted peach-and-nutmeg pie. "I like the warm spice and that it's not playing backup," Leland says approvingly. "It was a risky move using as much as you did, but I'd say it paid off."

"It's an example of something simple done well," Juliet agrees before they move over to Courchesne, whose raspberry coconut is praised for its sharp flavor and good crust.

"Grant, remind us of your pie," Juliet says as she cuts a slice. My heart kicks up, aware that I'm next.

"It's pear with vanilla brown butter."

"The lattice work is quite nice," Leland says, prodding it with his fork. "Very even, and I like the extra width of the strips."

"Thank you," he says.

Leland flips the slice on its side, and Juliet scrunches up her face in sympathy. "A bit underdone on the bottom, it seems."

Grant says nothing, but the line of his jaw hardens a fraction as he watches them eat.

"Very cozy flavor, though," Juliet says.

"I disagree. I'm not getting any vanilla at all. It's all one-note pear. I would consider this an example of something simple done rather poorly."

Oof. Grant nods, once. That's a hard thing to hear about something that looks as nice as his pie does.

They turn to me, and there's no going back.

My heart is galloping as they cut their sample slice, and it doesn't matter that I magic every pie I sell in one way or another. This is on TV, and the stakes are as high as they've been for any murder pie I've ever made.

Maybe higher.

"Nice body to the filling," Leland says. "There's nothing worse than runny pie. Good choice to cook the apples first."

"It's the best way," I agree, hoping my voice doesn't betray my nerves.

The nerves are stupid anyway, but knowing that intellectually does nothing to soothe them.

"The caramel is excellent," Juliet says, after she swallows. "Truly top-notch."

"The cider makes all the difference," I say, ignoring the pang. "If you're ever in Massachusetts, Hollow Hill Orchard is completely worth the stop."

"No branding!" Kate barks from the doorway. "Keep rolling; we'll cut."

"I'll keep it in mind," Juliet says with a wink.

"The honey streusel is a little too sweet," Leland says.

"I find it well balanced by the sharpness of the caramel and richness of the pastry," she says.

"Which, by the way, I could eat by the bagful," Natalie says, pulling one of the crispy dough braids off the top of the pie. I almost cringe as she does it but manage not to, aware of the cameras.

On one hand, yes, it's a compliment that she wants to eat the whole crust, but on the other hand, I desperately need this pie to make it out of the room so it can be shared.

Luckily they move on to Freddie before Natalie can do more damage, and his chocolate-covered strawberry pie takes the same hit Grant's did. "Wet bottom," Leland declares. "The problem with putting cocoa in your dough is that it makes it hard to judge when it's properly baked. This is underdone by at least ten minutes."

"But it's tasty?" he asks hopefully.

"If you enjoy the taste of raw dough."

"It's a good flavor combination, though," Juliet offers. "The presentation is quite stunning with the mixed chocolate curls."

"And if we were judging on visual appeal, that would be one thing," Leland says. "But it's a baking competition, not a beauty pageant."

In front of me, Courchesne snorts. "Someone's feeling sassy," she whispers.

I bite my lip, wondering how much of that was my pie's fault and how much was Leland's natural mean streak.

He shakes his head. "Really, at this stage we should be past getting style over substance."

They move on to Nell, and I replay the magic in my head, wondering if my nerves affected the blend. It's possible, but so is the fact that Leland can be a dick and it's not like honesty has been a problem for him yet.

"Nell, this looks like fun," Juliet says.

"It looks a unicorn died in a preschool," Leland says. "You're sure you didn't trade pies with Freddie?"

Oh shit.

Freddie looks like he's been slapped, and Nell turns scarlet. An electric hush settles over the room.

"Tell me," Leland continues, "what do you think the rainbow crumbs add to it?"

"Flavor and color," Nell answers, but it comes out sounding more like a question. She clears her throat. "People like them when I use them on donuts."

"I bet they don't like them in this quantity."

I stretch on tiptoes, hoping to see her pie, but with the way Natalie and the judges are standing, I can't. Still, I know what she was doing, and the gelatin-based crumbles she was using sounded a lot like the freeze-dried fruit streusel I sometimes make.

"Well, let's give it a taste," Juliet says, before things can derail further, and I'm glad, because across the aisle, Grant looks ready to start another judge throwdown. I try to catch his eye, but he's too focused on Leland.

"The pineapple and mango are perfectly balanced," Juliet says. "This kind of filling can be difficult, but you've done a lovely job."

"The topping adds nothing," Leland says. "It's flash for flash's sake, and you're better than that."

There's a compliment buried in there, but his tone is enough to negate it.

Nell's eyes are bright with tears, and my heart twists, praying that it's not the magic making him extra cruel.

"If you had given this a top crust, maybe with some crystallized ginger, you could've had something here, but you ruined it with this," he says.

"I'm not a judge," Natalie says, popping a handful of crumbs in her mouth, "but I like it. It reminds me of those crumbly strawberry ice cream bars."

Nell nods gratefully. "That's exactly what they're supposed to be like."

"It's juvenile," Leland says.

"Leland, do lighten up," Juliet says. "On a summer days, seeing this out on the table would be a joy."

"I simply think, given what we've seen, that this could've been better," he says, and Nell nods like it's the truth.

It guts me.

I look away, searching the wall for the telltale gap that says Derek is watching and hoping he's not.

Between me and Grant, Leland has just put himself on enough shit lists. But if Derek saw how he was talking to Nell, we might well have another murder on our hands.

Chapter Thirty-One

I need to get my pie back. The balance is off, with too much honesty and not enough desire to help. Dammit.

I don't know what went wrong. I based the magic off a mix I used last year to get information out of a less-than-helpful secretary, but judging by Leland's completely brutal honesty, something is not quite right.

Part of my brain insists it's just him being him, but still.

Set crew descend like locusts on the stations, cleaning and resetting for the creative challenge while we break for lunch, and in the flurry, I lose track of my pie.

What I don't lose track of is Nell. As soon as they release us, she beelines for the exit, and I'm on her heels.

"Wait," I call. She stops but doesn't turn, and I trot to catch her. "Are you okay?"

She shrugs. "It's only pie, right?"

"He was a dick, though. You didn't deserve that."

Courchesne joins us, hooking an arm through Nell's. "Fuck him, yeah?"

Nell glances over her shoulder like he might be watching before she shakes her head and puts on a smile. "Yeah. Fuck him."

The curse sounds so unnatural coming out of her mouth that Courchesne and I both dissolve into laughter.

"That's the spirit," I say, taking her other arm, and we set off for lunch like we're heading to Oz.

Derek, Vic, and Gemma are already in the dining room, tucking into the pies when we get there.

Shit.

Gemma's damp hair smells of chlorine, and she raises a forkful of Nell's pie in greeting. "It's *eat dessert first* day."

"Every day is *eat dessert first* day around here," says Courchesne.

"This crunchy shit is like crack," Derek says, plucking a chunk of honey streusel off my pie with his fingers and tossing it in his mouth.

"Ew, use a fork," Gemma says, stabbing at him with her own.

"I'm not double dipping."

"You're touching it."

He very deliberately pinches off another section of topping and flies it toward her face airplane-style. She shrieks and laughs, threatening to bite his fingers when he shoves it in her mouth.

Vic rolls her eyes. "Thank god the other adults are here."

"Speak for yourself," Freddie says. "According to Leland, me and Nell are preschoolers."

Derek's head snaps around, eyes sharp. "He said what?"

"Preschoolers. Me and Nell both," Freddie says. "Because she makes unicorn pies and because I'm the lowest bar, apparently."

"You didn't see?" I ask.

Vic shakes her head, gesturing toward Derek and Gemma. "No, I got stuck having a pool party with these idiots."

"I resent that," Gemma says.

"No, you resemble it. It was nice and quiet until you two showed up."

Derek ignores her and goes to Nell, who is skipping pie in favor of proper food. After Leland's critique, I don't blame her. I try not to eavesdrop on his obvious concern for her.

"Hey, if we're sharing pies with the staff, maybe skip mine and Grant's," Freddie says. "In addition to being a preschooler, I'm also afflicted with a soggy bottom."

"It's still good if you eat around the bottom," Gemma says, and Vic slaps a hand over her eyes as Freddie cackles.

"What?" Gemma asks, eyes wide.

"Children. All of you," Vic says, abandoning the pies for the buffet.

The rest of us follow suit, joining Derek and Nell at the long center table. Now that the police have cleared out, we're back to normal seating.

"He had no right," Derek is saying. "It doesn't matter if he's the judge, he had no right."

"It's fine, really," Nell says. "I'm over it. Honest."

"You convincing him or yourself?" Vic asks.

She smiles sheepishly. "Can it be both?"

"I'm going to have a word with him," Derek says, pushing his chair away from the table. "Right now."

"No you're not," Courchesne says, clapping a hand on his back. "That's not going to help a thing."

"She's right," Nell says, reaching across the table for Derek's hand. "Really, it's fine."

Derek hesitates, clearly torn between wanting to play the hero and wanting to respect his damsel's wishes. Courchesne pats his shoulder. "Down, boy."

He relents, scooting his chair back in and giving Nell's hand a lingering squeeze. "Forget Leland," Derek says, running his thumb over the back of her hand. "Maybe he can't see how incredible you are, but I can."

He speaks like they're the only two in the room, and the rest of us look everywhere but at them.

Behind Derek's shoulder I see Grant and Matt walk in with Ainsley on their heels. She barrels past them for the buffet and stays only long enough to assemble a salad, not even glancing at the pies on offer.

Next to me, Gemma points her fork at Ainsley's retreating back. "If anyone wants a word with Leland," Gemma says in an impish singsong, "I'd just follow her."

Oh no.

No no no.

"You're going to stab someone," Vic says, pushing Gemma's fork down. "And what is that supposed to mean?"

"That's why she doesn't hang out with us," Gemma says. "She's too busy with her boyfriend."

"She doesn't hang out with us because she's a raging bitch," Vic counters.

"And because she's banging Leland. True story."

I stand up, fast enough to draw attention that I don't acknowledge. "I'm going to run some pie to housekeeping," I say, praying no one volunteers to help. I need to get rid of my pie before anyone else can have a bite.

I should've known better. Honesty magic is a tricky thing, and I rushed it. I didn't work it in the right way, and now it's doing nothing but removing people's filters. That's not what I need right now. None of us do.

"Ask Daisy," Gemma says. "She knows."

"Why am I not aware of this drama?" Freddie asks.

"That can't be ethical," Matt says, dropping into a seat at the far end of the table.

"Neither is keeping secrets," Vic says.

"That's not true," Nell says, with surprising conviction. "Sometimes secrets are good."

"Secretly banging a judge isn't," Gemma says.

I arrange a trio of pies along my arm, Courchesne's and Tony's closest to my elbow and mine at the end, where it will be easy to discard.

"Here," Grant says, reaching for it. "I'll give you a hand."

"You just got here," I say, deftly maneuvering out of his reach. "Eat your lunch, really. I've got it."

He shrugs, cocking his head at the table. "Appetite's kind of spoiled."

"Okay. Grab that one," I say, nodding at Nell's. "Mine's all picked at anyway. We can't serve it."

I toss it unceremoniously into the bin and leave before I get sucked in by Gemma's drama.

"Is that true, about Ainsley?" Grant asks, once we're in the hall.

"I don't know," I say, telling myself it's not a lie. But I'm not stupid, and neither is Grant.

* * *

"Bakers, welcome back to your final pie challenge," Natalie says. "The judges would like to see what you can do with savory pies today, and to make it fun, we're making them mini. Think appetizers. Think tapas. Think big flavors in little bitty bite sizes. Leland and Juliet would like to see thirty miniature pies, stuffed with a trio of savory fillings, and each type should be encased in a unique dough, so bakers, do your thing!"

This time I'm careful.

This time, all that matters is the magic. I don't even care about placing or pleasing the judges as I measure out flour into three bowls. I cut my butter into cubes, driving intention down the knife with each slice.

When Natalie arrives with the judges, I stop working. I can't afford to be distracted when my hands are in the dough.

"Daisy, tell us about your pies," Juliet says.

I tap the edge of the bowl that holds my tried-and-true traditional dough. "I'm doing vegetarian game-day themed pies, and the buffalo cauliflower will be wrapped in my flaky all-butter dough. The loaded potato skin is getting a rye crust, and the pulled jackfruit-pork is going in a cornmeal crust. That one's more tender than flaky, but the flavor is great with the barbecue sauce."

"And you find jackfruit to be an acceptable substitute for pork?" Leland asks.

"Almost to the point that I have trouble eating it," I say. "The texture is so close that it doesn't seem vegetarian."

"I doubt the flavor carries that illusion," Leland says.

I give an airy shrug. "Let's be real. The main flavors of pulled pork are smoke and sauce and fat. I don't need meat to make that work."

"Well, you have your work cut out convincing me," Leland says, as if that were ever not true about any challenge.

"So, game day," Natalie says conspiratorially. "Exactly what game are we talking about? Football?"

"Supposedly?" I laugh. "My only knowledge of the Super Bowl is that it requires snacks, and I'm always down for snack events. I figure there will be enough people doing fancier flavors, like wedding apps, so I thought this would be something a little different."

"I believe you're the only one going full vegetarian," Juliet says. "Very daring. We'll leave you to it."

I wait until they're deep into their next conversation before returning to my doughs. I don't narrate for the camera even though I know I should. As I work the butter in, I work in the magic. Helpfulness blends with the flours, and candor catches on the grit of the cornmeal. I'll work openness but not radical honesty into the fillings. All I want is to prime the pumps of information, not turn them on full blast. It's impossible to control what comes out then.

Sure, a spontaneous confession could cut things to the chase, but I don't want to be the reason people start sharing all their darkest secrets. The only ones I care about are the ones that have to do with Bryan's death, and as I season and stir my fillings, I try to work that specificity into the magic, knowing it's not always that straightforward. All magic, whether it's a pinch of comfort or a heap of murder, can only work with what's in the recipient. It's magic, but it's not a miracle. I can't make someone feel anything they don't already have the capacity for, same as I can't kill someone who doesn't have it coming. If the magic were more manipulative, then I probably wouldn't need murder pies. I could bake my way to better people, but that's not how it works.

* * *

"Daisy, please present your bake," Natalie says.

I've made more than I need to, but I only arrange the required thirty in their black-and-white-check paper–lined plastic boats. It's not a fancy display, but it's festive, and absolutely something that would be a hit at a casual party. They were when I made them for Juan's Super Bowl party anyway, and that's what I remind myself of as I bring them up, trying to ignore that I'm following Tony's gorgeous trio of English-inspired pies with their naturally dyed hot water crusts.

Natalie and Juliet look delighted when I set down my tray, and it's not like I expected Leland to anyway.

"The sauces are a lovely touch," Juliet says, indicating the small pots.

"Blue cheese for the cauliflower, horseradish for the potato skins, and ranch for the jackfruit," I say.

The pies themselves are half-moons rather than round to make dipping easier. I have half a dozen extra of each back at my bench, something I played off as a miscalculation for the camera but is really to maximize sharing later.

They start with the cauliflower, splitting it in half to share. "Oh, look at that color," Juliet says approvingly. "Gorgeous." She samples a small piece and coughs, covering it with a laugh. "And quite a lot of heat."

"Hence the sauce," I say sheepishly.

"I like the punch," Leland says. "If that were on a wing, I'd be thrilled." He dunks it in the blue cheese and pops the rest of the pie in his mouth in one go. When he swallows, he says, "You know, I want to wish this was chicken, but I'm not sad that it's cauliflower either."

"Well, wait until you try the jackfruit," I say, unable to bite back the grin.

"Let's not get ahead of ourselves," he says wryly and moves on to the potato, which is loaded with scallions, cheese, and sour cream.

"It's almost like an American samosa," Juliet says. "And that should be an awful thing, but this is not awful at all. I could eat a dangerous amount of these."

"The rye is nice there," Leland admits. "Good crust. They would, however, be better with bacon."

I give the camera a mock-exasperated look. He may say that, but he still finished the whole piece.

"And now this." Leland holds up one of the jackfruit pies like it's an alien artifact, and I'm sure editing will turn it into a comedy moment.

It's fine.

Last laughs and all.

They split it, and Juliet says, "Smells like the real thing." She raises her half as if in a toast. "Shall we?"

I watch Leland's face as he chews, but it betrays nothing, because of course it doesn't. That would be out of character. He dips the second half in the ranch and finishes it before commenting.

He stares at me long enough to make me nervous. I swear, the man does unwavering eye contact like nobody's business.

"That," he finally says, "is not pulled pork."

Something in me deflates, but I try not to show it for the cameras.

"It is, however," he continues, letting a wicked smile light his eyes, "a pretty damn good substitute."

"It really is," Juliet agrees. "And the corn crust is perfect with it. Very well done."

"Thank you," I say, returning to my station content. Even if I get eliminated, I didn't screw up on pie day. I can go home proud.

Chapter Thirty-Two

For the first time, I'm genuinely nervous when we line up for judging. It's stupid, I know. I'm happy with my pies and that should be enough, but the reality is, it's not.

"Bakers, it has truly been a good day to pie," Natalie says. "The judges have been very impressed by many of the entries today, but one baker has consistently stood out with their exceptional crusts and creative twists on the classic flavors."

I find myself reaching for Nell's hand in what has become our ritual judging posture. The teaser hasn't given anything away. It could be me, yes, but it could just as easily be Tony, with his peach pie and showstopping British mini pies. I wouldn't even begrudge him the win, not with pies like that.

"It is my pleasure to announce that this week's Top Baker is Daisy," Natalie says, and Nell drops my hand, throwing her arms around me.

I couldn't wipe the smile off my face if I wanted to.

And yes, it's happiness, but also relief.

Frank would probably evict me if I didn't at least win pie week. He'd never admit it, but he loves the attention my last pie win brought the diner. And more than that, I think that little shriveled-up walnut he calls a heart is a little bit proud too, but he'd be on his deathbed before saying it out loud.

It doesn't matter, though, because in this moment, it's him I most want to share the news with.

But I'll happily make do with the new friends around me. I release Nell as Natalie's face takes on a somber look.

"Now, for the hard part," she says. "As much as I wish we could bring everyone to the next round, we must say good-bye to another baker. Grant and Nell, please come forward."

The shock on Nell's face is mirrored by the twist in my chest. She beat me in the cheesecake round, and her savories were solid. Surely she can't be out just because Leland thought her fruit pie was too colorful, can she?

She steps forward, and across the gap, Freddie is staring at me, brow furrowed in a mix of confused concern, like he doesn't understand why he's not up there. I give a tiny shrug, equally unsure. His trio of empanadillas were excellent, but his cheesecake was cracked, and he was sharing the spotlight of shame with Nell during the fruit round.

"As we get further along, it gets harder and harder to narrow it down," Natalie says. "Nell, despite your early win, you struggled during the craft challenge, and the judges found your savory options uneven. As for you, Grant, the judges were concerned with the quality of your cheesecake and didn't think your creative entries were quite creative enough."

In the pause, I forget how to breathe.

"Nell," Natalie says, and my hand flies to my mouth. Nell drops her head, and I can barely believe it. "You may return to the group. Grant, I'm sorry. Please hand in your apron."

* * *

"It's rigged," Vic declares, raising her glass for emphasis.

"It has to be, right?" Freddie agrees. "I mean, yay for me and all, but do you think they already know the winner?" His eyes light up. "Do you think it's me? Maybe that's my character, the unlikely winner!"

"Doubtful," Vic says.

"I deserved to be up there," Nell says. "Leland hated my fruit salad pie."

"He hated something about all of my pies," Freddie reminds her.

Nell swirls her drink as she mulls it over.

"Do you think it was punishment?"

"What'd you do that needs punishing?" Vic asks. "You're, like, Queen Innocent Sunshine."

She shakes her head. "Not me. Grant. Because he fought with Bryan?"

It's occurred to me too, but I don't say so, not yet, because the implications are larger than the judges being pissy at a contestant who didn't toe the line.

If the police have learned something somehow connecting Grant to Bryan's death, then it would make sense to eliminate him from the show before he was forcibly removed. It's going to be hard enough editing Bryan's absence, never mind if a contestant had to drop out this late in the game.

And it's not lost on me that we haven't seen him since the day wrapped. Sure, he's taciturn on the best of days, but even with everything that's going on, I can't help wondering if there's more to it.

* * *

I start with the easy option: I knock on Grant's door.

There's no answer.

I press my ear to the heavy wood but hear nothing.

That doesn't mean much, given how thick the doors are and how lush the sound-dampening carpeting is.

It's even odds that he's in there ignoring me.

Which, fair. It's late and he had a shit day. Still, I need to talk to him.

I return to my room, once again cursing that our stupid landlines don't connect to the other rooms. I rip a piece of notepaper off the pad on my desk and write *Can we talk?—Daisy.*

No point beating around the bush.

Before I can change my mind, I duck back into the hall and slip the note under his door.

As soon as I do, I realize I've trapped myself. I can either use this time to see what the rest of the estate can tell me or I can wait for Grant.

I decide to give him thirty minutes, then explore.

The knock at my door is soft, almost tentative, and when I open it, I'm surprised to see it's not Grant standing there, but Nell.

"Can I come in?" she asks, looking uncomfortable.

"Yeah, of course." I step back, giving her room. "Are you okay?"

She sits on the edge of the bed, her hands fluttering in her lap like worried birds, and my heart kicks in concern.

"Nell, what is it?"

"Derek told me," she says.

It's a complete sentence, like I should know what she means.

And then I do.

"About the spying," she confirms. "He told me you guys were listening in."

I groan. Stupid, stupid honesty magic. "I'm sorry. I was just trying to find out what was going on. I wasn't trying to pry into your life or anything."

"It's okay," she says.

I sigh. "It's not. That cop was out of line, and you had to talk about some personal stuff, and it wasn't even relevant to what I wanted to know. I'm sorry, really."

"It was, though. Relevant."

My breath catches, and I'm aware that it's not Derek's confession that brought her here. It's her own. "What do you mean?"

Her hands are still, like now that she's saying this, she can relax. "When he asked me about my mom's death. He wasn't out of line."

I'm quiet, giving her space to fill the silence on her own terms.

"I feel like I can tell you this because you'll understand," she says. "Because of your mom. I know it wasn't the same, but you know how hard it can be."

I do.

"At the end, it was harder. She was in pain every day, and it made her mean. Really mean. We never had a great relationship when I was growing up, but I was trying, you know? Leaving the past in the past?" She swallows hard. "She kept telling me to put her out of her misery. That's how she phrased it. She said if I wasn't such a coward, I would do the right thing. She wanted to die, and if she couldn't, she wanted to make me suffer with her."

My stomach clenches, knowing where this is going and wanting to stop her but needing to hear in equal measure.

"There was a visiting nurse who came in, but I was pretty much managing her care full-time. She couldn't do anything for herself. Not bathe or go to the bathroom or open her pill bottles."

It's like all the air is gone from the room.

"I opened them for her," she says. "All of them. On purpose."

She doesn't cry, and she doesn't apologize or justify it. She just lets the truth hang there like a poison berry.

"Oh, Nell," I murmur. I want to tell her I understand what it's like to kill a parent, but I don't. I can't.

"If physician-assisted suicide was legal everywhere—like it should be—I never would've had to do it," she says, suddenly angry. "But I had to."

"It sounds like what she wanted," I say. "I'm so sorry you were put in that position."

"It's not even over, though, that's the worst part. She's gone, and the only thing I inherited was the kind of medical debt they make memes out of." She exhales a sad laugh. "This show is my way out. I don't care about fame, I care about the money. The prize could get my head above water on the bills and maybe leave me enough for a few months' lease on a small storefront. I want to open a donut shop."

This last part is said in a rush, like it's the real confession here, and I smile. "You'd make a killing."

She looks shocked for a moment at my choice of words, then laughs. "Yeah, I think I would."

I hate to ask what I'm about to ask, but the magic is obviously doing its job, so I have to. "Was there anything you didn't tell the cop about Bryan's death?"

"Like did I dose him with prescription drugs?" She shakes her head. "No. I didn't. But they made it sound like someone did."

Chapter Thirty-Three

"Bakers, welcome to what is perhaps the most dangerous week of the show: caramel week." Natalie gives the camera a mock-terrified look before continuing. "This week you will be working with the most fickle of sugars at temperatures that can melt your flesh—so not only must your recipes be on point, so must your attention to detail, because one false move could have you cara-melting down."

She's exaggerating, of course, but she's not wrong. Molten sugar is no joke.

"For your first challenge, the judges would like you to make six individual crème caramels. They should be silken smooth and topped with a perfectly cooked sauce. I'm sure I don't need to remind anyone that today's results determine who will make it into the semifinals, so bakers, do your thing!"

At this point, the bare-bones recipe isn't a surprise. *Make caramel. Make custard. Bake.* Lovely.

"It's just flan, right?" Freddie asks.

"I think it's French flan," Courchesne says. "Note the accent mark."

"You're not comparing notes," Natalie reminds us in her cheerful camera voice.

"It's flan," Freddie repeats, but it's unclear if he's trying to convince the camera or himself.

It doesn't matter what it's called. It's custard. I can do custard. I just need to focus—and not on the fact that Grant ignored my note or that Nell is carrying a secret as big as some of mine.

I preheat the oven to 325. "I'd rather cook it at a lower temperature for longer," I explain to the camera, "rather than risk having it separate."

I start with the caramel, since I don't want it to be hot when I pour the custard into the six ramekins they've given us. The last thing I need is a curdled crème.

I swirl my pan as the caramel darkens. It doesn't take long before the acrid scent of burnt sugar fills the room.

"Shit, shit, shit," Freddie says, dropping his pan in the sink. He turns the water on, and it hits the pan with a steamy hiss.

That smell isn't going anywhere anytime soon.

I pull my pan off the heat right as it gets to the edge of amber and drizzle the hot syrup into the ramekins. So far so good.

Natalie arrives as I'm whisking eggs, asking if I've ever made crème caramel before.

"No," I say, "but I've made plenty of custards, so hopefully that'll get me through."

"Good luck," she says, and I'm pleasantly surprised to feel I don't need it.

I finish the crème part of my caramel without a mishap, and when I sieve it, just to be safe, it pours through the fine mesh without a lump in sight.

I split the vanilla-flecked liquid between the ramekins and arrange them on a sheet pan before telling my camera, "Going in."

I slide them in and set the timer for twenty minutes. Based on custard pies I've baked in the past, I know it's probably not enough, but I'd rather underestimate than over.

As I tidy my station, I notice Freddie filling a tray with water before setting his ramekins into it. Shit.

I look behind and see Tony has done the same.

"Oh, I'm screwed," I say, not bothering to hide my annoyance from the camera. "So screwed."

"Ten minutes, bakers, ten minutes!" Natalie says, letting a beat pass for the cameras before saying, "Remember, you're coming out of the oven and directly into the refrigerators, one in each. We'll pick up filming after the next round with plating and move right into judging from there."

We chorus our acknowledgment, and soon calls of "Coming out!" draw the cameras to the ovens.

I pull my bake, cringing at the surface texture. "Not good," I say, and that's what I get for treating it like a crustless pie. I transfer the ramekins to a small baking sheet and put them in the freezer, hoping for the best, but not remotely expecting it.

* * *

We break just long enough for the crew to reset, and I'm too jittery to relax. It's enough time to get some air and a drink, but that's it, and I feel trapped between the contest and the need to find answers about Bryan's death. I sneak a look at my cooling crème caramels, wondering again if getting eliminated might not be for the best. As it is, I'm going to have to make myself scarce at dinner if I want to do any investigating.

For a split second, I consider throwing it completely. My crème caramels are a mess, and I could deliberately bomb the next two challenges and write myself a one-way ticket to all the time I need.

And it's tempting.

But no. When we regroup, Natalie takes her place with Leland and Juliet and announces, "For the craft challenge, the judges would like to see a caramel nut tart. This can be sweet, it can be salty, it can be in the crust of your choice, but the primary elements must be caramel and the nut or nuts of your choice. Bakers, you have two and a half hours to do your thing!"

That's all it takes to change my mind. Sure, a tart isn't technically a pie, but it's close enough that I can't in good conscience throw it all away.

Natalie switches to her off-camera reminder voice, saying, "We'll break at the end of this round for an early lunch to give your tarts a chance to set, then we'll reconvene for judging both morning challenges before moving into the creative."

I tighten my apron strings as if strapping on armor. Surviving caramel week's schedule is going to be a miracle in itself.

I gather my crust ingredients, narrating as I go. "I'm doing a short crust base, which is similar to my pie dough, but I'm adding in some almond flour to carry the flavor all the way through." I chunk my butter up like I would for a pie and drop it into my flour. "The biggest difference is method, though. When I make pie dough, I leave big flakes of butter in the flour, but the shortness of this crust comes from mixing it in more. That way the tart will have enough stability to hold the filling." I demonstrate, working the butter into the flour until it takes on a sandy texture. What I don't say is that I'm working the same helpful magic into the dough as yesterday. It doesn't even feel strange doing it on camera anymore.

I roll the dough into a round and am pressing it into the pan when Natalie arrives with the judges. "Ooh, I smell almonds," Juliet says.

"I'm doing a cherry almond tart," I confirm.

"That's a classic combination."

"Are the cherries going in the filling?" Leland asks skeptically.

I want to say no, they're going in my tea, but I nod. "They'll be finely chopped and just enough to add a pop of flavor and a little bit of chew."

"That's the second one we have using something other than nuts," Leland muses, directing it somewhere between Juliet and the camera. "This is a caramel nut challenge, remember, not fruit and nut."

"It's just an accent," I say, but as they leave, I'm doubting my choice. The cherries were the thing that made the tart work, in my opinion, but maybe they're too much.

Dammit.

No. Fuck it. I pop the crust in the freezer to set and dump the dried sour cherries onto a cutting board.

Leland Graham does not get to convince me I don't know what I'm doing.

* * *

"I think I screwed up," Nell moans as we break for lunch.

"I heard you get the fruit lecture too," I say. "Screw it. I think banana walnut sounds awesome."

"It's only in the crust," she says, like she's trying to convince herself it's okay. "I blitzed banana chips with flour. I didn't think that was risky."

"It's not," Courchesne says, joining us. "He's just trying to psyche you out. If you want to talk about screwing up, I'm pretty sure I have enough bourbon in mine to drop Freddie."

"Hey, I resent that," he says.

"Seriously, it's a lot of bourbon." She shrugs. "Nothing I can do about it now, though."

In the dining room, I pause, scanning to see if Grant is there. "You guys go ahead," I say. "I want to check my phone."

It's not a lie, but it's also not the only thing I want to check. I find Kate in the office and collect my phone. A few texts from the diner crew, some pictures of Zoe that make my heart ache, and a message from Melly that says *I have news.*

Kate has her own phone to her ear and an exasperated look on her face as she bangs away at her laptop. It's as distracted as I've seen her, so I call Melly.

I have news is as bad as *we need to talk.*

It's not something that can wait.

She answers on the first ring. "Can you talk?"

"Sort of."

"Monitored?"

"Yes."

"Okay, just listen, then. I've been doing some digging, and first, my friend was right. Your tracks are completely covered. If someone very, very good was looking, then maybe the burner would be compromised, but not anything connecting to you."

Relief washes over me. "That's good."

"I'm not done. It turns out we weren't Matilda's first crack at"—she hesitates—"arranging things. She has posts on a few other forums, surface ones that can definitely be traced back to her."

"Okay." I keep my voice neutral, not wanting to draw Kate's attention.

"Still not done. I reached out to some reporter friends from that internship—one is down in your area—and, well, six degrees of separation got me someone on the crime beat with a reliable source inside. He said the cops—"

A slam from the office draws my attention from what she's saying. Kate has shoved her chair into the desk and is stalking toward me, finger pointed. "Finish and put the phone back in the drawer. Now."

She storms off, muttering to herself.

"Are you still there?" Melly says. "What's that?"

"Nothing. What about the cops?"

"The autopsy results came back. Tox panel showed a mix of alcohol and benzos, which he didn't have a script for. Cause of death was blunt-force trauma sustained in the fall."

"So he was alive when he went off the balcony?"

"It would seem so."

Down the hall, I catch echoes of Kate reading someone the riot act, and I know I don't have much time. "Melly, you're a genius. Keep digging, and if you find anything else, let me know."

"Will do. This teamwork thing is great, huh?"

I laugh. "Something like that. I gotta go."

"Kick ass, Pie Girl."

"Will do."

I end the call and go into the office, feeling like a trespasser as I drop the phone in the open drawer. The little lip of the lock is raised, and I have to force it closed. It sounds like a shot, but no one comes to investigate.

Kate has taken over every surface with computers, production schedules, and overflowing folders, and it's too much of an opportunity to pass up.

I check that the hall is still empty before riffling through the folders, looking for anything about the police visit. I get more information about network budgets than I care about, but nothing about Bryan. I scan the room, thinking there's got to be something. This is Kate's lair, after all, and Kate practically runs things.

There's a door opposite the hall entrance, and I jiggle the knob, surprised that it turns easily. On the other side is an office identical to Kate's that opens onto the reception area.

No one is at the desk.

Okay. Now this could be helpful. Heart hammering, I sneak through, keeping low. I'm hoping for a register, something that lays out who is where. If I can find out exactly which room is Bryan's, this snooping won't be for nothing.

There's a desktop computer on one end of the desk, the screen dark. I tap the space bar and it lights up, displaying a password box. Dammit.

I type *Longborough* and get an error message. Of course. That would've been too easy.

From the hall, I hear the machine-gun rattle of high heels, and my heart leaps up my throat. Shit. I can't go back through Kate's office, not if she's coming.

I hurriedly open drawers, looking for anything that will give me a hint about Bryan's room, when I strike a different sort of gold.

A box of key cards, all neatly packed in paper envelopes labeled with their room numbers. Except for the ones at the back, which are just marked *M*.

Master.

There are three cards in the envelope and I slide one out, pocketing it in my dress before I can talk myself out of it.

The clatter of heels is growing louder by the second, and I shut the drawer, vaulting myself up to sit on the reception desk. I spin, swinging my legs around and drop down in a puff of fluttering skirt before dashing straight out the main entrance.

Chapter Thirty-Four

The key card feels like a lead weight in my pocket as we return to the ballroom for judging. I completely missed lunch, forced to trek halfway around the entire estate before finding a way back in that wouldn't bring me past Kate's office.

It was worth it, though.

I might not have found answers, but I found access.

"Everything okay?" Nell asks as I pass her station.

I nod. "Just got stuck on the phone."

"Okay, bakers," Natalie says in her off-camera voice. "Crème caramels first. When I say go, get them from the freezer, and we'll pick up filming from the unmolding. Work at the ends of your benches to keep the shots tight. Go!"

We do as instructed, and the sight of my bake is enough to deflate some of the success I've been carrying from my impromptu heist. They're dark and uneven, and as I run a knife around the edges, I can tell they're too firm. The first one sticks, a sure sign that the caramel is overcooked.

It comes as no surprise when I place last, but Leland looks fairly shocked when it's Freddie he awards first place to. Freddie, for his part, does a well-earned victory dance that I'm sure will play well on camera.

The cameras pull Freddie and me aside for individual reactions, "It was a bad bake," I say. "I messed up with the water bath, and I'll just have to make up for it in the next round."

Across the room, Freddie is beaming at his camera as he talks, and I'm thrilled for him despite my poor placing.

It's funny, because when I first read the pitch for this competition, I was expecting it to be a more cutthroat version of the British show, but it's not.

Not if you don't count the dead bodies, anyway.

I'm pretty sure the British version doesn't have to deal with that.

"Okay, bakers, tart time," Natalie calls. "Fetch 'em and you'll have two minutes to plate, then back into the breach!"

The judges start at the front with Nell, and Leland is forced to admit that her banana-infused crust is really quite good. "The caramel is a bit bitter, though," he says, because he wouldn't be Leland without finding fault.

They move on to Freddie. "I went for a fancy interpretation of Snickers," he says as they slice into it. "Chocolate crust with a peanut caramel filling."

"Good chew on the caramel," Juliet says.

"And the chocolate crust is properly baked this time," Leland says grudgingly. "But I find the filling to be a little flat. If you're reworking a mass-market candy, you should be striving to elevate it, not simply change its shape."

"I could elevate the whole thing straight into my mouth," Natalie says, winking at Freddie, who takes Leland's comment in stride.

Courchesne presents her bourbon pecan without giving a hint that it's overboozed, and we're rewarded by Leland launching into a coughing fit.

"My, that is potent," Juliet says with a wicked grin. "I love it."

"It's far too much alcohol," Leland snaps, wiping his eyes. "And it's made it impossible for your caramel to set up enough. See how it's collapsing?"

"It's a caramel tart for the end of a bad week," Courchesne says breezily. "It's collapsing in solidarity."

"It's legless," Leland says. "And if you ate more than a few bites, you would be too."

Courchesne just smiles. "I'm not mad about it."

"Neither am I," Juliet stage-whispers, popping another bite into her mouth.

Then they're on to me, and it goes sideways as soon as Leland picks up the knife.

"Bit hard to cut," he says, leaning on the blade. "There's no way we're getting a fork through this."

"It's best eaten like a cookie," I admit.

Juliet smiles knowingly. "Like the one at Chez Panisse?"

"A riff on the classic," I concede, feeling embarrassed even though it's not strictly against the rules. After all, most recipes evolve from other ones. "In addition to the cherries, there's golden syrup to help keep the chew."

"It works," Juliet says, after she tries it. "I've had the original, and this is an excellent interpretation."

"It's good that you chopped the cherries as fine as you did. This way they're not upstaging the almonds," Leland says, and I almost sag with relief. It's not glowing praise, but it's not revulsion either.

I'm not out yet.

* * *

We're let out on a short break so we can check in with makeup for touch-ups while our stations are reset. Julian and the others are waiting with their kits in the atrium, and after I'm deemed fit for cameras, I beeline back to my room. The hall is quiet, and I slip the master key card from my pocket and hold it in front of my door's sensor. It unlocks with a solid clunk.

Bingo. Keys to the kingdom.

Inside, I stash the card in the pocket of one of the dresses hanging in the closet. Even though it looks identical to my real key card, I feel too exposed keeping it on me during filming.

I take a second to reset my ponytail in the mirror before heading back downstairs. I'm closing my door when a movement at the end of the hall catches my eye, a figure slipping through the door Tony showed me, the one he said Ainsley sometimes uses. I only have a glimpse, but there's no way that broad shoulder belongs to her.

It might, however, belong to Grant, and even though I know I should be going straight down to the ballroom, I want to talk to him alone. I hurry down the hall and open the door, the heavy sound of footfalls reverberating in the confined space. I crane my neck, trying to get a glimpse, but the stairs turn at sharp angles and it's impossible to see.

Keeping on my toes, I trot down the stairs, the rubber soles of my sneakers nearly silent on the treads. I pause on the last landing as light floods the stairwell from the open door below.

Framed inside is Leland Graham.

I swear, if Sherlock Holmes were real, he'd shoot me for being so dumb.

I wasn't following a possible suspect; I was catching a cheater sneaking a tryst between takes.

So much for Ainsley being over married men.

Chapter Thirty-Five

I let my mind wander as I make my cake layers, turning over the information from Melly.

At this stage, it's still only information, not answers, but it's something to chew on. For one thing, Bryan absolutely could've taken the pills himself, either on purpose or in a moment of stupidity. The fact that they weren't prescribed does put a check in the foul-play column, but still, it's not impossible that they were his. They're not exactly difficult to get a hold of, especially if you're already used to dealing with shady people.

"Going in," I call, sliding my trio of cake pans into the oven. I set my timer and start prepping the apple compote.

I run the stupidity theory first. There are two branches: one, if he'd had enough pills, he could've washed them down with booze in a misguided search for a good time, or two, he was trying to kill himself. I mentally cross the latter option off the list. People like Bryan—who are involved in the kinds of things he was—are narcissists, and narcissists don't kill themselves. I leave the recreational aspect on the table, but I'm not sold. Bryan was a lot of things, but I doubt he'd run the risk of ruining his on-screen persona with the massive hangover that concoction would induce.

I scrape the apples into a sauté pan and sprinkle them with sugar, cinnamon, and a pinch of salt. The filling isn't far off from what goes in the honey crunch pie, mostly because I see no reason to mess with what works. Especially since I have no guarantee that the showpiece part of this challenge will work at all.

But that's not worth worrying about yet.

The foul-play theory is next. If someone deliberately gave Bryan the pills, that means they would need three things: access to the drug, access to Bryan, and a motive.

Statistically, poisoning is a woman's means of killing, and it isn't lost on me that while magic, my pies could fall into that category. So much for bucking the trend.

Still, it means I can't discount anyone based on gender. It's possible they meant to simply overdose him but misjudged the amount needed. An accidental overdose could look like just that: an accident. If it didn't work, I could see the logic in thinking you could hide behind an intoxicated fall over the balcony too.

What's clear is that whoever killed Bryan doesn't want the credit for it. This isn't some serial killer taunting the police; it's someone hoping to get away with this one job.

I set my pan of apples in an ice bath to cool and check my cakes. The tops spring back when I touch them. "Coming out!"

I set them on my worktop, giving them a few minutes to cool in the pan while I assemble what I need for the hard part: spun sugar.

There have been more than a few times over the years that I've worried Frank was going to end our diner arrangement, but none were as close as the first time I attempted spun sugar. I had the sense not to do it in the pie van's kitchen, since molten sugar and tiny spaces is a recipe for pain, but I didn't have the sense to make sure Frank was gone for the night before setting up the diner for experimentation.

Let's just say it took a lot of elbow grease and forgive-me pies to make that right.

This time, I have a system.

I brandish my secret weapon for the camera. "This makes the magic," I say, twirling the spiky tool like a wand. It started life as a balloon whisk, but I cut the loops off, so now it looks more like a medieval torture device. Or a head-scratcher. "There's probably something official and French that proper pastry chefs use, but my bootleg whisk does the job."

I pour the dry sugar into a pan and set it over low heat, stirring gently as it melts. If I were going to magic it, this would be the time, but I can't risk it. This is temperamental enough without any mystical elements added in.

Leland and Juliet lurk just at the edge of my vision, and I force myself to ignore them, hoping they'll leave if they don't get a reaction.

As the sugar caramelizes, I stir in red gel coloring until it takes on the thick viscosity of blood. I give it a few minutes to cook once it's dyed, then pull it from the heat.

Here goes.

Using the deformed whisk, I stir until it starts to cool. Leland and Juliet are still watching, and I'm painfully aware of the camera's proximity. The last thing I need to do is accidentally get hot caramel on the poor operator.

"Stand back," I say, only half joking as I begin flicking the whisk over a greased bowl. Strands of translucent red caramel drape across it like spider silk, and I have to stop myself from doing a giddy dance. "It's working!"

"You sound surprised," Natalie says, sidling up to watch.

"Pleasantly," I say, keeping my eyes glued to the task. I keep going until I have the entire bowl covered, then I spritz my hands with pan spray and begin gathering it into a ball. Working quickly,

I taper the end and add indents in the top and bottom. I set it aside and flick a few more strands across the bowl, shaping these into a stem and leaf. Yes, it would be better if they were brown and green, but I'm not a wizard.

I set them into the top of the sugar apple and exhale for perhaps the first time since I started.

* * *

Courchesne is called first for judging, and she sets the bar high.

Literally.

Decorated with painterly splotches of gold-leaf caramel frosting, the cake itself is six layers of alternating chocolate and caramel and is topped with a towering sugar sail.

"It's simply stunning," Juliet says. "The icing looks like something from a museum."

"The sugar work is a bit thick," Leland says. "But outside of here, I doubt anyone would complain."

"Then why are you?" Natalie quips.

"Because this late in the competition, we expect perfection," he says, enunciating the last word.

"And this is very close," Juliet says, sampling bites from each of the layers.

"It's visually stunning, but having so many layers can make it difficult to serve."

"I'd be fine taking it whole," Juliet says, and Courchesne looks rightfully thrilled when she returns to her station.

Next to Courchesne's, Tony's honey-and-pistachio cake looks understated, but still elegant.

"I would've liked to see more advanced sugar work," Leland says, pulling one of the pistachio-flecked caramel shards off the top. "Very nice flavor, though."

"It's definitely an interesting profile," Juliet agrees. "But I'm afraid I'm not getting much of the saffron. To me, saffron is one of those ingredients where if you're going to spend the money on it, you want to know it's there. I do love the honey caramel, though."

Freddie's caramel latte cake, which is shaped like a mug and topped with a heap of spun-sugar steam, gets high marks for flavor and presentation, but Nell gets marked down on both.

"The peanut butter is gluing my mouth closed and has completely overpowered the caramel," Leland says.

"It is a shame about the tails," Juliet says, indicating the spiky caramel-coated peanuts lining the edge of Nell's cake. "If you had finished all of them, it would've been a very nice display."

"Some of them fell, and I just ran out of time," Nell explains. "I'm sorry."

"So that leaves us Daisy," Natalie says, and I bring my cake forward.

"The apple is lovely," Juliet says, touching it gently. "Very pretty."

"Unfortunately, it's the only thing that is," Leland says. "There's rustic and then there's rushed, and I think it's clear which this is."

I bite the inside of my cheek, refusing to react as they slice into it.

"Oh, that tastes just like fall," Juliet says.

"The apples are good, but I feel like we've already seen this from you," Leland says. "It's one thing to have a signature, but it's another to be stagnant with it."

I nod, aware that the camera is watching and return to my station, telling myself it's fine.

It's fine to be done.

Really.

I need the time to investigate anyway.

When they line us up for the final judging, I believe the words I'm saying.

Almost.

"Bakers, what has been a sweet week for some has gotten sticky for others," Natalie says. "But I am so pleased to share that this week's baker is the person who dazzled us with a textbook-perfect crème caramel and whose cake was the stuff of our caffeinated dreams. Freddie, congratulations, you are this week's Top Baker."

He cheers, and there's a flurry of congratulations that Natalie waits out. "But now we must say good-bye to the baker who will not be joining us for next week's semifinals. Daisy and Nell, could you please step forward?"

Chapter Thirty-Six

My heart is broken.

It's stupid to feel this crushed about a contest elimination, but I can't help it.

The look on Nell's face before she took off her apron reprints onto my eyelids every time I blink.

I feel like I robbed her, and it's awful.

She's sitting at the end of the table with Derek, who holds her hand without a care for who sees. If nothing else, I know she'll have good company for the time left at Longborough, but it doesn't erase the ache. All I can think of is the light in her eyes when she told me about her donut-shop dreams.

"You hear the cops were back?" Vic says, and I welcome the distraction, if not its meaning.

"For what?"

"Dunno," she says. "Just saw them in the hall this morning while you guys were shooting."

"They weren't doing more interviews?"

"Didn't talk to me," she says with a shrug, and it's so casual that I strike her off the list of potential poisoners. No one, not even Vic, could be that blasé in the face of possible police scrutiny.

"They were here a while, though," Gemma says. "They were taking pictures outside."

"Of what?"

"The spot Bryan died? I think? I was watching them from the west library."

That's interesting. The crime scene people would've taken pictures when they were here. I can't imagine what they would need more for, especially after everything has been cleaned up.

Unless it hasn't been.

As much as I want to leap from the table to go see, I resist. I don't want to draw attention to myself, or worse, invite a tagalong.

Instead I ask, "Has Grant been hanging with you guys today?"

"Negative," Vic says. "I think he's still salty."

"I think that's just who he is as a person," Freddie says.

"Rude," Gemma says.

Freddie shrugs. "Tact is just not saying true shit."

"Maybe, but someone should still check on him," I say, and even though I don't mean it to, it comes out sounding ominous. I guess two deaths in as many weeks will do that.

"I'll do it," Tony says, getting up from his spot near the head of the table. "I'm going up anyway. Good night, all."

For a split second I'm torn, wanting to stop him, wanting to be the one to talk to Grant first, but there's no way to do it without making it weird.

Besides, darkness will be falling fast.

* * *

When Freddie makes the move to transition the dinner crowd to the bar, I excuse myself under the pretense of needed phone time.

"But I'm man of the hour," he protests. "You can't abandon the party in my time of glory!"

"I'll join you later," I promise, grabbing a plate of leftover tart slices on my way out. There's only one slice of mine left, but it'll do.

My first stop is my room, where I stash the pastries before heading back down the stairs. I go out the main entrance and walk straight into a wall of humidity that would've destroyed our spun sugar had we been outside.

It feels like another storm is coming—if not tonight, then soon.

For now, though, there's still enough light to see by, and I turn right, cutting off the path that leads around the gardens.

The library's tall leaded windows are easy to pick out, illuminated softly from inside. I continue on. I'm looking up at the balconies when a flash of yellow catches my eye.

Fluttering off the corner of the third balcony is a torn strip of yellow police tape.

Bingo.

I move back, closer to the hedges, to get a full view. The balcony is on a corner, which means the room is the last on the hall and three floors up.

I scan the ground, looking for anything the police might've been interested in seeing again, but there's nothing obvious.

Maybe it's the balcony itself. Maybe they needed photos of the grounds to be used in court?

I squint up at the balcony, but aside from the scrap of yellow plastic, no one would ever know that a man fell to his death from it. The French doors leading inside are dark, as they should be, but the rooms to the right are lit up, and I can see a figure moving within, too small to be Leland.

Juliet, then.

If there was a struggle, she would've heard it.

I realize that's the interview I needed to hear. Not Tony's or Nell's, but the person who had the best chance of hearing what happened. I curse myself, wondering if there's a way to ask her without being too obvious. Sure, with any luck, the pie magic will still be working, but it's not like I can go knock on her door and ask if she heard anything suspicious without looking incredibly suspicious myself.

Still, at least now I know exactly which room is Bryan's.

And I have a way in.

* * *

Back inside, I take the long way, avoiding the bar. The last thing I need is to be waylaid.

I trot up the stairs, pausing outside Grant's door, but all is quiet.

I retrieve the plate of tarts from my room and go back across the hall. I knock, calling, "Grant? It's Daisy. I come bearing gifts."

Silence.

I repeat the knock, and this time there's movement from inside.

I step back, suddenly unsure of how to approach this and wishing I knew half as much about investigating murders as I do about committing them.

The door opens, and I hold the plate up like an offering. "I have snacks."

He grunts but opens the door wider, which I choose to take as an invitation.

"How are you doing?" I ask, brushing by him.

"Don't worry, Tony already did the wellness check," he says, letting the door close behind us.

I set the plate on his desk and give him the slice of almond tart. "Still, sugar has never made a situation worse."

"Except diabetes," he grumbles, but takes it anyway. He looks like he needs it.

"Fair enough," I say, watching his throat bob as he swallows. The effect won't be instant, but piled on top of yesterday's pie magic, it won't take long. "We were just worried. It's bad enough Ainsley shuts herself away. We wanted to make sure you didn't do the same."

"You were talking about me?"

"Not in a bad way," I assure him. "Just a concerned way."

"I'm fine. This was a lark, not my entire identity."

It stings the way he says it, even though I don't think he means it to. "It's kind of a lark for me too," I say, although I feel a million miles away from the time that was the truth. Now it's the thing that has the potential to change my entire life, for better or worse.

He takes another tart slice—Tony's ginger macadamia—and drops into the chair. "But not completely?"

"I guess not," I say, leaning my hip against the desk. "It's all gotten more intense than I expected."

"The competition or the rest?"

"Both."

A heavy silence punctuates the word, echoing the truth of it. It's as good an opening as I'm going to get.

"The police were back today," I say.

"I know."

"Did they talk to you?"

"They did."

"And?"

"And what?" He folds his arms across his broad chest, and I have a flash of talking through the mechanics of murder with

Derek, about how leverage could make it work but strength would make it easy.

No one knows I'm here.

Everyone is down in the bar, celebrating with Freddie, except for Tony, who is two doors down, and maybe Ainsley.

"Go ahead," he says, the words practically a challenge. "Ask."

"Did you have anything to do with Bryan's death?"

"You mean his murder?"

"Yes."

"No," he says, shaking his head. "I did not."

"Then what did they want?"

He opens his arms, palms up. "An easy target."

"What does that mean?"

"I'm the obvious suspect. I got loud with him, and then he died." Something shifts in his face, betraying an internal struggle I can't quite read.

"What?" I ask it gently and without judgment, an opening that invites the magic to come through.

"You should go," he says, slamming it shut. I bite back a growl of frustration. The magic should be compelling him to be helpful, not resistant.

Unless he somehow thinks getting rid of me *is* helpful.

For him.

I ease myself away from the desk, some visceral part of my brain warning against sudden movements.

"Okay, yeah," I say. "I wasn't trying to bother you. Like I said, we just wanted to make sure you were good."

"Nothing to worry about here."

Right.

Obviously.

Chapter Thirty-Seven

The one thing I didn't think to pack for this experience was a ninja suit.

And I'm regretting it.

My choices are either pajamas—loose shorts and a tank top that's barely up for the job—or a dress. Neither is the height of stealth wear.

I pick the darkest dress I have, a navy-blue shirtdress with white piping down the placket. It'll have to do.

It's late, the party in the bar long since broken up. I did, as promised, make an appearance, but I only had half of the drink Freddie insisted on getting me.

I need to be clearheaded.

By the time I made it down, Nell and Derek had gone, and I try not to think about her next door, knowing she doesn't have to get up on time tomorrow.

I, however, do, and the fact that it's now approaching two o'clock already has me planning the morning caffeine run.

Still, if I want to be stealthy, there's no better time like the dead of night.

My sneakers are silent on the plush carpet of the hall as I make my way across the estate. I use the atrium passage to bypass the main hallway, figuring if anyone is manning the fort, it will be at the front desk.

The west wing is a mirror of our own, with an identical staircase leading up from a grand foyer. I race up the stairs on tiptoes, feeling exposed without any nooks to duck into.

I pause at the end of the hall, orienting myself. I'm above the library, so Bryan's room should be the last on the left.

I creep down, heart in my throat. The amber glow of the hall lights has been dimmed to account for the late hour, but it's still enough illumination to make it impossible to tell if there are lights on under the other doors.

It's two in the morning and we all have an early day ahead. Surely everyone has the sense to be sleeping.

Everyone not currently engaged in crime, that is.

Breaking and entering should be harder than flashing a card at a scanner, but that's the wonders of modern technology for you.

The light flashes green as the lock clicks open with a *thunk* that seems to echo in the silence. I slip inside and wait for my eyes to adjust. The only illumination comes from the French doors, the soft glow from the moon letting me see outlines of furniture and little else.

This is the part I didn't plan through. Without my phone, I'm flashlightless, and turning on the main lights is a risk. It's unlikely they'll be noticed at this hour, but not impossible.

Shit.

I take a gamble that the rooms all share a similar layout, move to where my bathroom would be, and silently thank the architect for this lack of imagination when I find it. I turn the light on, closing the door halfway so it slants a beam into the rest of the room. It's not great, but it's enough for now.

The bed is neatly made and the side tables free of clutter. I check their drawers, but all that's left is a notepad bearing the estate's logo and pencil.

Instead of a writing desk like I have, this room has a pair of club chairs with a low coffee table, which is also bare.

The entire room is spotless, ready for the next guest to arrive.

Damn efficient housekeeping staff.

I cross to the French doors, finding them unlocked. I ease one open and step out. It's the same as mine, as all the balconies flanking the upper story, with the tall stone railings.

But this was the one that led to a death.

I go back inside and stand at the main door, taking in the room as a whole. I take a moment to channel my inner Sherlock, trying to see the truth of what happened.

I can picture it: Bryan, sitting in one of the leather club chairs, a bottle of something expensive on the table. A glass.

Maybe two glasses.

Maybe the killer was a guest before they became an enemy.

I reconfigure the mental picture: a shadowed figure in the chair opposite Bryan, sharing a drink.

Sharing pills?

That doesn't make sense. If Bryan was going to do recreational drugs with a guest, I don't see benzos being the top choice.

So if the pills weren't his, they were brought.

I play out a different version. The guest arrived with the bottle and perhaps the glasses too, because who doesn't like a guest bearing gifts? Even Grant let me in for nothing more than a plate of tarts.

Okay, so the guest arrives with the drinks and the pills. Are the pills already in the alcohol? No, because then the guest couldn't drink and that would look suspicious.

Shit.

I wish I knew what was found in the room after his body was discovered. Two glasses or one? A bottle?

Or was the alcohol consumed elsewhere? Not at the bar, because that's where we default to every night, but perhaps one of the smoking rooms?

I fast-forward past the drinks for now. I'll have to ask Melly if her contact has access to that kind of detail. I try to picture the next phase.

Did they move to the balcony willingly, and if so, why? To smoke? Stargaze?

I shake my head, dismissing it. Not willingly. That feels wrong.

Okay. I reset the scene in my head, Bryan and the mystery guest in the chairs, talking, drinking, maybe arguing? About what? The contest? His shady personal life? Could someone else have had the same dirt on him I do?

I let the question marinate, moving forward. The potent mix of benzos and high-proof alcohol wouldn't have taken long to kick in, and I realize that's the thing I need to figure out.

If the killer moved fast enough, was persuasive enough, they could've gotten Bryan onto the balcony on his own two feet. He would've been, to use Leland's term, pretty legless, but there definitely would've been a window of time where those legs could have gotten him outside.

That keeps the leverage aspect in play. If Bryan made it out to the balcony upright, maybe propped himself against the railing for support and was too out of it to put up a fight, I could get him up and over. It wouldn't be easy and he probably wouldn't go quiet, but he would go.

On the other hand, if he ingested enough pills to knock him out, that's a different story. One with a far narrower set of suspects. Sure, I could drag him from the chairs to the balcony, but I couldn't get him over. Not from the ground, not as dead weight.

But there are several people here who could.

The thought chills me even as I know I'm getting ahead of myself. Without knowing whether Bryan moved himself to the balcony, it's pure speculation, but isn't that what most detective work is right up until it isn't?

Before I can run my suspects through my imagined scenario, a muffled thump sounds from outside, making me jump. There's a dull crash, followed by muted words I can't make out.

I dash to the bathroom, turning off the light and plunging the room back into darkness. The French door is still open onto the balcony and will be a clear giveaway that someone's been here if it's noticed.

Shit, shit, shit.

I have no escape route until I know the hall is empty.

The voice becomes louder, the slurring words taking on a coaxing tone as another voice, a woman's, shushes the first.

It's coming from the balcony next door.

I ease out of the bathroom as the woman's giggle echoes in the clear night air.

Juliet? Having a balcony rendezvous? God, it's so Shakespearean I almost laugh.

And then I stop, because it's Leland's voice, clear as day, that says, "No one will see, I promise."

"You're so bad," the woman says in a southern accent I would recognize anywhere.

Not Juliet.

Ainsley.

Chapter Thirty-Eight

I was wrong about the room order. It wasn't Juliet I saw moving around inside earlier; it was Ainsley.

I leave as soon as I realize what I'm overhearing and hightail it back to my room, too wired to sleep.

I have nothing tangible to show for my snooping, but that doesn't mean I'm not on the right track. Because thanks to Leland's penchant for outdoor sex, I now have a potential witness I can actually talk to.

If I can figure out how to find the time with the semifinals looming.

Ainsley doesn't show at breakfast, and when I knock at her door, there's no answer. I could let myself in, of course, but that seems like overkill. She could be sleeping off her late night or still in Leland's room, waiting for everyone to be occupied with filming before sneaking out.

Still, impatience makes me prickle.

I return to my room to wait for Julian and practically drag him inside when he knocks. "Make me pretty and give me your phone."

"Okay, Bossy McBosspants, maybe it's time to switch to decaf?" But he does it, setting my makeup and handing me the phone. "Be quick," he warns. "I only have Tony, and you know he needs nothing except a dust of powder."

"Hey." I catch his hand before he can leave. "Thank you. Seriously. You've been saving my life with this."

"Anything for love," he says, breezing out before I can correct him.

I dial Melly. "I need a favor, and I don't have a lot of time."

"Good morning, sunshine," she says.

"Sorry, lack of sleep. But I need to you get in touch with your contact and see if you can find out what was in Bryan's room the night he died."

"Like an evidence log?"

"Yes. You said he had benzos and alcohol in his system. I want to know if there was a bottle found and how many glasses were there."

"Okay," she says. "Anything else?"

"Anything that feels relevant, but that in particular."

"Got it," she says. "I'll text you. This number or your own?"

I hesitate, not wanting anything to hit Julian's phone that could be a problem. "Mine. But be subtle."

"Subtle is my middle name," she says, and it's so far from the truth that I almost laugh.

"Don't worry, I got you."

"Thanks. I owe you."

"Damn right you do."

* * *

"Welcome, bakers, to pâtisserie week and most importantly, the semifinals!" Natalie says, her voice echoing through the ballroom. It's strange to be down to only four of us. They have us staggered across the stations, giving the cameras plenty of space to move. It seems impossible that only a week ago we had twelve bakers in here and as many cameras.

Abigail and Kate are both supervising as Leland and Juliet stand serenely at the judges' table. There isn't even a hair out of place to hint at Leland's illicit shenanigans.

Cheating bastard.

Natalie continues, "For the first challenge, the judges would like you to create a dozen of the miniature French classic, petits fours. These should be filled with strawberries and cream and topped with a poured white chocolate fondant. As always, this will be judged blind, so we'll say good-bye to Leland and Juliet for now." She waves them off, and Abigail follows them out. "You have two hours, so bakers, do your thing!"

"I swear," I say to the camera as I look over the recipe, "I have never made as much cake in my entire life as I have since being here."

The recipe is the usual nonsense: *Make sponge. Make fondant. Fill, ice, and decorate.*

Decorate. That's specific. At least I know what a petit four is and that they're supposed to be pastel and pretty.

I can do pastel and pretty.

Chapter Thirty-Nine

There's pastel and pretty, then there's pastel and absolute perfection. And mine were not perfection.

They were better than Freddie's neon offering but nowhere near as good as what Tony and Courchesne delivered, so I really need these blackberry lemon éclairs to work.

After hearing Courchesne lay out her yuzu and passion fruit combo, I'm afraid mine sound a little bit boring, but I'm not about to offer that up when the judges stop at my bench. No need to put ideas in their heads.

"Is choux something you're experienced with?" Leland asks.

I'm sure he knows the answer. "I had never made it until I started practicing for this challenge," I admit. "And there were a lot of practice batches."

"We'll see if it paid off," he says, and I have a flash of annoyance so sharp that I'm tempted to work some vengeance magic into the dough just out of spite.

It's strong enough that I immediately stop mixing. I know better than to let impulsive emotion dictate the magic, no matter how much the lack of sleep is getting to me.

"Get it together," I mutter, adding the eggs to the mixture in small pours and telling the camera, "The thing about choux is you can't trust the recipe. It might say six eggs, but depending on the weather or the whims of the pastry gods, it might be five or it might be eight and a half."

I stop after each addition to check for the telltale ribboning of the batter. It takes most of the egg but not quite all.

I transfer the mixture to a pastry bag and pipe six-inch strips of batter onto the parchment-lined baking sheet, smoothing down the little peaks left at the ends with a dab of water.

"In they go." With any luck, they'll puff up into hollow golden logs, but with choux, you never know where luck will land.

* * *

They puff.

They aren't even deemed boring, despite Leland being critical of the texture difference between the curd and cream filling.

"I think alternating lemon cream with blackberry cream would've worked better," he says.

"E-clair, ick-clair," I say before my brain kicks in. "I like it my way."

Natalie chokes on a laugh, and even Juliet looks amused at Leland's expression.

Stupid sleep-deprived brain.

"Your opinion is both noted and obvious in your choice of execution," he says archly. "But the critique stands."

I manage to keep my mouth shut as they head off to Courchesne, but barely. All I want to do is lay my head on the bench and sleep.

Which is when I realize, for the first time today, where I'm standing.

Chloe's station.

The fog of exhaustion lifts, replaced by guilt at not noticing before. In all of the commotion of the contest and solving Bryan's murder, she has somehow slipped from focus.

I'm vaguely aware of Leland praising Tony's Black Forest éclair and Juliet commenting on the particular difficulties of working with chocolate choux, but my attention is on the corner of the bench. There's nothing visible there, no sign still lingering of Chloe's fall, but that's the problem.

Out of sight, out of mind shouldn't apply to a person.

* * *

When we break for lunch, I grab Freddie, holding him back as Tony and Courchesne head to the dining room. "How do you feel about raiding the espresso machine?"

"Depends how you feel about adding vodka."

"It wasn't that bad," I assure him, hooking my arm through his. "But I won't tell if you don't."

"It was definitely that bad. He called them soggy and limp. Do you know two adjectives you never want applied to you? You guessed it. Soggy and limp." He tips his head back and moans. "I'm fucked."

"Probably not if you're limp," I say, dragging him forward. "Or soggy."

"I hate you."

"You don't," I say, reaching for the bar door but finding it locked.

Freddie shakes his head. "Passages, remember?"

I follow him down the hall into one of the lounges. He finds the sliding panel so quickly that I wonder just how often he's been using it.

Inside the bar, Freddie lets himself behind the counter like he owns the place.

"How many?" he asks.

"Would three be wrong?"

"Sweetie, for you I'll make it a quad."

I settle onto a stool while he pulls the shots, moving with practiced ease. "Barista?"

"Since high school," he confirms, reaching into the refrigerator for milk. The machine gurgles and hisses as he works with his back to me. "If the cake thing doesn't work out, people will always need coffee."

He turns, sliding me a mug filled to the brim and smelling like heaven. On top, in frothed milk and Instagram-worthy detail, is the distinct image of a very limp penis.

It completely breaks me. I dissolve into laughter, my exhaustion amplifying the absurdity by an obscene magnitude until tears stream down my cheeks. It only gets worse when Freddie grabs a bottle of top-shelf vodka and pours it into his own limply decorated drink.

He offers me the bottle but I shake my head, gasping for air.

"I think it would do me in," I sputter. "Unless this is your strategy to eliminate the competition."

"My limp and soggy éclairs are doing that work for me," he says, returning the bottle to its home and tidying up the evidence of our drinks.

"What'll you do if you win?" I ask, the laughter gone as quickly as it came.

"Same as everyone else," he says. "Stop worrying about shit."

Chapter Forty

I wonder what that would be like, not worrying.

Probably nice and probably not in the cards for me.

But at least for now, I don't have to worry about falling asleep on set, and that's an improvement. I leave Freddie at the dining room, but not before scanning the faces of who's inside.

No Grant, no Ainsley.

Perfect.

I don't bother bearing gifts this time, not when there are even odds I'll be left standing in the hall.

I knock on Ainsley's door, hard enough that she can hear even if she's on the balcony. "It's Daisy," I call. "Can I talk to you?"

There's the shuffle of movement inside and the door opens, revealing an irritated-looking Ainsley. "What do you want?"

"Just to talk," I say, regretting that I didn't bring something to sweeten the offer.

Preferably something with a hint of magic.

She sighs. "Fine, come in."

I'm not sure how to approach the questions I need to ask without sounding like a weirdo, but before I can say anything, she says, "Congratulations, by the way. On making the semis." It sounds like it costs her something to say it, and I'm oddly touched.

"Thanks. Have you been watching at all? With the others?"

She shakes her head, looking pained, and I realized Leland must've been the one who told her about the semifinals. It's exactly the opening I need.

"You're still seeing him?"

She shrugs. "Need something to keep me busy."

"That's sort of what I'm here about," I admit. "I've been thinking about Bryan's death a lot—"

"Oh god," she huffs. "Please tell me you're not one of those true-crime chicks. You think you can solve a murder before the police?"

"Kind of?" I figure it's better to let her think that than to tell her I'm usually more into the committing side of the equation.

"And what, you want a sidekick?"

The laugh bubbles up before I can stop it. "Definitely not." Even if I did, she would be my last choice, but I don't say that. I do have some tact, after all. "I was just trying to puzzle something out. I know Leland and Bryan were room neighbors. Were you with him that night?"

"I don't see how that's your business or even relevant." She shifts her weight backward, her posture taking on an instinctive defensiveness.

So she was there.

"Did you hear anything? An argument? A struggle?"

"Hello? Have you seen these rooms? They're practically soundproof."

But not completely. Last night proved as much, especially if balcony doors are left open. "Nothing?" I ask. "No scream?"

"You're morbid, you know that? There's something wrong with you." She shakes her head. "Seriously, I don't want to talk about this. You should focus on the real reason you're here and be thankful you still are."

I wonder if it's possible she really didn't hear anything, and then I remember seeing Leland slink out of our hall. "Were you with him here?"

"Ugh. Look, we always use his room. There are fewer people around, so we're less likely to get caught, okay? We learned that the first day. Is that the kind of detail that's gonna break your case wide open? The logistics of my affair?"

"Always?"

"Yes, god." She huffs, and I realize the anger isn't just anger. It's embarrassment.

I raise my hands in surrender. "Okay, sorry. You're right. But please, think back. Try to remember that night and if you heard anything from next door. Anything at all."

"You know what I heard? Leland's phone." She spits the word out like bitter fruit. "Said it was important and I had to go."

Part of me snags on the unfairness of the judges getting to keep their connection to the outside world, but I let it go. It's not what's important. "His wife?"

"Well, I don't think he'd kick me out to talk to his insurance adjuster, do you?"

"Fair enough. For what it's worth, that sucks. I'm sorry men are—"

"Men?" She snorts. "Yeah, me too."

* * *

"Bakers, welcome to your last challenge of the semifinals. For this round, the judges would like you to dazzle us with mirror-glazed entremets. These layered beauties should have at least three distinct elements and be finished with a coating shiny enough for Leland to admire himself in. You have five hours, so bakers, do your thing!"

I'm buzzing with a cocktail of caffeine, curiosity, and nerves, but for now, it's the good kind of buzz. It has the sharp kind of energy I get when diving into murder-pie orders, when focus matters more than anything.

The clocks are ticking down on both the contest and the crime.

Some of my best recipe development happens when I'm doing things unrelated to baking, like showering or walking Zoe, so hoping for the same effect, I set all the details of the murder puzzle to percolate in the back of my mind while focusing my conscious attention on the task at hand.

"Apple again?" Leland asks as he arrives with Juliet for establishing shots.

"Apple again," I confirm. "I'm doing a spiced biscuit base with layers of caramel mousse and apple gelée."

"It does sound yummy," Juliet says.

Leland sniffs. "It sounds reductive."

I meet his disapproving gaze without blinking. "The thing I like about apples is how versatile they are. They're equally at home in simple pies or lavish cakes."

I have no respect for him at this point. I can't, not when he's sleeping with a contestant half his age and lying to his wife about it, but I don't let it show.

At least, I hope I don't.

I'm going for confident-chef vibes here, not ragey-killer, but when he breaks eye contact first, it feels like a win.

Lavish is definitely the word for this cake. When I was practicing it, Frank had a conniption and accused me of trying to turn his diner into some artsy-fartsy French bistro, but it was worth it, because now the elements come together with ease.

So much ease, in fact, that I'm tempted to work a little delusting magic into it, just to mess with Leland's evening plans. The thought immediately brings back images of Freddie's espresso art, and I have to stifle a giggle.

But fuck it.

It's not delusting, exactly, but a dose of do-the-right-thing that goes into the mirror glaze. It would be more effective spread throughout each layer, but still, maybe it will be a nudge in the right direction.

"Okay, bakers," Natalie calls as I'm putting the finishing touches on my display, "you are down to one minute on this semi-final challenge. One minute!"

I step back, proud of the piece in front of me. Assembled using half of a ball pan, it's a perfect dome covered in shiny red mirror glaze. A shimmer of luster dust highlights the shape, and a single gold leaf sits on the top. Simple, effective, and dare I say, elegant.

Unfortunately, so are the others.

Courchesne's purple, gray, and black galaxy glaze is swirled with a milky white aurora, and when it's cut, it reveals a bold rainbow of layers.

"Oh, that's a delight," Juliet says.

Courchesne walks them through the tropical-inspired flavors she used, and it's enough to make me wonder if my three little layers are going to cut it.

"It's harmonious on the palate," Leland says, "but visually, I would like more cohesion or an identifiable theme."

She cocks her head, and even though I can't see her face, the set of her shoulders gives away her annoyance. When she speaks, her voice is measured but laced with iron. "Like I said earlier, the outside represents the ace flag colors, and the inside is pride. The theme identifies as queer."

Freddie turns and catches my eye, and I have to immediately look away to avoid losing it.

"I understand the intention," Leland says. "It's the visual execution I find wanting."

He clearly has no idea how much he's going to regret this when it airs, and I have exactly zero sympathy for him. In the doorway behind them I can see Abigail furiously tapping away at her phone and shaking her head.

"Hold!" she barks, marching forward. "Leland, rephrase that so you don't sound like a raging bigot on national TV, please."

"I'm not being a bigot," he protests, looking genuinely taken aback. "It's a valid point and hardly the first time I've pointed out color issues."

Abigail gives him a withering stare and he sighs, shaking his shoulders out and resetting.

Abigail stabs a warning finger at him and steps back. "Roll!"

"It's harmonious on the palate," Leland repeats, "but the colors are bolder than this dessert typically calls for."

Abigail circles a finger in the air, indicating the show can go on.

"Typical is overrated," Courchesne says sweetly as she gathers her entremets and returns to her bench. With her back to the judges, she pulls a face that will definitely not make it on air while we pretend not to notice.

Tony goes next with a Bordeaux-colored entremets decorated with an arc of blackberries, blueberries, and purple basil.

"This is simply stunning," Juliet says, cutting it to reveal a gradient of rich purple layers.

"I don't know that the basil adds much on top, but that's the worst thing I can say about it," Leland says, after trying a bite. "This could sit comfortably in the highest-end shops of Paris. In fact, I would love the recipe."

Of course that's the act I have to follow, but at least Juliet is gracious about it.

"That's a lovely glaze," she says. "It looks very inviting."

Leland cuts a wedge out, and I'm relieved to see all of my layers are still clearly delineated. Even he nods approvingly. "Using the mousse to surround the gelée was clever," he admits. "It makes for an interesting slice despite relatively simple elements."

"Excellent mousse," Juliet says. "Although the base is a little firm."

"Overall, though, very passable," Leland says. "Especially for an apple."

Back at my station, I whisper to my camera, "A week ago I would've taken that as decent praise, but at the semifinals?" I shake my head as Freddie brings his orange-and-magenta entremets up.

Leland looks at it for a long time, long enough to put us all on edge in that trademark way of his. "You know," he finally says, "when you said orange, I was concerned. But looking at it now?" He shakes his head. "It's actually gorgeous."

Freddie's shoulders drop with relief.

"It's like a sunset," Juliet agrees. "Exquisite use of color."

They slice into it, revealing layers of almond dacquoise, chocolate mousse, and chili mango compote.

"Attractive interior," Leland says as he presses his fork through it. As soon as it's in his mouth, he's spluttering, holding his hand out to stop Juliet from doing the same.

"Jesus," he chokes. "Exactly how much chili did you put in there?"

"Half a teaspoon?"

"Are you sure? Did you even taste it?"

"It's the same amount I use at home," Freddie says, sounding bewildered.

Juliet, looking intrigued, loads her fork with the mousse and dips it in the compote. "Oh, that is fiery," she says. "The addition of another sweet milky layer, like a white chocolate bavarois, would have helped balance it out. I like the idea of this combination, especially with the chocolate, but I'm afraid the proportions are a bit off."

"A bit," Leland scoffs. "That's weapons-grade heat."

"I'm sorry," Freddie says, retrieving the cake. His forehead is furrowed as he goes back to his station. He drops the entremets on the bench and swipes a finger through the compote. His eyes widen in alarm when he tastes it. "Fuck me."

As the judges deliberate, we all, even Tony, crowd in for a taste before the set crew takes it away.

It is, indeed, a startling amount of spice.

"I don't get it," Freddie moans. "It's gotta be the brand of pepper. Or it's mislabeled. This isn't how it should be."

"Dude, why didn't you taste it?" Courchesne asks.

"Because I was rushing. And because I can make it in my sleep."

"I would maybe not share this one," she says. "You know, for the safety of others and all."

Freddie takes the cake and unceremoniously dumps it in the bin, then points at it. "That's going to be me next. Just you wait."

Chapter Forty-One

For the first time since we started, we're not allowed to choose our spots in the final lineup, and that's when I know I'm in danger.

I started between Freddie and Courchesne, but before we begin filming, Abigail points to Freddie. "Other end. The rest of you are fine."

The judges come back in with Natalie, and Abigail gives the signal to roll.

Natalie surveys us for what feels like an eternity, then says, "Before we begin, you should all be extremely proud of yourselves to have made it as far as the semifinals. You have competed against some of the best bakers in the country, and it is now down to the four of you. This has been another difficult week of judging, particularly for the honor of Top Baker. It is, in fact, the closest it's ever been, but I am pleased to announce that Tony, you are once again Top Baker. Well done."

He purses his lips like he's trying to keep the smile in and nods while Natalie pauses for the camera to capture reactions.

"And now," she continues, "we must say a heartbreaking goodbye to someone we have come to know and love over the course of the competition. Freddie and Daisy, could you please step forward?"

I do so numbly, not even surprised. Freddie looks like he might cry, and as we take our spots, I link my arm tight through his.

"This week we saw struggles with color on the petits fours and uneven execution of éclairs, but unfortunately, the deciding element came down to flavor. Daisy, the judges have commented before that they want to see growth beyond the apple garden. And Freddie. Your use of spice knocked the judges' socks off today, and not in a good way."

His arm tightens on mine in the long silence that follows.

It could go either way.

I played it safe and boring. He at least took a risk and had design on his side.

Natalie steps forward, hand out. "Freddie. Please hand in your apron."

I throw my arms around him before he has a chance to remove it. "I'm sorry," I whisper.

"You're not the one who almost killed the judges," he says, laughing despite the circumstances. It quickly turns choked, though, and he curses. "I'm going to cry about cake on TV, aren't I?"

"Please don't, or I might too," I say, letting him go.

"And then I will," Natalie says with a sniffle as she accepts Freddie's apron. "We're truly sorry to see you go."

* * *

Vic is waiting in the atrium when we leave the ballroom, along with Gemma and Matt. She claps an arm around Freddie and hauls him in for a squeeze.

"My, how the mighty have fallen," she says, but there's no barb in the words, only affection. "Top Baker to one of us losers, all in a day."

"Everyone is buying me drinks," he announces. "In vast quantities. After I go cry."

Arrangements are made to meet for dinner, and we go our separate ways. I'm halfway to my room when it sinks in.

I made it.

I'm in the finals.

I have a one-in-three chance of leaving here with more money than I've ever seen in my life.

It's overwhelming enough that I almost don't register the phone ringing when I flop down on the bed. "Hello?"

"There will be a full-cast meeting in thirty minutes. Please be punctual."

Kate hangs up without saying good-bye, and I groan. So much for the nap I was hoping to take before dinner.

* * *

There's a hushed uneasiness as we gather in the dining room. No one has been told the reason for the meeting, only that attendance is mandatory.

I don't think I'm the only one scanning the room, searching for missing faces, fearing the worst.

Leland, Juliet, and Natalie stick together off to the side, but they look relaxed. If something is wrong, they're not showing it.

Abigail blows in with Kate on her heels. "Thank you all for coming," Abigail says. "First, I would like to congratulate our three finalists for making it this far. Well done." It's the most emotion we've seen from her yet, and that's including the aftermath of both deaths. "I wanted to take this time to go over the plan for tomorrow, since it's going to be a departure from the norm."

She holds up a hand, forestalling any speculation.

"The reason we have kept all of you sequestered here for the duration of filming is because tomorrow you will all be back on set." Surprised glances are exchanged, but no one dares interrupt.

"Don't get too excited. Those of you who have already been eliminated will not be returning as contestants. You'll be returning as guest judges."

"Oh fuck yeah," says Freddie, throwing his arms out. "Payback's a bitch, but I take bribes."

"You absolutely do not," Abigail snaps. "In the morning, the finalists will assemble as normal and begin filming, during which time the rest of you will gather here for a more detailed briefing about what we need from you. While you won't be on set for the full day, you are to remain nearby and make yourselves completely available. Tomorrow is not the day for long walks in the woods or leisurely lie-ins. We have a show to wrap, and it's all hands on deck. Finalists, be prepared for a long day, because we'll be staggering elements of the final two challenges and breaks will not be on the normal schedule. I suggest you all get a good night's rest."

She leaves before anyone can ask for more details, and the kitchen staff ready the buffet. There's a frozen moment where no one seems to know what to act on first: the food or the information.

Grant breaks first, getting up for food, and as everyone follows, chattering about the next day's upheaval, I realize this is my best chance. I slip out the door before I can get caught in a conversation or fit of conscience and run upstairs. I retrieve the master key from my room and take a few steadying breaths. My heart is racing and not only from my run up the stairs.

I cross the hall and tap the key to the sensor on Grant's door.

It feels wrong, but the police are interested in him, which means I am too. Besides, there's something he's hiding from me, and if it's the key to unlocking this, then I need to find it.

His room is neat, the bedding rumpled as if he was recently lying on top of it, but nothing is in disarray.

I know he eats fast and is unlikely to socialize, so I don't have time to waste. I start with the bathroom, where a zippered leather pouch sits on the counter. I rifle through its contents, but it's only a barbershop's worth of beard care products. No pill bottles. I check under the sink and in the drawers, but nothing. If he doesn't keep them in the bathroom, then maybe the bed tables, where they'd be easily accessible. The drawers of each are empty aside from the estate stationery and information sheets, but in one of the lower cabinets I find a bottle of whiskey, a heavy-bottomed rocks glass set upside down atop the neck.

My pulse beats in time with the seconds ticking by as I pull it out.

Half-full.

I check the corners of the cabinet—empty—and return the bottle.

Would half a bottle have done the trick? If they shared it? I'm not a big enough drinker to know for sure, but factoring in the pills, I think it's possible.

It's also possible that Grant likes to drink alone. I remind myself the whiskey itself isn't proof. Right now, it's only a coincidence.

It's the pills that matter.

I find Grant's suitcase in the closet, most of his clothes still in it. I move the piles out, making a mental note of the order, and run my hands along the case's interior mesh pockets. Nothing.

I repack the clothes and put the case back in the closet, turning in a circle to survey the whole room. Maybe the cops are wrong and he's the wrong lead. But I think back to the night I came to talk to him, the cagey look on his face as he fought the magic. He was hiding something.

He was sitting on the edge of the bed, and he was lying to me.

The bed.

I lift the pillows and move the duvet, knowing there's no way to reset it exactly the way I found it but past caring. If people are hiding something, their subconscious mind tends to draw their attention to it, and Grant had kept his ass glued to this bed.

I sit where he sat, taking in his view, but all I'm facing is the door. He would've seen me, the desk, his closed closet door.

And then I know, like the princess with the pea, that he didn't have to watch his secret to keep it safe. He knew it was safe because he was already guarding it.

I sweep my arm beneath the edge of the mattress, and midway down I find it, cold and hard beneath my fingers.

I extract the bottle, and one lone white rectangle rattles in the bottom. The label has been picked off, but when I shake the pill into my palm, there's no question.

* * *

I don't hear the lock click.

I don't hear the door open.

I don't hear Grant until he's on top of me, grabbing my arm and hauling me up. The pill falls to the carpet without a sound, but I manage to keep the amber bottle clutched in my other hand.

When he sees I have it, he drops my arm, covering his face with his hands. A low growl escapes from the space between them.

I back away from him, holding the bottle to my chest. "It was you." I shouldn't be surprised. I mean, I'm in his room because I suspected him, but to have the proof in my hand makes it painfully real. This man—this man I liked, who I shared kitchen space with—not only killed a man, but he put me, Melly, and my very livelihood in jeopardy. The fear at getting caught morphs into a burning rage. "What were you thinking? Why?"

"I should be asking you that," he snaps. He rakes a hand down his face, pulling hard at his beard. "God, why did you touch it? Your prints are all over it now. Fuck."

I realize he's right. I've been handling evidence in a murder case without gloves. It would take nothing for him to shift the blame to me. I was going to kill Bryan Miller, and now I'm going to take the fall for *not* doing it.

My back hits the door and I reach for the knob, trying to work out if it's best to turn the bottle in or destroy it, but I realize it wasn't triumph in Grant's voice, it was frustration.

My hand stills. "Talk," I demand.

He drops to the edge of the bed, the same place he sat the last time I was here, and braces his elbows on his knees. He bows his head, and when he speaks, it's with a weariness I feel in my sleep-deprived soul. "It's not mine."

"Not your prescription?"

"Not my bottle, not my Xanax, not my anything."

"But you just happen to have it." It comes out more like a statement, but he answers it anyway.

"It showed up in my bathroom."

"When?"

"Yesterday."

"And then the police came?"

He nods. "Coincidence, right?" The way he says it makes it clear he believes it was no such thing. "I thought they were going to search my room, but they just grilled me about my medical history and recreational drug use. Look, I almost told you this when you were here before, but I didn't know how. I didn't know if it would help, if you'd believe me, or if it even mattered. I felt like I should tell someone, but I didn't want to involve anyone either."

"Why didn't you tell the police?"

He scoffs. "Right. Because they would absolutely believe a bottle of random pills magically appeared in my room."

"What about the whiskey?" I ask.

"What about it?"

"Did that magically appear too?"

He shakes his head. "I know how it looks, drinking alone, but it helps me sleep. I bought the bottle from the bar. You can ask."

"Why didn't you get drinks with the rest of us?"

"Because it was awkward for me, all right? You guys all have this group thing going on, and well, I didn't really fit in that. Why does it matter anyway?"

"There was booze and benzos in Bryan when he died. Now those same things are here. If they're not yours, whose are they? Why would someone plant pills in your room?"

"Because I'm the obvious suspect. I'm the one who fought with him, remember?" He heaves another sigh. "Look, the whiskey was all me, I admit. I'm not proud of it, but it's the truth. I swear I have no idea where the pill bottle came from, though."

"Why did you keep it?"

"I was trying to figure out what to do with it. If I threw it out and it was found, it still has my prints on it, you know?"

I search his face, looking for any hint of deception, but I'm so tired I don't trust myself. He's convincing, but killers often are.

I would know.

"Are you going to call the cops?" he asks.

"Not yet."

He meets my gaze. "I didn't kill him."

"But someone did."

Chapter Forty-Two

When I leave Grant's, the encounter catches up with me like a tsunami. As the adrenaline recedes, my knees get that wobbliness that comes after a near miss with something deadly. I wait at the top of the stairs until I get my bearings.

I'm in dire need of my phone, food, sleep, and some damn answers.

With any luck, some answers will be on my phone, so I make Kate my first stop.

She sighs when she sees me, like it isn't her entire fault we have to go through this nonsense, but hands me my phone. I power it on, and notifications ping one after another on the screen.

Half of them are optimistic good-luck messages from Noel and the diner crew that almost make me tear up. Of course they would assume I made it to the finals. I wish I could tell them they were right.

Two of the messages are Melly's. Finally.

So you know those glasses I was looking at? I found two pairs but only one had amber on the bottom.

I roll my eyes. Subtle, my ass.

The next one is equally bad: *I finally got the bottles cleared out. Not one to be seen in the whole room.*

I text back *Good to know* and power the phone back down.

Two glasses, no bottle.

I turn that over as I make my way to the dining room.

Two glasses suggests a guest, but why would the killer leave his glass behind? Surely it would have DNA on it.

Unless it was wiped.

Or not used.

If only one glass had dregs in the bottom, it's possible only one drink was poured.

I push open the dining room door and find it empty except for the kitchen staff closing up the buffet. One of them notices me and stops. "Oh, I'm sorry. We thought everyone was finished."

"I'll be two seconds," I say, grabbing a plate. "Sorry."

"No worries," she says, stepping back. "Everything is still hot."

I take a scoop of the cheesy polenta and veggies, barely caring what's in it is as long as it's calories.

"Anything else?" the cook asks.

"Nope, thank you." I turn for the table, then spin back around. "Wait, actually, yes. Just a question, though. Is there a separate dining room somewhere else? Where judges eat?"

"Yes, on the other side of the estate. It's a meeting hall, but we often set it up for serving when we have concurrent functions."

"Does it have a bar?"

Her expression remains polite, but concern clouds her eyes. "There's an adjacent lounge with a small bar, yes. I'm sorry, may I ask why you're curious? Has something not met your standards here?"

"Oh no, not at all," I assure her. "This has been fabulous. I was curious is all. I can't imagine keeping a place this size running."

I thank her and let her return to her work, adding the new info to the mix.

It explains why we never see the judges at the bar with us, and it explains how Bryan could've gotten a drink without having a bottle in his room.

Of course, someone could've brought a bottle, say, from their own room.

Someone like Grant.

* * *

What is meant to be a brief appearance at the bar turns into an hour and a half, but I can't be mad. It's the usual group, and everyone has that slightly wild last-day-of-school vibe. Even Tony comes down, clinking Shirley Temples with Gemma, and although he watches more than he participates, there is a happy contentment to him that I suspect is only half related to getting Top Baker again.

Freddie, for his part, has moved straight from disappointed to devilment and is intricately plotting how his reign as guest judge will be the thing to change his life when I finally call it a night.

Our hall is silent, and I'm giving serious thought to a long bath as I pull my key card out. The bubbles and fancy oils will be worth the risk of falling asleep and drowning.

But the plan evaporates as Ainsley slams through the door at the end of the hall, tears streaming down her face.

She looks as startled to see me as I am to see her like that, and the anger that flares across her face is almost feral.

"Are you okay?" I ask, pocketing my key and approaching slowly.

"Obviously not," she snaps.

I nod. "Okay, yeah. I meant, is there anything I can do?"

She shakes her head, rifling through her bag for her key and dropping it. It makes her cry even harder.

I pick it up and she snatches it, sniffling hard. Her hands shake so much that the sensor has trouble reading it and she slams it against the door, hard enough to hurt.

"He fucking dumped me," she says. "Said it's over. That I was a mistake." The last word breaks on a sob.

"I'm sorry."

"Are you?" she sneers. "Because last time I checked, no one gives a shit about people who have affairs."

"I'm sorry you're hurting," I say honestly. What I don't say is that it's probably my fault, mostly because I'm so surprised the do-the-right-thing magic actually worked so well on someone like Leland. When you're so used to doing what you want, doing what's right can be hard, even with help.

"Yeah, well, fuck him." There's a wild recklessness in her eyes that is a one-way trip to badness. "He wants to see hurt, I can show him hurt."

"You don't want to hurt him," I say, trying to keep my voice soothing, but she continues like I haven't spoken.

"Fucking bastard. I'll show him. He thinks he can just throw me away? I can destroy him. I'll tell everyone about Chloe."

At that, every nerve in my body snaps to attention.

Time stops.

Even Ainsley freezes, the shock of her own words written across her face.

"What do you mean?" I ask carefully.

She shakes her head, all emotion drained from her. "Nothing."

"Ainsley."

"It's nothing," she says, setting the key on the sensor with deliberate care.

"It's not."

"Good night, Daisy," she says, slipping into her room and closing the door.

The lock engages like a gunshot.

My first instinct is to go find Leland and make him talk.

The only thing that stops me is the fact that I just saw firsthand how dangerous emotion can be, and I can't afford mistakes. Not now.

I have enough awareness to recognize that I'm too enraged to be rational with him right now. But the itch to bake an undiluted honesty pie and force-feed it to him is hard to ignore.

Chloe.

In all the concern about my own involvement in Bryan's death, I've let Chloe become exactly what they called her: a tragedy.

But that's wrong. I knew it at the time and I know it now.

She is the key.

I pound on Ainsley's door long enough to accept that she's going to ignore me. I could let myself in, of course, corner her and try to force her to talk, but I can hear laughter as others come down the hall, and I'm not ready to make a spectacle. Not yet anyway.

I return to my room and fill the tub with an obnoxious amount of bubbles, hoping to soak away some of the agitation. I have all the pieces, and I have one day left to make the connections.

The problem is that there are too many coincidences.

Like the coincidence that I'm here, I was going to kill Bryan, and he died before I could. That's a real one.

The fact that two people have died of different causes during the same show is the one I have a problem with.

Because it's not a coincidence.

It's a connection.

Chapter Forty-Three

The answer comes to me in the night, in that space between dreams where brain cells can't get in their own way. I've been so busy focusing on why someone here would want Bryan dead that I almost forgot why I needed to kill him.

Bryan the celebrity chef and Bryan the man were two very different people, but tigers can hide only so many stripes.

It's not about who Bryan was to anyone here. It's about who he was as a person.

If running Pies Before Guys has taught me anything, it's that women tend to kill for safety, as a last resort.

But men? Men kill for greed, for lust, for power.

And sometimes, like Tony, they kill by mistake.

* * *

I wake more rested than I have a right to.

"Feeling nervous?" Julian asks when he finishes my makeup.

"Feeling ready."

And I am.

The gathering on the stairs feel empty now that we're down to three.

"You know," Courchesne says, "I love you both, but it's on now."

"Damn right," I say, and she has no idea how true it is.

Tony grins. "Good luck. To both of you."

"To all of us," Courchesne corrects.

"All of us," he agrees, the hint of a smile on his lips.

Below us, the cameras gather and we separate, waiting for the final signal to begin our last walk down.

* * *

"Welcome, bakers, to the final round of *Bake My Day*!" Natalie says, voice booming with enthusiasm. "You have conquered your cakes, dazzled us with desserts, and blindsided us with innovative baking. Each of you should be exceptionally proud, but don't get too comfortable, because things are just heating up. Leland and Juliet still have some challenges up their sleeves as we tackle iconic American desserts. Or at least desserts named after iconic American places. It's a loose theme." She winks as Leland and Juliet join her. "For the warm-up, these two would like you to begin with something that has an equally loose grasp on its own identity: the Boston cream pie. Is it a cake? Is it a pie? I don't know, but you have two hours to make it, so bakers, do your thing!"

"What it is is an abomination," I say when Natalie gets to my station. "Pie is sacred. You don't slap some custard in a cake and call it pie."

"Strong feelings on the official state dessert from Miss Massachusetts herself," Natalie says in a mock-sportscaster voice. "And do you think those feelings will affect your bake? You realize it's one of Leland's favorites, right?"

"Everyone's allowed to be wrong sometimes," I say with an extra-innocent smile.

Natalie laughs. "Ooh, shots fired in the first round. I better leave you to it."

As soon as she's gone, I'm in it, magicking the everloving shit out of this impostor pastry. The mix I need is more complex than I want to put into a single bake, plus I have no idea how they're staggering guest judges. I brush that concern aside, not wanting doubt to leech into the magic.

This is the final. The last day.

The bakes need to be perfect and so does the magic.

Most of it goes into the filling, a simple vanilla custard that gets sandwiched between two layers of yellow cake.

Natalie calls a five-minute warning as I'm pouring my ganache over the top. It's thin enough to run down the sides in irregular drips.

"Time! Bakers, bring your Boston cream confusions to the judges' table!"

We do as instructed and then wait as Leland and Juliet come in.

Natalie grins. "Bakers, congratulations on finishing your last ever warm-up challenge. That should be a relief, but today Leland and Juliet aren't the only judges you have to impress." She pauses as Matt, Gemma, Ainsley, and Grant come in. "Perhaps you'll recognize them?"

There are smiles and waves as they join Leland and Juliet.

Ainsley stands as far from Leland as possible but gives no other indication that there's any history between them.

More than history.

Secrets.

They work through the cakes, and I don't even care that my drippy ganache is criticized.

I care that it's eaten.

"I think this one is stunning," Gemma announces when they get to Courchesne's, in a voice that's close enough to Juliet's to make me wonder if it's a deliberate imitation. "I like the sharp edges."

"Traditionally the ganache is poured," Leland says.

"I like it too," Ainsley says, a hint of defiance in her voice. "It's the best looking."

In the end, it's Tony who takes the literal cake, with Courchesne in second and me in third. It's obviously not an ideal place to be starting from, but I have two games I'm trying to win today, and one matters more.

Chapter Forty-Four

We break so set prep can work, and with only three of us, it's quiet on the patio.

I spent part of the night debating whether I should call Rensler and share my theory, but in the end, I didn't. For one thing, it's the last day of filming, and while this contest isn't the most important thing in the world, it isn't nothing either. There is a life-changing amount of money on the line, and if Matt and Derek were my cofinalists with their doctor and banker salaries, I might care less about that, but none of us here are privileged enough to throw that kind of payday away. Justice matters, but letting the contest play out won't bring anyone back.

It will, however, give my magic time to work.

Natalie calls us back in, and we take our places. In her off-camera voice, she says, "Remember, staggered elements for the next two challenges. We're starting with the first half of the creative, then we'll take an early lunch and come back for the craft before finishing the creative. Yes? Good." She visibly shifts personas, clapping her hands and becoming more animated. "Bakers, welcome back to your final final challenge. Once again we have a misnomer, for this dessert is neither fully baked nor from Alaska. Named in honor of the great frozen state, your baked Alaskas should feature two types of ice cream set atop a flavorful base and encased in decorative meringue, so bakers, do your thing!"

I immediately start rough-chopping mint to go in a pan of cream. "The most important thing is making sure the ice creams set," I say to the camera. "So I'll start there and do my brownie after."

For now, Juliet and Leland are the only judges in the room, and when they get to me for the overview, the sharp scent of mint is permeating the space.

"Something smells good," Juliet says. "Tell us about your baked Alaska."

"I'm calling it malted mint shake," I say, feeling a sudden swell of affection. I was planning to explain the origins, but I didn't expect to be punched in the ribs by feelings as I did so. "It's a combination of malted vanilla and mint chocolate chip ice creams, which are Frank's favorite. He owns the diner I make pies for, and he put up with a lot while I was getting ready for this show, so I wanted to do something in honor of him."

"I'm sure he'll be very proud you've made it this far," Juliet says. "I can't wait to try it."

Leland, not one to be sidetracked by feelings, peers into my simmering pot. "I see you're using fresh mint?"

"I am, but I'm also using a touch of gel color, because in Frank's mind, it's not mint if it's not green." I don't tell him the rest of what's going in there. No need to spoil the surprise.

"And you find it works well with the malt?" he asks, pinning me with that stare of his.

"I do."

He waits for me to flinch, but I don't. "Well, we'll see, won't we?"

"We will."

* * *

When Natalie gives the twenty-minute warning, that's our signal to wrap things up. My soft-set ice creams are swirled together in a plastic wrap–lined bowl, both brimming with as much magic as malt and mint. I press a circle of fudge brownie onto the top and pop it in the freezer.

The break for lunch is called, and again, it's just the three of us. I didn't count on that, but I suppose now that the others are technically judges, it makes sense. Still, it would've been nice to have an idea how the Boston cream magic is getting on—if at all.

Focused magic is hard in a way my regular magic isn't. If I'm baking for the farmers' market or the diner, the magic I pour into the pie is generalized, evoking roughly the same thing in everyone. Sure, everyone metabolizes it differently, but a happy pie makes a happy person.

This cocktail of magic is different. Part of that is the honesty element. Honesty magic can get out of hand very quickly, and the last thing I need is everyone confessing their deepest secrets on camera, so I focused it, like the magic that goes into murder pies. A murder pie is perfectly safe for anyone to eat, with the exception of its intended, because it's so carefully tailored.

Today I need that kind of precision, but I need it to cover two very different people, just to be sure. That's the part that makes it complicated.

That and the whole final-round-of-a-televised-baking-show thing.

That's a factor too.

* * *

"Bakers, welcome to part two of your final day," Natalie says when we return from lunch. "For the craft challenge, we're wading into muddy waters with a recipe with as many variations as the US has states. For this round, the judges would like to see your interpretation of a Mississippi mud pie. Now, there's some debate on what makes a proper mud pie, but for the sake of this challenge, the judges would like you to include a dense element, a creamy element, and a crunchy element held together in a crumb crust, and the primary flavor should, of course, be chocolate, so bakers, do your thing!"

And this is very much my thing.

Natalie may think chocolate is the star of the show, but she's wrong.

It's magic.

As I work, everything—the cameras, the judges, the ballroom itself—disappears, and it feels like being home. I work the magic into every facet of the pie, stirring it into my chocolate grahams with the butter, sifting it into the cocoa for the fudge layer, and whisking it into the eggs that thicken my custard.

It's even in the whipped cream, spiked with hazelnut liqueur and an extra dose of the do-the-right-thing that went into yesterday's entremets and this morning's Boston cream.

Even as I talk to the camera and banter with Natalie, most of my mind is on the magic.

It's on Chloe.

And it's on blackmail.

* * *

"Bakers, that is the end of your final craft challenge," Natalie announces, Leland and Juliet at her side. "It's do-or-pie time, so move your bakes to the end of your bench, and let's welcome our team of guest judges!"

Freddie, Vic, Nell, and Derek stroll in like they own the place, flanking the judges on both sides, and we're all grinning at each other like we've been separated for weeks instead of hours.

They descend on Courchesne first.

"Remind us of your take on the mud pie," Juliet says.

"I went Elvis-style," Courchesne says as Leland portions himself a large piece. "I have a brownie layer at the bottom topped with peanut butter pudding and a caramel banana crumble on top."

"I'm sold," Derek says.

"Perhaps we try it first before making such judgments?" Leland says archly.

For a moment the only sound is forks scraping the plate, then a groan.

"Still sold," Derek says. "That's bomb."

"It is very good," Juliet agrees. "Although it's so rich I'm not sure I could eat more than a few bites."

"Good. More for me," Derek says.

"The topping works very well," Leland concedes. "The dried banana and caramel are almost peanut-brittle-like, and that kick of salty-sweet helps cut through the richness."

"Thank you," Courchesne says, swatting Derek away as he tries to double dip his fork back into the whole pie.

They stay on that side of the aisle, moving on to Tony next.

"My inspiration came from my grandmother's favorite candy, Almond Joy," he says. "The crust is almost equal parts desiccated coconut and chocolate cookie crumbs, and there's also coconut in the custard. The almond comes through in the mud cake and again as garnish."

"It's very sophisticated for a candy bar," Juliet says. "That chocolate is very dark."

"Too dark," Leland says. "Which isn't something I'd usually say, but the cake and the crust together are edging very close to bitter. Taken individually with the coconut custard, they're excellent, but together it's overpowering."

Tony nods, accepting the feedback but not apologizing.

"I dig it," Vic says. "I like a chocolate that doesn't fuck around."

Natalie laughs, and Juliet hides her smirk with another bite before saying, "I think I agree with Vic on this one. Again, a small sliver would do, but I would enjoy every mouthful."

At that, Tony smiles, just enough to reach the corners of his dark eyes.

And then they come to me.

Nell stands close enough to nudge my arm, and it feels like all the times we've stood for judging, only today the stakes are so much higher.

"Daisy, tell us about your pie," Leland says, and I'm tempted. I'm tempted to tell him exactly what's in it and exactly why, but I don't.

Not yet.

"I went with a twist on one of the classic interpretations," I say, watching Leland's knife sink through the layers. "I grew up eating the coffee ice cream version, so I took that and upgraded it to hazelnut latte."

Freddie swoons dramatically. "I already want to marry it."

I grin, continuing, "The crust is plain chocolate with hazelnut fudge on the bottom, mocha custard in the middle, and a hazelnut whipped cream on top."

"The piping is lovely," Juliet says, noting the rosettes and starbursts.

"Whipped cream is so much more forgiving than royal icing," I say with a laugh.

"We're judging more than looks," Leland reminds everyone, and I try not to tense up as they put the first magic-laden bite into their mouths.

Freddie groans in a way that would put Harry and Sally both to shame. "This. Is. Divine."

"Why thank you," I say, grinning.

"I feel like I could eat it for breakfast," Nell says. "Like, I know I shouldn't, but it's like morning coffee in food form."

"It's very nice," Juliet says. "Lovely balance of flavor."

Leland sniffs. "I would like more crunch. The hazelnuts are getting lost in the fudge."

"Don't care," Freddie says, forking another bite in his mouth. "It's cold. It's coffee. It's the pie of my dreams."

"Well," Juliet says, "I think we'll have our work cut out for us ranking these."

"I should probably take this one," Freddie says, "you know, to make sure it's consistent all the way through."

"Don't you dare," I say. "Sharing is caring, remember?" I say it lightly, but a thrum of worry runs through me. If this pie doesn't get shared, my chances of things going my way are cut in half.

Freddie gives the pie a longing look. "You give me life and snatch it away."

"Come," Juliet says, ushering everyone off. "Let us discuss the merits of pie. Thank you, Daisy."

They leave and Natalie calls an hour break, but not before someone from the set staff gathers the three pies for delivery to the dining room.

Perfect.

Chapter Forty-Five

"Bakers, it's time to whip it, and whip it good," Natalie calls. "And by *it*, I of course mean meringue, because it's time to get these Alaskas baked!"

By now the pie magic will be kicking in, laying the groundwork for the finale, but that doesn't mean I'm done.

As I scrape the seeds of a vanilla bean into my egg whites, I work more magic in, a desire for release and unburdening. The pinch of cream of tartar is accompanied by a bigger pinch of indignation, a risky ingredient that I'm counting on affecting one person and one person only.

I whip it all with a cup of sugar, sweetening it until it will be impossible to resist.

As Leland and Juliet look on, I fetch my ice cream from the freezer. When I press the brownie, there's hardly any give, which is a good sign.

I work the plastic wrap loose, tugging the edges until the ice cream dome releases. The surface is mottled where the two flavors have melded together, but it's frozen solid, and that's all that matters.

Ignoring Leland's scrutiny, I upend the meringue over the top. The beauty of this is in the chaos. Toasted meringue doesn't need to be precise to be pretty. Using the back of a spoon, I swirl sweeping spikes across the surface, making sure all of the ice cream is covered. If it isn't, it will melt the minute I put the torch on it, and no one wants a melty Alaska.

"Fire in the hole," I call, brandishing the butane torch like a weapon as the camera zooms in. It ignites with a hiss, and I make sweeping passes across the meringue, sealing the magic in. I keep the flame moving, going for golden brown rather than blackened.

It feels a little like alchemy.

"Two minutes, bakers, two minutes and you will have reached the end of your final final challenge," Natalie says.

I give the Alaska one more pass and set the torch down.

It's either enough or it isn't.

There's nothing else I can do.

And as I move the dessert to the end of my bench, I'm okay with that.

"Bakers, your time is up," Natalie says. "Step away from the sweets."

We do, and in the moment where the judges take their places at the table and the three of us are eyeing each other's offerings, it sinks in.

It's over.

Courchesne realizes it the same time I do because she's crossing the aisle, arms out, and I'm already halfway to her. We fall into a hug and then we're swallowing Tony in it too.

Because we're here.

We made it.

All the way to the end.

* * *

There's a flurry of activity as the rest of the bakers pile in and line up behind Leland and Juliet.

Tony is called first.

"Please tell us all about your baked Alaska," Juliet says, inclining her head to include other bakers in her use of *us*.

"I went with roasted strawberry and mascarpone ice creams on top of a lemon basil sponge," he says without embellishment.

"Digging the porcupine effect," Vic says.

"It is very unique," Juliet agrees, admiring the piped spikes of darkly toasted meringue. "Almost like modern art."

Leland cuts into the Alaska, removing a wedge of neatly layered cake and ice cream. "Very nice," he says, sliding the rest of it down to Natalie for further portioning. "I like the definition between the layers."

Shit, was I supposed to do that? After the entremets I thought we were done with layers.

I let it go. There's nothing to be done about it now, and besides, layers and swirls both taste the same in the mouth.

There's a beat where everyone is focused on the flavors and some of the bakers murmur comments at each other, but it's Leland who clearly has an opinion. He pins Tony with a hard-eyed stare.

"That," he said, "is one of the best ice creams I've had in my life. Seriously. The roasted strawberry is bold and jammy, and the mascarpone gets out of the way to let it shine."

"It really is lovely," Juliet says. "I wasn't sure about the basil in the lemon, but I think it really elevates the whole."

Freddie waves his fork at it. "If you swapped the lemon for chocolate, it would be the bougiest Neapolitan ever."

"I'm glad it's not," Leland says. "Very nice work, Tony."

As he returns to his station, set prep whisks in to remove the judges' dirty plates and replace them with fresh, and they're so fast it's like watching a race car pit crew work.

"Courchesne, please bring up your baked Alaska," Natalie says when they're finished.

She sets it on the table and doesn't wait to be asked for an explanation. "I like to call this my Bourbon Street peach cobbler," she says. "It has a vanilla pound cake base and is topped with peach and bourbon vanilla ice cream. I used Russian piping tips on the meringue to mimic clouds of whipped cream."

"I do like the look of all those ruffles," Juliet says.

Leland is ducked down, inspecting it from all the angles. "The browning is uneven because of them, though." He tips the platter for the camera. "See here, this is still sticky."

Courchesne nods but doesn't say anything. After Tony's flawless bake, anything could be a deal breaker now.

They cut into it, revealing abstract splotches of pale peach and creamy white.

"I didn't layer," Courchesne says. "I did individual scoops that I pressed down because I wanted the cobbled look of the cobbler to carry through."

"I think it works," Juliet says, taking a bite. "Mmm. As does the flavor. The warmth of that bourbon is wonderful."

"Ooh, and strong," Nell says. Behind the judges, Derek makes a show of taking Gemma's plate.

"Twenty-one plus only," he says, flashing that Hollywood grin as he dances away from her grabbing hands.

"It is strong," Leland agrees, sobering everyone. He gives Courchesne a stern look. "This isn't the first time you've had a heavy hand with the alcohol."

"I am from New Orleans," she says with a shrug.

He continues like she hasn't spoken. "However, it is the first time it's worked in your favor. It's strong, but with the peaches and that buttery base, it works."

She gives a cheeky bow that earns a laugh. "Why thank you."

And then it's me and it's not just the contest on the line.

It's everything.

* * *

When I was researching baked Alaska recipes, I learned that they're sometimes called bombe Alaska, and that feels fitting. After all, it's not just a dessert I'm carrying to the judges' table on shaking legs.

It's a bomb.

I leave that part out of my explanation, of course, simply reiterating the inspiration for the flavors.

"Classic swirl on the meringue," Leland remarks as he cuts through the shell. "Well toasted."

I don't need him to tell me that the slice he removes isn't as pretty as the previous two, but he does anyway.

"Muddled coloring," he says, letting the cameras get a close-up. "The ice creams were marbled while still soft?"

I nod, nerves choking my vocal cords.

"The point of two flavors is to have two distinct elements," he says, leaning on the *distinct*.

If only he could imagine how distinct it really is.

"The brownie on the bottom is divine," Juliet says. "It's like pure fudge."

There are murmurs of agreement from the bakers, and Freddie raises his fork for another declaration.

"Okay, if Tony's was almost bougie Neopolitan, this is a bougie ice cream sandwich and I am here for it."

"The malt comes through very nicely on that vanilla," Juliet says.

"But it completely melded with the mint," Leland counters. "Which, to be fair, does seem very nice. The shaved chocolate is a welcome change from chips, but I haven't gotten a big enough bite on its own to fully appreciate it."

"Malted mint works for me," Matt says, shrugging. "It gets my vote."

Natalie waves her hands dramatically, cutting him off. "Let's save the voting for deliberations," she says, ushering them out. "Off you go now."

"Yes, I believe we have a very difficult decision ahead of us," Juliet says, thanking me for my Alaska and not even realizing how right she is.

Chapter Forty-Six

It feels like it takes forever for the judges to return, and for the first time since the beginning, there's a silent tension as we wait.

I brush my hand across the edge of my worktop, remembering Chloe and reminding myself that it doesn't matter who wins.

What matters is the truth.

"It's time," Natalie says, and we gather, we final three, to await our fate.

Abigail and Kate flank the door as the judges and bakers file back in.

Courchesne's hand finds mine, and I reach for Tony. His cool fingers close around mine, and we all exchange nervous, hopeful looks.

No matter how this goes, we made it this far.

Gemma and Nell stand off to one side, each holding the corner of a giant cardboard check with that life-changing sum written on it.

I scan the others, looking for hints of the winner, of the magic working, of anything that will end this electric anticipation.

It is, of course, Natalie's job to do that. "Bakers," she says, "it has been a long and sometimes sticky road, but the time has come to reveal who will be crowned the ultimate Top Baker. First, I want to say this has been an incredibly difficult—but delicious—decision as you have all worked so hard to get here. But I am absolutely thrilled to announce that our winner is—"

This pause is the longest yet, and in it I see all the outcomes.

The win, the loss, the magic.

The lives changed and saved and ruined.

"—Tony! Congratulations!"

I drop his hand as his own fly to cover his face, and the rend in my chest is not from losing. It's from knowing what this means to him, that he made it, that maybe now he can believe he's more than a man who made a terrible mistake.

Because he is, and though he doesn't know it, his story held the key I needed to unlock the truth of what really happened.

I hug him before I can stop myself and so does Courchesne, and then it's a crush of congratulations as the other bakers swarm around us.

It's joy, pure and simple, because it really didn't matter who won, because how can you be upset when the winner is your friend?

Cameras circulate as we carry on, catching the moments and snippets of chatter that will no doubt end up in a montage at the episode's end.

I notice that Grant and Ainsley stick to the edges, but Juliet and Leland work through the crowd, commenting and congratulating everyone on their efforts.

I maneuver myself out of the crush and circle around a camera. The operator is the same guy who filmed me at Frank's what seems like ages ago now.

"Please keep filming, no matter what," I say as I go by.

I position myself near Ainsley and Grant, and for a moment I see the celebration from their perspective, from the outside, and I hate what I'm about to do to it.

I hop up onto the judges' table, and even though I loathe being a spectacle, I have to appreciate the efficiency as heads turn and voices fall silent.

Abigail is marching toward me, but before she can stop me, I say, "I want to take a moment to remember Chloe."

The hush that falls is complete.

"I think it's safe to say when we signed up for this that we knew it would be hard, that we would be pushed to our baking limits. But Chloe never got a chance to see how far she could go. She came here wanting to make her students proud, and instead, she was taken from them. It might have been an accident, but it was not without malice."

There's a stirring, and I know it's now or never.

I have an audience.

I'm safe and cannot be silenced the way Chloe was.

The magic will either be enough or it won't be.

"Chloe did not die alone."

"Get down," Abigail barks. "Cut cameras!"

I trust they won't. The possibility of capturing a scandal is always film worthy.

And this is going to be a scandal.

"Four people knew what happened that day, and two of them are dead." I pull a Natalie and pause before dropping the real bomb. "Two of them are here."

That stops even Abigail in her tracks. The cameras are up, capturing the looks and whispers being exchanged among the bakers.

Ainsley and Grant are the only ones who aren't participating. Grant's jaw is set, his eyes hard as he glares at me.

And Ainsley.

Ainsley is at war, the magic playing across her face as she looks between me, the floor, and Leland.

"It's time to do the right thing," I say. "That's all I'm asking. Do the right thing."

"You have no idea what you're talking about," Leland sneers.

And there it is, that flash of indignation at being asked to simply do what's right. It's not a smart emotion, it's selfish and narcissistic, and I am sick of men who think the rules don't apply to them. It was easy to bring it out, a small dash of amplification in the mud pie, and now Leland has revealed himself.

"Don't I?" I ask, teasing the magic forward.

My worry was knowing it couldn't be a murder pie. Not for this. The fundamental ingredient in a murder pie is the need to stop, by any means necessary, and Bryan was already the natural stopping point.

This is an untested blend, designed to play equally on the conscience and the ego, because with someone like Leland, the former can't be counted on.

"I have a theory," I say, deliberately goading him with my tone. "I think it started as an accident. I think when you discovered Chloe knew about your affair, you tried to shut her up."

It's not Leland who answers, but Ainsley. "Yes."

He whirls on her, but Derek and Matt are already moving, positioning themselves between the two. Derek holds a big arm out to Leland but doesn't touch him.

"Ainsley?" I prompt.

"It's true. We were sleeping together, and Chloe knew."

"And you fought with her," Gemma says, like she might've forgotten.

"But I didn't kill her."

"Because Leland did," I say.

"She fell," he protests. "I never laid a hand on her."

"But you were there, weren't you?" I ask, knowing the answer.

"What'd you do? Crowd her? Threaten her? She was trying to get away from you when she fell, wasn't she?"

"I didn't kill her," he repeats, voice low and dangerous.

"But Bryan thought you did, didn't he? He saw and he thought he could extort you, right? What did he ask for?"

Abigail steps forward. "Leland? Is this true?"

Leland barks a bitter laugh. "Yes, it's true. He was going to blackmail me with something I didn't even do. He wanted access to my plane in exchange for his silence."

"You have a plane?" Vic asks.

Courchesne shushes her with a whispered, "Not the point."

"Do you know what he was going to do with it?" I ask, aware that's also not the point but still curious.

Leland sneers and shakes his head in disgust. "I've heard rumors."

"What rumors?" Juliet asks.

"About the girls."

"That's enough," Abigail barks. "I don't want rumors, I want the truth."

"We all do," I say, turning back to Leland. "What happened?"

"I told him to fuck right off," he says, chest puffed out like his ego might save him.

"And?"

"He said if I didn't comply, not only would he tell the police about Chloe, he'd tell my wife about Ainsley. We married without a prenup. She would destroy me in a divorce."

I manage to keep the disgust off my face, but barely. "So you killed him."

I say it like a fact, not a question.

The unburdening magic should be building, turning the truth into something he's desperate to share, but he's silent for a long time, fighting it.

Abigail turns to Kate and murmurs, "Get the police here. Now."

Kate speeds off, her heels echoing in the silence.

"He deserved it, didn't he, Leland?" I ask, poking at the indignation.

"Fucking right he did. I was the damn victim, but I had no way to prove it."

I don't remind him that Chloe was the ultimate victim. I need him to keep talking.

"Tell us how you did it."

"It should've looked like suicide, with the pills and the whiskey," he says. "No harm, no foul. But then the damn cops wouldn't let it go."

When he doesn't continue, I prod him. "So you needed someone else to take the blame."

He shrugs. "Had to try." Ainsley is staring at him like he's a pile of rotten fish guts, but he doesn't even notice. "It should've worked."

"Except I saw you," I tell him. "You were in our hall, and it wasn't Ainsley's room you were leaving, it was Grant's."

Leland turns to Grant and tips his head. "If it matters, it wasn't personal."

Grant's eyes flash with fury. "You planted drugs in my room. I'd say that's pretty fucking personal."

Matt shifts, ready to intercede if needed, but Grant just drags a hand down his beard and blows out a hard breath. "This is some bullshit."

"That," Abigail says, "is the biggest understatement I have ever heard."

Chapter Forty-Seven

With his entire confession on camera, Leland has the grace to not fight the arrest, but he still looks indignant as Rensler tightens the cuffs, like he can't believe he's meeting the consequences of his actions.

I feel worse for Ainsley, who may not be the nicest person but also isn't a monster. She's taken in for questioning, the police squawking about obstruction of justice and impeding investigations, charges that I hope don't stick.

I think she's learned her lesson and then some.

Kate is sent with her, both as a representative of the network and to make sure the original footage is kept safe.

As for the rest of us, we're sequestered and given a hand-crampingly large stack of fresh NDAs to sign because, in true show biz fashion, the show is still going on.

And who knows, judging by the gleam in Abigail's eye, all the added drama might even be a bonus. After all, part of the new agreement includes clauses about making ourselves available for any subsequent promotion, interviews, or official documentaries as requested.

Tony, for his part, gets to keep his prize money regardless of what happens to the show. He earned it.

It's late by the time we're released and we all have packing to do, but when Freddie suggests one more gathering at the bar, no one says no.

Grant surprises everyone not just by joining, but getting the first round. "A toast," he says, raising a glass. "To Tony, for winning. To Nell and Derek, for starting something sweet. And to Daisy, for seeing the truth of things. Thank you."

There's the tinkle of touching glasses, and everyone shouts their addendums, toasting themselves, the bar, and each other.

At the end, Tony keeps his glass raised. "To new friends," he says, "even for those of us who struggle making them."

"Aagh," Freddie screams. "If you make me cry, we can't be friends anymore! No, wait, that's a lie. You can buy my friendship. You're a rich man now."

Tony smiles, and it lights his whole face for the first time since he's gotten here. I know it's not the money doing it, although I'm sure it helps. It's that he's found a new way to define himself, one that's about growth and not just guilt.

It's a good look on him.

"Well, I'm still hoping for a network deal," Courchesne says, knocking back the rest of her drink. "Not gonna lie. I might've been beat, but I'm still the Real Ace of Cakes."

This earns another toast, and so it continues, long into the night, and it's wonderful enough to make me feel like everything will be okay.

Epilogue

The show airs a full six months later than it should've, but it airs.

One of the major streamers got wind of the scandal, and a deal was struck that had all of us back together multiple times for interviews about the behind-the-scenes drama. A fast-tracked companion documentary detailing the sordid life and death of Bryan Miller will drop the minute the season finale ends for viewers hungry for more.

Frank has gone all out for the premiere, setting up a projector and inviting more people than we can comfortably fit in the diner to the viewing.

Juan and I spent the day prepping snacks, which are on the house tonight. Frank says it's because the event will bring in more business on the back end, but I don't buy it.

I think he's enjoying the spotlight.

Noel, for his part, is taking advantage of the crowd to test out some new summer cider flavors and seems as happy to be home as I am.

Melly shows up, of course, and is still trying to get me to spill about the results. She gets the same reaction everyone does at that request, an enigmatic smile and open-handed shrug.

Before we left, Abigail reminded us that if we thought the police were scary, they had nothing on the studio lawyers, and I believe her.

I sit on the long counter between Noel and Melly, something Frank would normally never allow, but it's too crowded for anything else.

As the opening music sounds and Natalie's voice-over introduces the show, I'm hit with a flood of emotions. Pride at doing something so outside my comfort zone, affection for faraway friends, and contentment that it's over.

Show biz is definitely more trouble than it's worth.

The intro cuts away to our very first walk down the stairs, and the diner erupts into cheers as, on screen, we make our way to our stations.

As we do, we're introduced on voice-over, with scenes from our home segments spliced in. The kitchen staff whoop when our familiar workspace appears for viewers around the country to see.

On screen, Natalie welcomes us to our first warm-up challenge, and I laugh as Frank gives me shit for making my cookies too damn big.

I might not have won, but right now, sitting on this counter, in this diner, it feels like I have.

* * *

Since the show wrapped, an angel investor has dropped enough start-up money in Nell's lap to get her donut shop off the ground. I have a feeling that angel has a particularly devilish smile, but he did it the right way, with no strings attached and no need for recognition.

Derek Langley is definitely one of the good guys.

The same streamer doing the documentary also poached Courchesne, and she's busy filming the first season of her own show. Freddie is already scheduled to guest star.

Vic decided if she couldn't afford a storefront, she could at least afford a van, and Grant helped her outfit it with a full kitchen and custom cabinetry. One of these days we're going to team up and bring the mobile *Bake My Day* pie-and-cookie experience to the masses.

Tony's first cookbook is due out next year, but he's mostly channeling his love of baking in a less flashy direction. His New Beginnings Bakery is staffed entirely by ex-cons and at-risk kids, and his quiet passion has made it a sanctuary of second chances. Matt even connected him with a psychiatrist friend who provides pro bono mental health care for all the employees.

Ainsley wasn't charged with anything more than stupidity, but she doesn't keep in touch with anyone from the show, which I get. I wouldn't want to be reminded of that time if I were her either.

Gemma, for her part, is excelling at pastry school and has the kind of social media following that will make her an instant hit if she decides to go the cookbook or TV route, and she's young enough to try anything. Juliet keeps in touch with her and has promised to mentor her throughout her education.

And then there's me.

I have a diner in desperate need of pies and a Pies Before Guys in-box full of requests to go through, and I wouldn't have it any other way.

Recipes

Create Your Own Cookies

Cookie Base Ingredients

1 cup butter (room temperature)
¾ cup brown sugar
½ cup granulated sugar
2 teaspoons vanilla*
1 egg
2¼ cups all-purpose flour
1 teaspoon baking soda
1 teaspoon salt
2–4 cups mix-ins**

Method

1. Preheat oven to 350.

2. Cream together butter and sugars, then add vanilla and egg. Mix to combine.

3. Add flour, baking soda, and salt and mix on low until just combined.

4. Add mix-ins and mix until just combined.

5. Scoop cookies onto tray and bake 8–10 minutes (or a bit longer if you prefer your cookies crisp).

Notes

* Vanilla can be subbed or supplemented with other extracts to complement your mix-ins.

** Don't limit yourself to chocolate chips! Think about spices, nuts, dried fruit, sprinkles, marshmallows, candy—even other cookies!

Combo Ideas

Peanuts, caramel bits, and crushed banana chips

Mini marshmallows, chocolate chips, and crumbled graham crackers

Dried cherries, lime zest, and white chocolate

Crystalized ginger, dried mango, and chili powder

Maple extract, chopped maple candies, and dried blueberries

Concoct Your Own Quick Bread

Quick Bread Base Ingredients

3 cups all-purpose flour*
1 teaspoon salt
1 teaspoon baking soda
1⅔ cups buttermilk
Flavor add-ins**

Method

1. Preheat oven to 400.

2. Combine all ingredients in a large bowl and mix gently with spoon/spatula until it starts to come together.

3. Turn out onto your work surface and knead gently until cohesive dough is formed, but do not overwork.

4. Shape dough into a ball. (If you prefer two smaller loaves, split in half first.)

5. If adding a topping (e.g., finely grated cheese, coarse sugar), pat dough with wet hands and sprinkle topping over surface.

6. Using a knife or bench scraper, score dough with a deep X.

7. Bake 35–45 minutes (20–25 if baking two small loaves) or until a deep golden brown.

Notes

* Feel free to play with the flour—sub in some whole wheat or rye to make it your own!

** For add-ins, get creative! You can use spices, cheese, fruits, nuts, veggies, chocolate—anything you want! The amount you use may vary based on personal preference; just remember that wetter add-ins might extend your baking time.

Combo Ideas

Caramelized onion and gruyere
Jalapeño, bacon, and cheddar
Dried figs, walnuts, and dark chocolate chips
Sun-dried tomatoes, olives, and asiago
Pecans, orange zest, and dried cranberries

Design Your Own Donuts

Brioche Donut Base Ingredients

2¾ cups all-purpose flour
¼ cup sugar
1 tablespoon instant yeast
1¼ teaspoons salt
½ cup milk, heated to 105 and allowed to cool to room temp
1 teaspoon vanilla
2 whole eggs + 3 yolks
10 tablespoons softened butter
2 quarts neutral oil, for frying

Method

Day 1:

1. Combine dry ingredients in the bowl of a stand mixer* fitted with a paddle.

2. Add milk, vanilla, and eggs/yolks, and mix until a shaggy dough forms.

3. Working in small batches, add butter, mixing thoroughly after each addition.

4. Switch to a dough hook and beat on medium-low for ten minutes to develop the gluten.

5. Transfer to a large greased bowl and cover. Refrigerate overnight.**

Day 2:

1. Tip dough onto a floured surface and roll out until ½ inch thick.

2. Cut donuts into desired shapes. (If you don't have a ring cutter, simply use two rounds of different sizes. If you have no cutters, use a knife or pizza wheel to cut squares or rectangles.)

3. Gently gather scraps and reroll, cutting out as many more donuts as you can. (Pro tip—any wonky scraps taste just as good as proper donuts when they're fried up!)

4. Cut out as many parchment squares/rectangles as you have donuts (excluding holes) and arrange donuts on them. Cover loosely and let rise until doubled in size. (Timing will depend on the temperature of your kitchen.)

5. While they rise, prep your glazes*** and decorations.

6. Heat oil in a large pan over medium-low. You want to keep it between 325 and 350 degrees, so adjust heat as needed while working.

7. Working in batches, gently slide the donuts (parchment square and all) into the oil. The parchment will separate quickly and can be fished out with tongs.

8. Fry for approximately two minutes per side, using a skimmer or slotted spoon to flip them halfway through. They should be golden brown with a pale ring around the center.

9. Cool donuts on wire racks set over paper towels.

10. Glaze, fill, and decorate as desired.

Notes

* This dough is best prepared in a mixer but can be done by hand if necessary. Begin by working ingredients with a spatula or wooden spoon in a large bowl until the butter is incorporated, then turn out onto your work surface and knead by hand. (Depending on proficiency, this could take up to 20 minutes.)

** This step can *technically* be rushed by proving dough at a warmer temperature for a shorter time, but I highly recommend making this a two-day process.

*** Depending on what you use for glazes, they might set up a bit before your donuts are ready for dunking. If that happens, just give them a good stir or a blast in the microwave to loosen them up.

Finishing

The possibilities for donuts are absolutely endless. They can be filled, frosted, and flavored any way you imagine. The ideas below will get you started, but use what's in your repertoire to make them your own!

Coatings

Powdered sugar
Granulated sugar
Cinnamon (or any spice!) sugar
Fruity sugar (Mix powdered freeze-dried fruit with granulated sugar. A little fruit goes a long way here!)

Fillings

Jam
Curd
Pastry cream/pudding/custard
No-bake cheesecake
Stabilized whipped cream

Frostings

Powder sugar glaze
Chocolate ganache
Flavored icing (Shortcut: Store-bought frosting makes a quick and glossy icing—simply microwave and dip!)

Garnishes

Cookie crumbs
Candy
Freeze-dried fruit
Sprinkles
Cereal

Acknowledgments

As always, the first slice of the thank-you pie goes to my awesome agent, Rebecca Podos, for believing in murder pies from the very beginning. Can't believe we're here for seconds!

And of course, there should be an absolute mountain of thank-you pies for everyone at Crooked Lane. Faith Black Ross took a chance putting murder pies on their menu, and for that I am forever grateful. Thanks also to Rebecca Nelson, Melissa Rechter, Madeline Rathle, Dulce Botello, and Molly McLaughlin for their work in getting this book to print—publishing would fall without the hard work of the production, marketing, and publicity staff and interns. Also thanks to Rachel Keith for once again making sure I know how words, commas, and days of the week actually work!

I would also like to thank Stephanie Singleton for creating such a fabulous cover and Tanya Eby for narrating the audiobook to perfection.

Thank-you pies all around for everyone who blurbed, supported, or otherwise cheered on this wacky series of mine, including, but nowhere near limited to, Olivia Blacke, Alexia Gordon, Catriona MacPherson, Melissa Bourbon, CJ Connor, and Michelle

Cruz, and all the bloggers, reviewers, and booksellers who recommended it. You're all the best!

Thanks again go to Erika for the unwavering enthusiasm and book talks – huzzah for tiny in-person book communities! And, of course, to Adam, who likes seeing his name in print and continues to eat the things I bake with unwavering trust. True love!

And finally, thank you to all the readers who picked up the first book and still came back for seconds. I am beyond thrilled that my weird little murder-pie books found their way into your world!